Lady Poore

Recollection of an Admiral's Wife

1903-1916

Lady Poore

Recollection of an Admiral's Wife
1903-1916

ISBN/EAN: 9783337166526

Printed in Europe, USA, Canada, Australia, Japan

Cover: Foto ©Raphael Reischuk / pixelio.de

More available books at **www.hansebooks.com**

RECOLLECTIONS OF AN ADMIRAL'S WIFE

1903—1916

BY

LADY POORE

THIRD IMPRESSION (SECOND EDITION)

With a Portrait

LONDON

SMITH, ELDER & CO., 15, WATERLOO PLACE

1916

TO
ALL THOSE SAILORS AND SAILORS' WIVES
WHO HAVE HONOURED ME
WITH THE TITLE
OF
FLAG-MOTHER

NOTE

*My readers will be disappointed to find in these
"Recollections of an Admiral's Wife" very few
references to the views and doings of the Admiral
himself. This reticence is due to the fact that the
Admiral is on the Active List of "The Great Silent
Navy."*

I. M. P.

CONTENTS

CONTENTS

x

CONTENTS

PART III

ENGLAND, 1911—1916

CONTENTS

PART I

ENGLAND, 1903—1908

RECOLLECTIONS OF AN ADMIRAL'S WIFE

CHAPTER I

FINDING A HOME

It was on the 30th of August, 1903, that I became the wife of an Admiral. In other words, my husband relinquished the command of H.M.S. *Jupiter*, which he had held for eight months, and was promoted to flag-rank on that day.

I had been spending six cold and blustery weeks at Ambleteuse, a quiet little *plage* a few miles beyond Wimereux, and joined him at Torquay when the Home Fleet dispersed after manœuvres. He was far from being elated by his promotion, which was automatic, although the fact that he had become a rear-admiral at the age of fifty was due to two special promotions for war service and three years as commander of the Royal Yacht, *Victoria and Albert*. He had been thirteen years a captain, the average period in those days, but for an admiral he was young and had every prospect of being employed.

In his thirty-seven years of service he had not once been in a home squadron until appointed to the *Jupiter*, and cared but little for his first experience of the chilly waters and foggy atmosphere which surround these islands, but the actual moment of departure from a ship he liked and the exchanging of the captain's four narrow stripes for the rear-admiral's one wide and one narrow caused us both a pang of regret. We had had bad times as well as good in the thirteen years, but he knew he would never again experience the peculiarly keen delight which a captain, proud and happy in his command, enjoys—a delight shared to a considerable extent by his wife. If we could have one slice of our time together over again we should agree in encoring the years, 1896–1900, when he commanded successively the cruiser *Hawke* and the battleship *Illustrious* in the Mediterranean.

From 1893 to 1896 he had had the *Tourmaline* on the North American and West Indian stations, and plenty of good times did we both have out there, but the poor little ship could neither sail nor steam, and no sailor can love a " lame duck " with the devotion a mother lavishes upon a crippled child. Nelson always found his ship and his ship's company the best in the service, but I doubt if Nelson himself could have waxed enthusiastic over a ship actually struck off the fighting strength of the

Navy as inefficient when he assumed command of her.

Still, there is undoubtedly something in the position of any captain in the British Navy, no matter how insignificant his command, which differentiates it from all others. He is " under God " responsible for his ship and his men. She is a unit, contemptible perhaps in herself, but forming part of the greatest and best of navies, and as such is precious and beloved. No commander-in-chief can have quite the same feeling of intimate possession when in charge of ever so fine a fleet as that which animates and inspires a young lieutenant whose obsolescent torpedo-boat is the apple of his eye and the core of his heart. Even the midshipman of the dinghy will scheme and steal for his boat, so that she may be the smartest and most efficient of her humble class and justify his devotion by becoming agreeably notorious among her fellows. Since the Navy is very conservative in certain things this is probably the case still. It was so when my husband at thirteen and a half was sent for by his commander and told to " find " a brass yoke and rowlocks for his boat—the dinghy. He " found " them within a week and learnt that stealing for the good of the ship is no sin but a virtue—so long as the thief is undetected.

After bidding good-bye to the *Jupiter* we started off on a round of visits, and only settled down in our flat at Knightsbridge when autumn was well advanced. To us, who had been wanderers for so many years, London was still full of charm and crowded with surprises, and for the first few weeks we enjoyed life extremely. When winter set in my husband treated himself to a month's hunting with the Blackmore Vale, but I remained in town, and as the days grew shorter and the fogs thickened my affection for London cooled into a tepid liking punctuated by attacks of acute disgust. Then, as the freshness of my wallpapers and chintzes faded, I fell out of love with the flat which had seemed so pretty in the previous spring, and I never got used to finding smuts on my dressing-table when I rose in the morning, smuts on my nose when I came in from shopping and paying visits, and smuts in my white hair after driving home in a hansom from a play or dinner.

And yet I enjoyed the dinner-parties particularly, for at that season there is time and room for the entertaining of people neither rich nor great, but possessed of good spirits and a liking for good talk. Bridge had not yet superseded conversation, and we could accept the invitations of our friends in the confidence that we should not be expected to pay for our dinners afterwards, or draw down upon ourselves the contempt of adversaries and re-criminations of partners by our infamously bad play. It was pleasant, too, to feel that my very limited stock of dinner-gowns caused neither heart-burnings on my own part nor comment from my fellow guests, as they must in a limited circle where " hardy perennials " are unfavourably received.

FINDING A HOME

I am certain that neither Mr. Cope nor Mr. Sargent, nor Lord Morris nor Sir Alfred Lyall cared whether I wore black or white, and when I sat next one of these interesting and famous men I was equally regardless since I knew myself to be at any rate tidy and inoffensive.

I cannot now recollect any noteworthy speech made by one of them. They seemed to me to talk like ordinary people, only better, and Lord Morris had so whimsical a way with him and was so entirely free from the self-assertiveness of the *raconteur* that anything he said seemed to me to have a special charm. We were talking of the spread of teetotalism on one occasion, and he remarked, " Well, I don't doubt that teetotallers are very well-meaning people or that they have done a great deal of good, but I find them dull. Indeed, I can't, with the best will in the world, picture to meself a party of teetotallers *rollicking round the parish pump*."

Early in the new year of 1904 we both fled to purer air—my husband to Paris, where he established himself in a French family and worked hard at the language in which he had passed for interpreter fourteen years previously, and I to Switzerland.

At Easter we returned to the flat, but the spring was spoilt for us by bad news of our boy, a midshipman in the *Glory*. He had only been six weeks on the China station when he fell ill with enteric, and for ten black days we were almost without hope. But the skilful treatment of Surgeon Mowat,*

* Drowned in the transport *Royal Edward* in 1915.

supplemented by the unwearying care of Sisters MacPherson and Inness at the Naval Hospital at Hong Kong, pulled him through, and our relief and thankfulness were such as any parent of an only child, sick to death and half the world away, can appreciate.

I think it was during this time of suspense that we both felt the intolerableness of London as a home, and when the reports from Hong Kong passed from mere hope to reassurance, we decided to buy a house in the country if one could be found to suit our purse and perhaps fifty per cent. of our requirements. We made a fruitless excursion into Hampshire, but had the luck to hit upon the very thing in the *Country Life* we bought to read on our journey back from Brockenhurst. My husband went down next day to Winsley, liked the house, and fell in love with its surroundings. Together we visited it, and, finding ourselves in perfect agreement as to its desirability, its purchase was concluded without loss of time.

That our new home was in Wiltshire added enormously to its attractions in my husband's eyes, since there have been Poores in the county since Roger Poore became Bishop of Salisbury in 1102, and Herbert and Richard, who successively occupied the same position in 1194 and 1217, chose the site and planned the building of the cathedral which is the Mecca of the family.

Since Rushall was sold in 1830 by Sir Edward Poore (my husband's grandfather), there has been no family place in the county, and Cuffnells in the New Forest was sold by the next Sir Edward (my husband's father) in 1855. As a very small boy my husband had lived at Knighton, on Salisbury Plain, and later with his dowager-grandmother in the Cathedral Close ; and every inch of a Wiltshire down, every stone of Salisbury Cathedral, is dear to him.

Knighton was bought from my husband by the War Office in 1898, and then, of all the acres that had once belonged to the Poores, only about four hundred remained. The little old manor house at Durrington is still his property, but it is set in the midst of camps, and can hardly be classed as a desirable residence in the language of the most sanguine agent. We were not coming back to the original home of the Poores, but we had found a home, and it was in Wiltshire.

CHAPTER II

UNACCUSTOMED SURROUNDINGS

BEFORE we took possession of Winsley Corner (erstwhile Winsley Chase, a designation too high-sounding to accord with its modest acreage), my husband was whisked off to play his part in the Naval Manœuvres, in which, with the *Ramillies* for flagship, he commanded a small squadron. September 1st, 1904, found us the enraptured owners of the spot " beloved over all."

But a week earlier my husband had been offered the post of Rear-Admiral in the Mediterranean, where he was to relieve the late Admiral W. des V. Hamilton in November, so we had to bestir ourselves to get things in order before he reluctantly turned his back on Winsley and headed for Gibraltar. Meanwhile Roger had made a good convalescence and was appointed to the *Ariadne*, flagship on the North American and West Indian station. He and his father left England within a few days of one another, and I confess I found the possession of a permanent home but a poor compensation for being bereft of both my menfolk. Still we had had two delightful months, and, although the uncertainty as to when I should " join up " once more with my husband was not a little depressing, I was left with plenty of occupation for the winter.

Winsley Corner is twenty-five miles from Salisbury itself, but we can look eastward across the downs on a fine day as far as the Plain, and to the south we have the long woods of north-east Somerset, from Clay Hill to King Alfred's Tower, for background, while the steep slopes of Westwood and Freshford, well-clothed in beech and yew, occupy the middle distance. Four hundred feet below us the silver curves of both river and canal mark the bottom of the hill that drops with precipitous haste from our very doorstep.

A big clump of beech and birch, walnut and fir—
too wild for a grove, too small for a wood—some
fifty yards below the house-front casts a welcome
shade on lawn and garden, and breaks our landscape
into two pictures. It breaks also the force of those
violent gales which tear across from the Bristol
Channel eighteen miles away, but there are equinoc-
tial periods when the opening of the front door lets
in such a blast as (to borrow the phrase of our
predecessor) " blows the parlourmaid backwards up
the front stairs." Yet the trees and shrubs and
flowers bear these buffetings bravely, and seem
indeed to grow all the stronger in our deplorably
poor soil, as though fresh air were more essential to
their well-being than the " rich loam " so dear to
gardeners.

We soon found out that it was sheer waste of
time, labour and temper, to try to grow anything
which did not enjoy these conditions, and though
the greedier of hardy perennials and hybrid-
perpetual roses are unsatisfactory with us, we have
in April and May the loveliest of gardens, where
masses of rock-plants invade the paths, huge poppies
wave their scarlet and blood-red flags, tulips flourish
in grass and border, and flowering shrubs other than
peat-lovers show more blossom than leaf. After
midsummer only the unfailing good nature of
begonias and geraniums and the lavishness of
rambling roses redeem the garden itself from shabbi-
ness, but its setting is always delightful. Even in
the blackest months of winter drifts of fallen

beech leaves make warm patches for the eye, weary of gaunt tree trunks and pallid fields, to rest upon. Through the naked boughs gleams the silver crescent of the canal, and steel-blue pools of Avon peep between the shock-heads of pollarded willow that fringe their banks.

The house itself is just what we want, for it contains a reasonable number of good-sized rooms catching every ray of sunshine afforded by our capricious climate, and out of forty acres the ten we keep in our own hands give us enough amusement, anxiety and occupation for every day of the year.

To us, homeless for the first nineteen years of our married life, the pleasure of owning a house and garden, some trees and a few fields, has been very great. To unpack everything for once; to collect and store our books; to improve, or add by degrees, fixtures and fittings, and even build a few more rooms; to replace, arrange and re-arrange furniture and hang all our pictures *at last*—all these doings, quite commonplace in themselves, appear of immense importance to people previously homeless. The choice of paint and paper, carpets and curtains, is a serious matter when one is decorating, or making habitable, one's very own house, and the fact that Economy rears her ugly head on every possible occasion and Patience is an oft-needed virtue only serves to make the slow realisation of the ideal home more enthralling. Naturally hasty, I feel sure wealth would have been disastrous to me, for I should have bought a thousand things that took my fancy, only to find I did not care for them twenty-four hours.later. It is astonishing what a safeguard a small income can be.

Behind our house, close but not encroaching, lies the dignified little village of Winsley. Its solid stone houses and cottages are enlivened with strips and patches of gay garden, and close around it cluster the comfortable homes of our few neighbours, homes not large enough to be called " places." It is a stone country, and but for the green of pasture and foliage and the russet warmth of lichened tiles, stone would be depressingly predominant.

If you were to ask a child in our neighbourhood to imagine a country without stone you would be expecting too much of him. Born of a race of masons and quarrymen, brought up in a stone house, trotting along the lanes to school between " dry " (*i.e.*, innocent of mortar) stone walls, and with a disused quarry for a playground, such a child would find it next to impossible to picture the flat and monotonous fertility of Holland.

A stone country such as this has a gracious loveliness quite unlike the austere beauty of a granite-ribbed mountain side. Ours is a softish stone after all, an imperfectly petrified clay called by some " bastard freestone," and our climate is mild enough to favour the natural growth of acacias and sycamores, beech and fir. The dripping mists of our deep valleys help to clothe roofs and walls with orange, white, and grey lichens and mosses of the pin-cushiony type, golden, green, and brown.

Stone-crop in the season paints each wall-top yellow; the small lilac toad-flax hangs wherever it can find roothold; wine-red ivy, five-pointed and veined with vivid green, pushes between the stones and clasps them in the close grip of knotty-dust-brown fingers; and tiny harebells and gay rock roses deck the coarse tufts of wayside grass below.

The older houses are covered with stone " tiles " (of all roofings the most picturesque in its irregularity and varied weather-staining), and almost all have the flat-topped porch formed of a slab of stone with scroll-shaped supports on either side. Rough " rockery-stones," as our people call them, are often piled on the porch-top with a little soil between them, and here house-leeks nestle and " snow in summer " is encouraged to spread its tufted carpet to the sun. A narrow path of broken flagstones, with pipings of bright green moss delicately out-lining the seams of its grey patchwork, leads from door to gate.

Red brick when it is old is beautiful, but it takes long to fade to the ideal ruddy hue, and there is a certain vulgarity in new red brick of which the very newest stone cannot be accused. As a background for a cottage garden of mixed flowers brick cannot compare with stone, which even gains forgiveness for certain painful shades of what seedsmen call *amaranth,* but women who know stigmatise as *magenta*; and magenta against red brick makes the teeth ache—the teeth of intelligent women.

There is little to admire in a stone-quarry when

it is being worked.   Blocks of stone, heaps of earth, cranes, tools, and toiling men are hardly picturesque ; but there is beauty in the band of tired quarrymen trooping homeward with the setting sun on their powdery faces and shabby stone-dyed garments, looking as though they were " done in pastel," and with even the familiar handkerchief of gaudy red subdued to a dull rose-madder.   And how can one speak adequately of the charm of a long-abandoned quarry?   It is the rock-garden of a god, a rough amphitheatre of shelves and ledges, and pits and crannies, sown by the birds or the winds, watered by the rain, and, let us hope, visited only by people who love it and take light toll of its ferns and flowers.   There are tall ash trees and sturdy hollies growing in the clefts, and trails of ivy dangle and sway like long rope-ladders twenty feet and more over its jagged edges.   Groups of green hart's-tongue star its shadiest slope, and underfoot there is a tangle of wild thyme and mint, ground ivy, speedwell, pansy, yellow toad-flax, wild geranium, and, best and earliest of all, sweet violets, purple and white. But the plant of all others which triumphs in an old quarry is the common clematis—" traveller's joy," or " old man's beard," as you please.   Here no one disturbs it, and it performs prodigies of gymnastics, flinging itself from tree to tree like a long-tailed monkey in the primeval jungle.   In early winter the quarry is frothing with its silvery tufts ; but it is not only in our quarries.   It surges over the tops of stone walls ; it pours its foaming cascades over steep grassy banks; it drapes sere hedgerows and garlands naked boughs; it swathes whole families of stunted and shivering trees in a drooping quilt of pale grey swansdown. Lovely is it in the tender green of May; lovely, too, in the white blossom of July and August; but lovelier far in the dying year, when every leaf is gone and puffs of feathered smoke poised above its dull brown stalks of tough and twisted cord alone remain.

One learns a new word now and then from the workers in stone. A " cock-up " is one of the stones set up on end to crown a wall, and a " coign " is, of course, a corner-stone. Once in a while a mason possessed of more imagination than his fellows rises to carving vases, sun-dials, or garden-seats. I have seen lions, too, strange, smiling beasts with long slender limbs, and tongues and manes painted red, which surprise the passer-by by peeping at him from a shrubbery; and surmounting the porch of the small square-faced house behind them there is a little grey mannikin in a cocked hat, obviously intended for Napoleon. There is a legend that a former owner of that house sent " Napoleon " into the nearest market-town in his donkey-cart the morning after a prolonged carouse. What Napoleon ? one asks, and why did he sit up all night drinking in our village inn ? No satisfactory answer is here forthcoming.

An attempt was made not long ago to establish a school of stone-carving in a neighbouring village, but the number of pupils dwindled instead of increasing, and now there is nothing left to commemorate the failure of a praiseworthy effort save a large vase, cleverly carved, which decorates the hall of the nearest technical school.

Granite and Bath-stone are not more unlike than the strenuous North-Countryman and his easy-going brother of the South ; but since nothing short of a permanent fall of twenty degrees in the average temperature could avail to toughen the fibre and stimulate the ambition of the Southern, one must needs accept him as he is—and he is a pleasant enough fellow, after all—along with the charm of the country which produces him.

CHAPTER III

TAKING ROOT

IT was odd to find ourselves forming part of a strictly civilian community with interests centred in the solid earth, and entirely unacquainted with our life and our associations, and I very soon cured myself of speaking of naval people and naval affairs, which were as foreign, and as unintelligible, to my neighbours as their environment and mode of life appeared at first to me. Being in a minority of one during my first winter at Winsley, it was very obviously my place to learn, but when the squadron under my husband's command was transferred to the Channel in 1905, he conceived and carried out a plan for giving about a dozen of our neighbours a glimpse of a life to which they were complete strangers.

The carpenter, his wife, sons and daughter-in-law, the stonemason's family of similar composition, and the blacksmith and his wife took advantage of an excursion to Weymouth and were my husband's guests at lunch on board the *Albemarle*. The visit went off with perfect success and gave my husband quite as much pleasure as those whom he entertained, and the account I received of it a couple of days later from one of the party was extremely funny. Everything he had seen and heard was bewilderingly new and strange, and his vocabulary did not comprise words in which to describe his experiences. It seems that when the visitors were going round the ship my friend got rather tired of climbing ladders (perhaps because a lifelong familiarity with ladders had caused them to pall upon him), and sat himself down in some part of the ship which from his explanation I was quite unable to locate. A young bluejacket inquired what brought him there, and on finding he " belonged to the Admiral's party," made the, I fear, quite apocryphal statement that all the men under the Admiral's command " loved him as a mother loves *his* child ! "

The ladies of the party were presented with cap-ribbons before they left the ship, and wore them when they landed at Weymouth, eliciting much delectable chaff from bluejackets on the esplanade.

I do not know whether their visit left a lasting impression on the minds of our friends, but, not long after, a farmer's son told me he would like to join the Navy, and in a flutter of importance I procured all the necessary information. After consideration the boy said he thought he would sooner be a Blue Marine, and went to Bristol with a view to enlisting, but a badly knitted collar-bone disqualified him for this service and he forthwith joined the R.A.M.C. ! Even this turned out badly, for he disliked his preliminary training so cordially that he was bought out without loss of time.   So ended my efforts as a recruiting agent for the Navy.

I went very seldom to Weymouth when my husband was there and saw but little of the *Albemarle* in consequence, but he was able to come over to Winsley for forty-eight hours now and then, and found it very good to have a real home to go to.

During the visit of a French squadron to Portsmouth I spent a few days there and was present at a great ball given at the Naval Barracks in honour of the *Entente*. It was good to be once more in touch with naval people, and I was glad when some of the Albemarles asked me to dine with them at a hotel and go with their party, as my husband was officially engaged elsewhere. A certain admiral had been told off to take me in to supper, but finding another admiral's wife much to his taste evaded his responsibilities and left me in the lurch, whence my husband ultimately rescued me, so that I did not depart unfed. He had to get away early, and if the calling of carriages had worked according to the beautiful and elaborate system formulated I should not have suffered by his loss. As it fell out it did not work at all, and, but for the humanity of a military stranger of great, but unknown, importance who despatched a fleet-footed orderly to find me a hansom, I might have remained standing on the pavement till daylight. But the ball was well worth a little inconvenience, for I met numbers of old friends, and the procession of royalties and grandees, both British and foreign, among whom none was fairer than the future Queen of Spain— then Princess Ena of Battenberg—was both interesting and amusing.

Next day we went to some international naval sports outside Portsmouth, where the meeting of old friends was of greater moment than the display itself, and when they were over we had the good luck to find an empty waggonette in which to return to the town, and the still better luck to pick up Sir Arthur Wilson—my husband's commander-in-chief —and his flag-captain, who were, for want of a conveyance of any sort, making their way home through a noisy crowd on foot in all the glory of uniform and decorations. Roger, whose ship was also at Spithead, had spent his afternoon in visiting French ships and eliciting by means of rudimentary and ungrammatical questions information which he was quite unable to comprehend. But he felt that, though a mere midshipman, he, too, had done something to further the " intended cordiality "—as the men called it—an " intention " which has now crystallised into solid friendship.

My husband's appointment was only held for a year, and in November, 1905, he was a free man, so far as any sailor can consider himself free while he is on the Active-list. He was made a J.P. for Wilts and a Poor Law Guardian, but, though conscientious in the discharge of his duties, they were not so heavy but that he could devote about seventy hours per week to the improvement and beautification of his still new home. For me the summer days were never long enough to hold the pleasing tasks I set myself, but the dark winter evenings were something of a trial then and are so still.

Country dwellers owning well-disciplined minds may accept the coming of the lamps on a winter's afternoon as marking the beginning of a period of unavoidable imprisonment within doors that will last till the following morning ; but it is not so with me, and when tea is over the longing to be out again draws me from the fireside, and, whatever the weather, I take the road. The darkening world that calls me offers no welcome as I step forth into the dusk. The group of beeches on the lawn, so friendly by day, stands stiff and black against a dull sky ; the distant downs have melted into a dim horizon ; only the lights on the far side of the valley twinkle a faint greeting across the misty blanket lying close down upon the water-meadows. A beam of ruddy light from the kitchen casement projects itself as far as the garden gate. Beyond that there is the narrow lane overhung with beech and sycamore, carpeted with muddy, trodden leaves, and leading on the one hand to nowhere in particular, on the other to the village and the plain. I seldom take the former direction after sundown, for the steep field-path is lonesome and the walled cart-track thickly hung with hoary brambles that claw one as one passes.

It is something far stronger than my cowardice that sends me out on these dreary evenings, since for me almost every route is beset with little terrors. First comes the mouth of a narrow footpath, high-walled, set at right angles to the lane and finished with a tall V-shaped stile. No one has ever pounced out upon me at this spot, but it is an ideal pouncing place, and I never pass it without a tremor. Where the lane curves towards the village I meet one or two people. If I can see who they are I greet them by name ; if not, I give them good-night all the same, for in these parts those who pass without speech after nightfall are held to be bent on no good. The light pouring from the forge doorway makes a wide splash of red on the road, and the smith is busy shoeing a great horse from the timber-waggon drawn up hard by before the " Seven Stars." The driver and his mate inside have left the dog in charge of team and timber, and the glow of the lantern hanging from the end of the longest log keeps passing carts at a safe distance from that huge battering-ram of ivy-wreathed fir. On I go past the silent school-house, along the yew-fringed churchyard wall, and, turning to the right, am soon outside the village and away on the road that winds across the plain. They say here that the ghost of a stranger once irretrievably lost in the maze of our serpentine lanes haunts them still. Driven to despair by their fantastic and meaningless loops and doublings and their frequent junctions with other lanes as wanting in objective as themselves, he lay down and perished in the snow.

The cows mercifully are all in bed and asleep by this time, and I tramp on securely for perhaps a mile without seeing a single bogey. Then a strange figure makes me pause. It walks, but it has queer drooping wings, and because I am ashamed to turn and run I face it until it materialises as old Grannie Smith carrying two pails of water suspended from a wooden yoke. She curtsies, pails and all, unhitches her buckets, and stands at ease. " Carr'ing water from the well, my lady," she explains. " 'Tis teejus work for a ol' body, but it do come easier like in the evenen—marnens my leg be crule bad. When I do get out o' bed of a col' marnen I caan't 'ardly move no sense. Blood don' sim to run, an' I do creak like a ol' door. 'Tis on'y pity for the poor beast as do force I to gi' the pig his meat." Then, as she prepares to get under way once more, she adds confidentially, " That there hearthrug you give I, my lady, I do on'y use he o' Sundays." " Oh, Grannie, how wrong of you ! And the flannel nightgowns, too ? " " Well, I be savin' of 'em up till Christmas. ' When the days they grows longer, the cold it grows stronger,' I've allus heerd say, so I be jes' savin' of 'em up. Good-night to ye, my lady." I look after the winged figure in helpless distress. She ought not to be carrying heavy pails of water—this lone and crippled woman—at the age of seventy-two, but if she did not keep going with incredible courage on what the State allows her she must exchange her poor home for the workhouse.

Deep in considerations affecting my new herbaceous border, a matter requiring nearly as much thought as the furnishing of a house, far more than the ordering of a trousseau, I reach the Bradford road and am on the point turning uphill towards the village, when three men, heading no doubt for the " Seven Stars," emerge from the gathering dusk within a few paces of me. They are shouting remarks of grave political import at one another as they straggle along—" a terrible and bloody revolution . . . never be downtrod no more . . . them useless Lords . . ." are among the phrases neither new nor attractive that reach my ear— and I hastily decide to go home by a roundabout field-path rather than share the high-road with rural Radicals, drunk or sober. Through a rusty kissing-gate I pass into a big square field, and have almost reached its farthest corner when out of the ever-darkening dusk loom the huge forms of Farmer Cleverly's three stout cart-horses. I dare not " shoo " the creature, nearly as big as a hippopotamus, which bars my passage to the stile. If I startle him he is sure to " galumph," a practice I fear and hate in loose horses. . . . Ah, now he moves on—the colossal roan—tearing at tufts of grass as he goes, and I, noiseless but with beating heart, glide swiftly behind his hairy heels and scramble with deep thankfulness over the welcome stile.

The black chasm yawning in the lane-wall hardly ranks as a terror after this encounter, and when I get back to my despised fireside I have what I should call an adventure to relate to my husband. He is unsympathetic, even slightly contemptuous about Farmer Cleverly's roan. " Why, those horses would never dream of touching you, even if you were to chase them." *I* chase them ! Heaven forbid !

CHAPTER IV

PAROCHIAL

LIFE at Winsley was as different from country life in the South of Ireland, to which for a considerable part of each year I had been accustomed before my marriage, as it well could be considering the slight disparity of latitude and longitude. The orderly ways, the sound and tidy cottages, the relegation of pigs and hens to yards and sties, and the Wiltshire accent and idiom made life at Winsley more like that described in the English story-books of my childhood than anything I had been used to at home. I missed the pretty speeches, the picturesque imagery and ingenious falsehood which made the Kerry peasant so interesting and attractive. No grateful beggar at Winsley called down ornate blessings on my head or prayed that " the Lard might lave the back-door of Heaven open " to me " at the lashte," and the description of the English beggar's ailments was franker, if less original. But on the other hand it was far easier to get a direct answer to a plain question ; open windows were the rule rather than the result of accidental breakage, and I found the clean faces and pinafores and well-brushed hair of the Winsley children more to my taste than the shaggy manes and shapeless turf-smoked rags of the gossoons and girleens of Ballybog. And yet I loved the bare feet of the Kerry children —feet on which they pattered so lightly over rough bohireen or tussocky bog ; I missed the great hooded cloaks of the older women, the little head-shawls worn by the girls, the tumbled, tawny locks that go with hazel eyes, and the blue-black tresses with the black-lashed blue.

The unexpected rarely happens, or so it seems to me, in a quiet country neighbourhood in England, but it is the rule in Ireland. You invite a man to spend a week-end, and he remains thirteen years ; you go out to buy a packet of postcards and return with a couple of bloodhounds on a string. Where in England can you find a squireen who turns his farm-servants into footmen in scarlet liveries and directs one of them to say grace before meat in the words, " For what Mr. L. A. is about to receive may the Lord make Mr. L. A. truly thankful " ? Nor do our English coroners pronounce such a verdict as " By the visitation of God under suspicious circumstances." But then we do not in England have members of two hostile factions returning wildly drunk and combative from the market-town, with murder, of which not one of the party is either willing or competent to give evidence, done on the way.

Such people simply do not exist over here outside a lunatic asylum ; in Ireland they are not only tolerated but as philosophically accepted as the scent of turf-smoke in the shirts home from the wash or the erratic behaviour of trains on small local lines when guard and engine-driver agree to stop and pick mushrooms, confident of the passengers' approval or, at least, consent.

But to set against the charm of the unexpected and the comedy it almost invariably provides, there are the trials brought about by the happy-go-lucky conduct of domestic affairs in my native land— entertaining to read of, but in actual and protracted experience painful, and even revolting, to the impatient or pernickety.

One cannot " have it both ways " ; and now, though I read every one of the Ross-Somerville books twice a year to keep myself Irish, I am content to dwell in England and conform to the orderly ways which have become dear and even essential.

After a while I found myself almost insensibly, or, perhaps I should say, unintentionally, launched on the tide of local " good works." The newly-established Parish Nursing Association took me for its first president ; and the Churchyard Improvement Society wanted a secretary. Later on I became secretary to the Women's Branch of the Bradford-on-Avon Tariff Reform Association, but my faith in the efficacy of Tariff Reform was rudely shaken by the experience I gained in Australia, and I could not conscientiously identify myself with it on my return.

The Churchyard Improvement Society, which started brilliantly, barely survived my departure owing to friction for which my successor was, happily, not responsible, but the Nursing Association has thriven and completely justifies its existence, and our nurse now lives in a nice little house of her own and is no longer, as heretofore, a lodger subsisting precariously on the goodwill and varying cookery of successive landladies.

Of all the introductions due to modern philanthropy the district, parish, or village nurse seems to me the most valuable.

The village nurse of fiction is a lady mysteriously bereft of helpful relations or friends, and driven by an unhappy love affair to disguise, or rather enhance, her remarkable personal charms by adopting the plain gown, close bonnet, and large white apron proper to the *rôle* she has assumed. She speedily becomes involved in a second love affair, even more embarrassing than the first. Spiteful tongues are busy with her name, unsympathetic district visitors hound her down, but, adored by the poor of the parish and seriously courted by a millionaire, she triumphs over every difficulty, marries the more desirable of the two suitors, and shames the district visitors and other narrow-minded persons by her patience and courage in adversity and her modest yet dignified bearing in prosperity.

None of our nurses, and we have had several since the first came to this village eleven years ago, has been at all like the nurse of fiction. They have been for the most part hard-working, capable women, suited for the position—no easy one—they have filled. A village nurse may have to pass the night in a house where dirt is as one of the plagues of Egypt — active, all-pervading, sparing none ; or she may have to listen to the language and endure the company in such a house of the prize bully and drunkard of the village for hours together ; or she may get neither food nor drink during a long night vigil which her sensibilities will permit of her tasting. It is better that she should not be of too fine a fibre. An exquisite refinement, a vivid imagination, an overflowing sympathy, will not wear well. Our nurses have been put to it now and then to get adequate rest and food (the printed rules of the committee notwithstanding) ; and a tough and hardy constitution, a stout heart and well-balanced nerves are their useful and obedient servants on such occasions. A sense of humour, which, unfortunately, is born and not acquired, will prove a priceless adjunct to the village nurse's equipment. Nurses such as ours can feel at ease in the poorest cottage, understand the prosaic point of view of the day labourer and his wife, tolerate their unequivocal language and make the best of actual squalor. They must be unafraid of cows and the dark, used to rustic ways, simple-minded, unimaginative, slow to speak, and discouragers of gossip. Our nurse is a Church-woman, but she is not " churchy," and the most hostile Nonconformist among her patients has to admit that she is a good Christian.

It is not easy to convince the rural population of the necessity for a village nurse, and some people who ought to know better tell you that her presence and practice in our midst must limit or imperil the exercise of neighbourly offices among the poor. But it is true that since nurses came to Winsley infants and young children are more scientifically and more satisfactorily started in life, and fresh air—the bugbear of previous generations of cottagers —is freely introduced into the bedrooms of the sick. Newly-sprained ankles are not now put under the pump, nor old cobwebs from the cowshed applied to gaping cuts. A patient whose case is graver than he suspects is counselled to see the doctor, and nervous people, who would send for the doctor on some trifling pretext, are cured out of hand by the rest or dieting advised by the village nurse. But the kindly neighbour is as welcome as ever when she comes in to tidy up a bit, or to get the children off to school betimes in the morning.

The collection of subscriptions towards the maintenance of a nurse in a large and straggling parish is no light matter. Until every one has been convinced by personal experience of the benefit to himself or his family of her skilled services his purse-strings are not likely to be untied. But it is pleasant to watch the gradual awakening of the rustic mind to the need of supporting this servant of the public. " I'd sooner never taste another bit of meat all my days than not to pay toward her sal'ry," says one poor woman. Old Mrs. E. is another appreciative subscriber. When her neighbour Mrs. F. was at death's door, and had no one more experienced than her twelve-year-old daughter to attend to her, the old lady made shift to climb the steep stair and adjure the sick woman to send for nurse. " Do 'ee 'ave 'er, my dear, do 'ee now, Mrs. F. She's not a ladybody. She come to see I when I were that bad with the rheumatics I couldn't neither sit nor lie. Rubbed me, she did, an' got me into bed that comfor'able! She's a good 'ooman, I tell 'ee." And Mrs. F., hovering on the threshold of a world where nurses are not needed in a professional capacity, gave a languid assent. Ten days later I heard from her own lips how tenderly she had been moved, and washed, and comforted, and fed by the strong, kind woman sent to her help. " There ! I felt diff'rent the very moment she come nigh me." And always once, sometimes twice, a day during the critical period, in rain or snow, fresh or tired, came nurse to the distant hamlet where Mrs. F. lived—and still lives to sing her rescuer's praises.

The doctors like nurse. They recognise in her a valuable ally and regard her as a person to be depended on. She is not always busy. Sometimes in the summer months work is slack with her, and she looks depressed until a man falls off the top of a hayrick and gives her an interesting " case " to attend to. We were remonstrated with on having a nurse at all in our parish of five hundred inhabitants. " There are only two in Bradford " (our market-town), " with a population of five thousand," said our critics. " Then we should by rights have only one-fifth of a nurse—which is impossible," was our obvious rejoinder. With the village itself and no fewer than six outlying hamlets to serve, the poor fraction would have a hard task. Ours is not a rich parish, and desperate efforts have to be made by the committee to raise funds out of which to pay the nurse. Each summer we have a village fête, where flying-boats and cocoanut-shies, Aunt Sally, skittles, quoits, athletic sports, a tea-tent, and competitions of various sorts bring in a surprising harvest in copper and small silver. The village rises to the occasion. Nearly all the food is given by the farmers' and tradesmen's wives, the field is lent by a kindly Nonconformist, Church-folk and Wesleyans treat one another to Aunt Sally shies at four a penny, and in the evening, by the light of Chinese lanterns, there is dancing on the trampled grass. Village lass and village swain perform a high-stepping polka, and when men are scarce girls will dance with one another. Nurse is the heroine of the hour. She flies in boats with a grave Poor-Law guardian, plays skittles with the vicar's churchwarden, and in the dance her hand is sought by many. After Easter there is the annual rummage sale, where fabulous bargains are to be had and all our old gowns and hats are displayed. Nurse herself is a stallholder. Everything, from a collar to a perambulator, finds a purchaser, and miracles of adaptation and renovation are performed on the cast-off goods of the " gentry " by their new owners. Meeting one's own last summer's hat upon an unknown head causes one a sensation incomparable with any other.

There is no doubt that nurse exercises a wholesomely civilising influence in the district. She teaches the rudiments of hygiene in a series of unimposing object-lessons in the houses of her patients. The right feeding of the baby lays the foundation of health in the man, and simple cookery for invalids practised at the least modern of kitchen-ranges—the open hearth—brings the cottage wife or maid to see the error of her culinary ways. And it is not only the humbler dwellers in the parish who benefit. When a chance visitor met with a serious accident to his eye, who but nurse came to the rescue ? And when the doctor arrived there was *nothing to undo*. For all who live more than two miles from a doctor the village nurse is not merely a comfort : she s a necessary.

CHAPTER V

" NOTHING TO LIVE FOR "

As entirely voluntary work I had taken upon myself the visiting of the old men in the Bradford-on-Avon workhouse infirmary. The old women had their sewing and knitting to occupy them, and an apparently limitless stock of grievances and gossip, besides the visits of ladies interested in their welfare, but the old men, unvisited, sat listlessly round the fire through the dull winter days, and in summer crept up to the top of the steep, square kitchen-garden where they perched like shabby old birds on the long benches set so that the sunshine could warm their chilly blood and rheumatic joints. I grew quite fond of the poor derelicts who had drifted into this not uncomfortable haven. Some of them were fairly resigned to living by rule and eating what was put before them, but in others the passionate regret for their lost independence burnt like a consuming fire. Among these irreconcilables one George (pronounced Jah-urrge) interested me particularly. He would not occupy himself with rug-making which, on somewhat the same lines as the Brabazon scheme, I had introduced into the infirmary, and while the other old men were ready enough to spin yarns as they gathered with me near the fire, George sat apart moody and rebellious. Even when we were telling ghost stories he took no part beyond saying contemptuously that a good man wouldn't want to come down here again from his comfortable place in heaven, and a bad man in " the other place " would never be allowed the indulgence of a night out. He " couldn't say " as to women. One day George appeared at our back door and asked to see me. " If so be you could let I have a couple of shillun I'd take it very kind," he said, without beating about the bush. " I bain't covetcheous. 'Tis for my first wik's lodgen. There's a grocer to Bradford wants a erran' boy and he's willun to gi' I a trile ; but them people at the lodgen-house wants pay in advaance, an I've not a penny, no, nor a farden, in the world. Come out of the House this mornen', I did, an' while I bin there my darter-in-law (her I lived wi') bin an' sold off ivery stick in the plaäce an' away wi' her Lard knows wheer, an' six wiks rent owen."

I asked him if he was fit to go to work again.

" Fit as iver I'll be. A man don't git no stronger after seventy year, an' I'm in my seventy-five."

George had got very thin and did not nearly fill the suit of clothes which had been put away for him by the Matron while he had been in the infirmary. His stiff sandy beard and bushy eyebrows now showed far more white than red, and the huge freckles had faded from his face and hands. He got the two shillings, and sixpence over for baccy, thanked me briefly and took the Bradford road, leaving me wondering whether some better scheme for the old fellow's maintenance could not be devised. Old age pensions only materialised after his death ; he was without near relations and too "independent" to attract friends. He had desperately resented his removal to the infirmary where he had suffered and waited, not patiently, but in grim silence, till discharged by the doctor. Neither his wife's death long years before, nor the death of his only son was comparable as an event with his consignment to the workhouse, an hour of dire anguish followed by the disgrace of two months spent among paupers. "I niver done no harm to no-one," was his complaint ; "niver were in prisun nor took up by the p'lice. But I were allays poor."

It was six months before I heard news of George and then I found his name in the local paper in a paragraph headed "Attempted Suicide of a Bradford man." It was George ! On the hottest day of the year, a Sunday, "George S., aged seventy-five, had made a determined effort to drown himself in the Avon." A passer-by, "much to be commended for his promptitude," had hurried to the spot and fished the old man out. He was unconscious, but not dead, and was carried *to the workhouse infirmary !*

He recovered, and the magistrates would not send up the case to the Quarter Sessions, but " very kindly " committed him to the workhouse. It was kind, of course, but the irony of George's fate was peculiarly cruel. A year later he was still an " inmate," pottering about over little jobs of gardening, building and pig-feeding, and, for a while, convoying a small workhouse boy to school at Winsley every day. They were kind to him at the Union, but he was restless, suspicious, discontented, weary of life. I never spoke to him of his attempt to take his life. It seemed indecent to pry into his feelings, and his motive was obvious.

But there was a sequel to George's sad little story—a little bit of Indian summer before he drew down the curtain with his own hands and went to a world where the self-respecting poor find all they need. It was the Christmas Fund of the *Westminster Gazette* that gave George the brief period of sunshine, of liberty and paid work that followed the dreary spell of life without hope, fire without comfort and food without relish. How he worked ! How gallantly he struggled on through a cold and wet winter doing odd jobs as long as anyone would find them and pay him for them ! He lived where he could, but he was cross-grained and unaccommodating, and he often changed his lodgings.

We had been nearly a year in Australia when a Winsley friend who had been good to George sent me a cutting from a Wiltshire newspaper describing how he had *again* attempted to drown himself in the Avon, and *again* been rescued and sent to the workhouse !

" Let me go ; I've nothing to live for," he said, as he struggled with his rescuers. They could not let him go, but a week later Death released him.

CHAPTER VI

GO-FEVER

" Sick she is and harbour sick—
O sick to clear the land ! "
—KIPLING.

AT this time our means of locomotion other than our feet consisted in the services of one useful horse which drew a brougham, a victoria, or a dog-cart, as circumstances dictated, but the desperate hilliness of the surrounding country made our visiting radius a small one, and when we had been to lunch with friends near Frome, or ventured as far as Corsham in the afternoon, the horse had to stay in bed and rest all the next day. This is one of the penalties paid by poor people for living in the country, but we had no doubts as to the wisdom of our choice and never once sighed for the joys of London, since they were inseparable from those disadvantages which had influenced us in leaving it. There I used to feel like a tired, elderly butterfly, for poor people must use 'buses, tubes and trains, buy their clothes at crowded sales, and sit, at best, in the Upper Circle when they go to a play ; and unless one is a positive fixture, not only willing, but able, to be regularly and punctually useful in a settlement, or as a workhouse and hospital visitor, it is not easy for the unskilled philanthropist to practise philanthropy in London.   In the country one can more easily choose one's own times and objects, which, as one grows older, is a comfort, and one feels less of an atom and more of an item in one's manageable, if restricted, circuit.

At any rate, my life at Winsley was pretty well filled with little things and was gradually becoming a sort of small-patterned mosaic, inoffensive, inconspicuous and quite unexciting ; but when three years had passed I began to wonder when, and if, my husband would be again employed.   He had acted as Chief Umpire in the Naval Manœuvres of 1906, and brought out his report in record time with the help of as good a group of assistant-umpires as any Navy List could have furnished (Captains Henniker-Hughan and A. Everett ; Commanders Phillpotts and Thorp) ; but for the fifteen months that followed nothing had come his way, and I could not bear to think his career ended, though he was never at a loss for occupation ashore and, mercifully, neither fumed nor fretted in seclusion. I do not think that I was quite free from personal ambition.   I felt it would be pleasant to have the chance and the scope accorded by circumstances to the wife of a Commander-in-Chief, and I certainly did not wish to sit still at Winsley till I died.

Besides I loved the sea in spite of being a bad sailor, and every day the " go-fever " in my heart grew stronger. I was plucking at my anchor, so solidly imbedded in inland soil, pining to get out· again into the wide world and see new places where the sun shines by habit and not by accident. Salt-water, hot sunshine and sailors and sailors' wives offered a complete and intensely desirable contrast to the life I had been leading for three years, and the fact that I had never since the age of eight remained for so long a period together in the same country seemed to explain, if not to justify, my restlessness. Mrs. Noah must have been deeply thankful when the Ark grounded on the top of Mount Ararat, but if I had been in her place I should soon have regretted the impossibility of shoving off again.

PART II

AUSTRALASIA, 1908—1911

CHAPTER VII

My husband went alone to Portsmouth early in December, 1907, to see Roger, who was an acting sub. at the Navigation School, and talk over his prospects. The naval doctors had decided that the *migraine* headaches he suffered from would definitely incapacitate him from performing his duties at sea since they temporarily affected his sight. So at twenty-one he was to abandon the profession most dear to all of us and start life afresh. A friend of mine at Southsea had asked me to spend a few days with her so as to see something of the boy, and it so fell out that my husband's train and mine passed one another near Salisbury as we journeyed in different directions one Friday afternoon. But an official letter was awaiting him on the hall table at Winsley which was to make a great difference in our lives—a letter which bore Lord Tweedmouth's signature in the corner of the envelope—and I was beset with doubts and hopes as I travelled to Portsmouth. Next morning I received a telegram from home saying, " Important letter will reach you at midday," and, devoured by impatience and curiosity, I watched the clock till the postman arrived. The letter told me that my husband had been offered the Australian Station, and would have to leave England the following month if, after seeing me, he decided to accept the post. That day I lunched at Government House with General Sir Henry and Lady Settle in a most complicated frame of mind. I rejoiced to see them again, for we had not met since 1899—1900 in Malta, and I believe I talked quite coherently, even on the subject of the new Territorial system with Lord Winchester, who was my fellow-guest. But, although I never hesitated for an instant as to the desirability of going to Australia, the long voyage, the question of finding immediate and suitable employment for Roger, and half a dozen other problems, both domestic and financial, occupied the greater part of my brain that day, and as I was pledged to secrecy they had to remain pent up in that limited space till my return next morning to Winsley. Small wonder that on leaving Government House I made two bad shots before hitting upon the particular football ground where I was to meet Roger and see a match in which several of his friends were playing. But I finally drifted in through the right gate, and, seeing no Roger, hovered modestly outside the enclosure until he should perceive and claim me. My forlorn position appealed to an official, who invited me inside the barrier, and presently no less a person than the commander-in-chief himself, attracted, let me hope, by my unassuming demeanour, advanced to the rescue. That he was Sir Day Bosanquet I had not the least idea, but I was glad and thankful to be " taken notice of " by a handsome and dignified elderly gentleman until Roger at length appeared. I can remember nothing about the match in which he was, of course, absorbed, but I met a number of old friends and returned to Southsea on top of a tram with some of them in a joyous confusion of mind and spirit comparable only to that of a field-mouse which, after hibernating for the fullest possible period, has woken up in a well-stored granary crowded with entertaining mice and lighted by electricity. Once more the Navy claimed me, and I claimed the Navy. " We are of one blood, thou and I," is the unexpressed thought which possesses my mind whenever I see even a single bluejacket on leave in the depths of our inland county. " There is salt water mixed with the blood of sailors," Admiral Grenet, once Italian naval attaché in London, used to say ; and some sailors' wives have it also I am sure—if only a few drops.

Next day found me back at Winsley, and from that time until I started for Sydney on February 26th, 1908, my days were filled with business and my nights chiefly useful for recapitulating all I had to do and remember. Lieutenant F. C. Fisher was appointed flag-lieutenant to my husband, and before they sailed in January he and I had many a consultation about footmen's liveries, stamping of note-paper and all the details which had to be thought of and executed quickly and finally. When one is going to the Antipodes for three years it is almost like dying, for one's home, one's garden, one's prospective tenants and one's pensioners (down to the thrushes and robins) must be meticulously arranged for if one is to start on one's long journey free from anxiety as to all one leaves behind. And then there was Roger, who had decided to be a planter in Ceylon, and " shoved off " shortly before I did.

Before my husband left England, the Austral Club entertained us at dinner at the Ritz, where we met a number of Australians, all as friendly and helpful as could be. The late Lord Jersey—once Governor of New South Wales, and with Lady Jersey deservedly beloved and remembered in that State—took me in to dinner, and both he and Sir F. Buxton (once Governor of South Australia), told me much that was of interest then and of service later. In a letter I received shortly afterwards from Lord Jersey, he said :

" I hope you and the Admiral will have a great time. . . . You will find the Australians open-hearted and generous, devoted to those who carry out the naval duties of the Empire and desirous of making every visitor to their land happy and at home."

CHAPTER VIII

LONDON TO SYDNEY

I WAS really thankful to be off when the moment arrived, and clutching a bunch of lily of the valley and *duplicate* copies of Mr. Locke's latest novel—all farewell offerings—I stepped into the boat-train for Dover. The knowledge that all I best loved was ahead of me (like the proverbial carrot hung before an unwilling donkey's nose), enabled me to start in good heart upon what, of all things, inspires me with loathing—a long sea voyage.

There was a capital cabin for me on board the Orient liner *Omrah* at Marseilles, and a warm welcome from my maid, who had come alive, but not unscathed, through the Bay.

The only face I recognised among my fellow-passengers at tea-time was that of Mrs. X. (*en route* for Naples) whom I had known at Malta eight years before. She was a most entertaining companion and helped me through the afternoon hours of the following day when I lay tired out in my berth. Her taste for adventure had led her into strange countries and company long after the passage of years and a certain plumpness might have been expected to keep her anchored at home. She had well-cut features and short curly hair, generally surmounted by a " pork-pie " hat of velvet that matched in colour her rigidly tailor-made coat and skirt. A fancy waistcoat of manly cut and a stiff white collar and tie completed her turnout. The story goes that she was invited to the coronation of the present Czar at Moscow, but on her arrival at the Russian frontier the custom-house people, most unjustifiably considering the possession of no less than thirteen fancy waist-coats a suspicious circumstance, deprived her of all but three. The ensuing ceremonies were thus shorn of much of their splendour and the ten detained waistcoats were only restored to her when she quitted the country.

The voyage would have been like any other long illness but for the fact that we had on board a most attractive and entertaining theatrical company bound for Melbourne. Their charming singing and dancing, the pretty, unpainted faces of the ladies and the unaffected cheerfulness of the whole troupe made the long hours shorter. I had never before been brought into contact with " the profession," and this opportunity cleared my mind of a great deal of ignorant prejudice, leaving in its place a very warm appreciation of the generosity and in-telligence of its members.

One of the chorus ladies—a particularly graceful and rather reserved girl—was attacked one day on deck by a minister of I forget what puritanical denomination, who told her it grieved him to see her spend so much time on the process of manicure which she was carrying on most decorously at the back of a ladder one hot morning. " Of what use are those white hands and polished nails, my young friend ? " he asked. " Do they feed the hungry, and comfort the sorrowful, and make garments for the poor ? " " They feed the hungry four times every day on this voyage," replied Miss C., adding mischievously, " and several people have told me they are very comforting to hold." Of course she did *not* tell him that they performed miracles of fine needlework. I have to this day a specimen of her skill in the shape of an exquisitely-made *camisole* (*anglicé* petticoat-bodice) which she gave me at Sydney in the following spring.

Mr. Tom Pain, now so well known at the Halls, found me one day in the writing-room just at that awful moment " when breakfast is a memory and lunch still unsecured." We had never spoken to one another before and he began with the question, " Are you going to Melbourne ? " I said, No, I was going to Sydney. " Where are you putting up ? " " At Admiralty House." " Oh, is that a comfortable place to stop at ? " I said I hoped so. The *Sydney Bulletin* was so fond of this story that it appeared (with variations) no less than three times in its pages.

At Colombo I had a few hours to spend with my boy. We lunched together at Mount Lavinia, drove about in rickshaws and parted at sunset on the coaly deck of the *Omrah*. One " carrot " had been devoured all too quickly, and the poor donkey felt very forlorn with the weary ten days' run to Fremantle, and the dreaded passage of the Bight still to be won through before she could secure the second.

At Fremantle I had only time to find out how good Australian grapes are and how treacherous and inadequate are sea-legs when first ashore, and after a hot walk through the flat streets with the Acting Governor and his A.D.C. (both possessing very long and useful land-legs) I was almost glad to return to the ship.

As we rolled round Cape Leeuwin I longed to make a joke about the " Bight being worse than the barque," but, though I had time and seclusion in abundance for this mental exercise, I reached Port Adelaide without succeeding. There I was met by Captain Boddam-Whetham, the Governor's A.D.C., who convoyed me to Government House, and I was so glad to see Sir George and Lady le Hunte that I never curtseyed to His Excellency ! I think it was Lady le Hunte's fault for welcoming me so warmly that I forgot for the moment Sir George was the King's representative in South Australia. It is so nice to be welcomed by an old friend after spending several weeks among strangers, however friendly. That afternoon, just before my train left Adelaide for Melbourne, whither my theatrical friends were going by sea, a telegram was brought to me wishing me " good luck from the ' Hooks ' " (the play they were to open their tour with was " Miss Hook of Holland "), and I started on my journey feeling warm about the heart. About noon next day—our train being very late—I found my second " carrot " on the platform at Melbourne. He had not *promised* to meet me there, for he has always disliked making promises which may never get beyond the abortive stage of good intentions, so it was something of a surprise. Together we drove off to Federal Government House where I curtseyed accurately, and most willingly, to the Governor-General and Lady Northcote and had a peaceful hour's *tête-à-tête* with my husband before lunch. Lord Jersey had been good enough to write and ask Lord Northcote to befriend us, and from that day to the moment of their leaving Australia, some six months later, no one could have been more kind and helpful ; and the staff were equally so. As for Lady Northcote, no novice ever had a more admirable Mother Superior (in status, not age) than I found in her. Both she and the Governor-General were as just and wise as they were generous, and though I sometimes heard them criticised for keeping up too much state, I always maintained my view that a Viceroy must be *plus royal que le roi*. Kings and Queens can unbend when and where they choose ; a viceroy must play the kingly part on every occasion unless he obtains a special dispensation to relax ceremonial.

The following appreciation of Lord and Lady Northcote, which appeared in the *Morning Post* of May 3rd, 1910, will give some idea of what they did in and for Australia :—

RECOLLECTIONS OF AN ADMIRAL'S WIFE

AMBASSADORS OF EMPIRE.

THE WORK OF A GOVERNOR-GENERAL.

LORD AND LADY NORTHCOTE.

General principles are best illustrated by particular instances. The record of a model Ambassador of the Empire will show what a Governor-General can and should do. Such a model was Lord and Lady Northcote of Australia. (The grammar of that sentence is exceptional, but the fact can be expressed in no other way, for the work of the one cannot be separated from the work of the other.) They identified themselves completely with the political, the social, the industrial interests of Australia, and so combined a happy sympathy with a great ability in every public action, that in the Commonwealth they are cited in proof of the good qualities of the Mother Country ; in London they are appealed to confidently as witnesses to the good qualities of the Australian.

The chief secret of such a great success was the practical quality of their sympathy with Australian life. It was not merely a matter of speech-making and lip-service. It was not confined to the faithful performance of the diplomatic and administrative duties of office. It was a whole-hearted identification with all the national ambitions, industrial and commercial, as well as political, of the Commonwealth. Australia was just beginning on an ambitious scale to weave wool into tweeds when Lord Northcote arrived as Governor-General. Those tweeds were good without a doubt, but they were not " fashionable " ; they had to meet the prejudice that " home-made " meant homely. Lady Northcote made it public that she thought Australian tweeds quite good enough for anyone to wear ; she had dresses made of them and announced the fact ; sent Australian tweeds to friends in the home country. The result was a " boom " in Australian tweeds ; one factory doubled its output within a year, and started to build new premises. Others prospered in like measure. Discussing the increase in Australian manufactures a year ago with a merchant, he said to me, " Yes, of course, the increase in the tariff, but you mustn't forget the Northcotes. They were as good as a ten per cent. increase in the tariff." In various other industries Lord and Lady Northcote took the same interest. Australian gem-miners, Australian metal-workers, Australian book-binders and many other trades found a great stimulus in their custom and the example of that custom. Lord Northcote was always preaching from the platform, " There is nothing that you people here of the British stock cannot do." He and Lady Northcote were always giving practical effect to that view by confining their patronage to Australian crafts. . . .

A visitor to the London house of Lord and Lady Northcote to-day will see a hundred and one memorials of this practical interest in Australian welfare. The place has throughout an Australian atmosphere. There are Australian carpets, Australian pictures, specimens of Australian metal-work—this latter of excellent quality though in some branches it was never thought of as a possible Australian industry until Lady Northcote gave the stimulus. In conversation, too, there is constant reference to Australia. I know several citizens of England who are " discovering " Australia through this returned Governor-General and his wife. To have confirmed the people of Australia in a profound respect for the home country, to now being engaged in educating the people of Great Britain to a profound respect for Australia—that is true work of Empire building.—F.

Melbourne's farewell to the Governor-General and Lady Northcote was ample proof that their fine qualities and their good services to the Commonwealth were appreciated in Victoria ; from personal experience I can only speak of the scenes which marked their departure from Sydney.

The great Town Hall was crowded with Lady Northcote's women friends and admirers, *protégés*, and beneficiaries, when she came on the Lady Mayoress's invitation to take public leave of them. Music, which she had helped and encouraged in a hundred ways, was not wanting, and flowers were everywhere. They were careful to give her as a souvenir something that should unite in its small compass an example of the arts, the crafts and the products of the country to which she had been a far-seeing and hard-working friend. A slender vase of Australian gold, beautiful in design and workmanship, was presented to her, and, brave and collected as she invariably was, her words of thanks that day were spoken with difficulty. Standing close behind her, I felt such a wave of sympathy and admiration pass over me that I grew hot and cold by turns.

Next day at the railway station a crowd of men and women of all conditions of life assembled to see the departure of the Governor-General and Lady Northcote, and we, of course, were there. But the cordial good wishes, the handshakings and adieux of their social and official friends could not compare as a tribute to their generous and painstaking kindness with the grief of a woman of the people who, with a small plush-clad child on either side of her, stood on the platform drowned in tears. I do not know what unpublished deed of helpfulness had made her constitute herself Chief Mourner, but I am sure the few whispered words and the friendly hand-clasp of the Governor-General's wife were what the humble admirer craved for.

We sometimes felt that the solemnities and dignities of his official position were little to Lord Northcote's taste, and that he was happiest when touring in the farthest reaches of the known, and peering into the untamed but reclaimable recesses of the Never Never Land. Any form of self-advertisement was utterly foreign to him, and the limelight tired his eyes. Only his conscientious devotion to duty combined with a deep and never-failing interest in Australia can have carried him through the years of his service to the Empire—a service in which his wife, with her almost masculine grasp of each situation as it arose, shared to an unusual degree.

I have spoken elsewhere of the power for good which a Governor's wife like Lady Rawson can exercise. The wife of a Governor-General possesses even more of this power, and when State-Governors or Governors-General unite with their wives in setting such an example as places them in the same distinguished category as the King and Queen they serve, their influence is far-reaching and enduring. It is not enough to make clever speeches, although a ready tongue is of great importance ; they must be examples of clean living, they must have a high standard of duty, honour and unselfishness, courtesy and usefulness, upholding all that is just and fine and seemly and discouraging vulgarity, folly and excess in any form. They should remember that there are numbers of people in each State or Dominion who hear and see and comment on almost all they themselves say or do—people who may never have the chance of going home, and will regard the King's representative and his wife as chosen specimens of the best England can produce, the fine flower of English character and deportment. When these accredited representatives fall short, dissatisfaction, and even disgust, is felt by the sound and loyal, who are alienated by their failure. That is quite bad enough, but even greater harm is done by the setting of a low standard before the young and unformed, or the " self-made," who would quite naturally have profited by the presence and practices of the best, yet accept the bad or indifferent as some people accept and adopt the current fashion in dress, however ugly. The selection of a Staff who will fitly support their Chief and maintain the standard set by himself and his wife is of the utmost importance.

Lord Northcote was fortunate in having for his private secretary Fleet Paymaster H. H. Share, R.N., now on Admiral Sir John Jellicoe's staff. He always accompanied the Governor-General on his more distant expeditions, and at all times and in all situations connected with his responsible position Mr. Share's *rôle* was so filled that it did not admit the possibility of an understudy.

With every conceivable precaution, as I thought, I once caused a typewritten copy of some verses, anonymously addressed by myself to Mr. Share, to be placed upon his office writing-table at Government House, Sydney, so that they might force themselves upon his notice when he sat down to tackle the correspondence of the day. My accomplice, Captain Stevens, A.D.C., did not play the game, for he disclosed their parentage, and from their subject I presently received a rhymed acknowledgment too complimentary to reproduce. My verses (which contain no exaggerations), will be found in the chapter devoted to such trifles.

CHAPTER IX

FIRST IMPRESSIONS OF SYDNEY

I RESUMED my journey to Sydney the same afternoon, and saw by moonlight for the first time the pallid, ghost-like stumps of gum-trees, ring-barked and dead, on either side of the railway line. My maid took them for tombstones until their number made such a theory untenable ; for there were miles of them. They are to my mind one of the most depressing evidences of civilisation. Past suburban stations with Scotch and English names which confuse the newcomer by their strange juxtaposition we ran through the early hours of a sunshiny morning into Sydney. There my old friends, Captain and Mrs. C. L. Napier met and welcomed me, and together we crossed the narrow strait separating Sydney proper from North Sydney and landed at the bottom of the garden of Admiralty House.

As we walked up the steep path we met a big black and white " willy wagtail," my first bird-friend in a garden full of birds. He was a delightful personage who flirted his tail and piped "Sweet pretty creature " from the far side of a bed of scarlet salvia, and my cup overflowed. It was the 1st of April ; and All Fools' Day, as I found it in 1908, is marked in my life's calendar in large clear red letters.

When we had made a tour of the house Mrs. Napier left me, and I enjoyed the almost forgotten luxury of a very deep, very hot, bath of *fresh* water. Even then I did not feel quite clean, but was able to look forward hopefully to becoming so before long.

It was five days before the flagship came into harbour, so I had time to learn the names of the footmen (luxuries who had hitherto been strangers within my modest gates) and to lose my awe of the *chef* whom we had inherited from our predecessors— a piece of good luck for which I can never be too thankful—before the house filled up. On the

Sunday following the arrival of the *Powerful* no less than fifteen naval officers called upon me about tea-time, and, much as I enjoyed being fully restored to the social atmosphere from which I had been almost completely exiled for five years, I admit I was somewhat bewildered, and shall ever remember with gratitude the kindness of Mr. Fanshawe, who helped me to pour out tea and to affix the right names to my guests—every one of them strangers. But to this day I call Mr. Locke " Mr. Bolt," when I meet him ! And all the time I had at the back of my mind the story of a certain Admiral's wife at Greenwich upon whom thirteen subs. called simultaneously one Sunday. She was not a conversationalist at the best of times, but in describing the situation to a friend soon afterwards she said, " I gave them all tea, and then, *as I had nothing to say, I said nothing.*"

Our first appearance in public was made on Easter Eve at the great Autumn Agricultural Show. My husband lunched with the president and committee at the show ground, and Lady Northcote very thoughtfully asked me to Government House so that I should go with her party. The show itself was excellent and the exhibitions of horsemanship (and horsewomanship) thrilling. No wise man finding himself for the first time in Australia will call himself a horseman until he has seen what the bushman can do.

But even more interesting to me than the show itself were the spectators. The smart gowns and pretty faces of the women, the lean, bronzed men from " out-back," the gay crowd generally—all were worth looking at, especially by such an ignorant stranger as I felt myself to be. If I had had the least notion of the burning interest taken in the new Commander-in-Chief's wife I should have been unbearably nervous, but in spite of some hints I was far from being fully alive to my new importance, and when I had been presented to that fine old sailor, Admiral Sir Harry Rawson (then Governor of New South Wales), who had already welcomed me by letter, I entered the arena feeling pretty comfortable and quite unconscious that no detail of my personal appearance, my unpretentious white garments and doubtfully successful hat would escape the sharp-eyed ladies of the Press.

But they were generous to a fault, and indeed from that day till the moment when I bade good-bye to Australia nearly three years later, the Press was far kinder to me than I deserved. One paper only, so far as I know, was thoroughly nasty. It was called *The People*, and I never saw but one copy of it, and that was sent me by the Editor. After reading what it had to say in my dispraise I felt as I do when by mistake I take up a hair-brush instead of my hand-glass and look into it. Then for one hateful moment I wonder whether I have suddenly turned into a hedgehog, or at best a " bearded lady." Even the *Sydney Bulletin*, whose bitter cleverness I had been taught to dread before I set foot in Australia, gave me no such shock ; indeed, it went so far as to say that I looked like a seagull at the first Government House Ball I attended—a compliment which gratified me extremely.

Those first weeks in Sydney were full to overflowing. The Randwick Autumn Races and three big balls all took place in Easter-week, and I made some dreadful blunders by speaking to people to whom I had not been introduced and calling others by names that were not theirs. But I did try very hard to cultivate a memory for both names and faces and was thankful to anyone who was unmistakable through some peculiarity in appearance. But freaks, frights and frumps are very rare in Australia, and pretty girls and women very common, so my memory was most severely tried.

I had but little time to spend in my delightful garden, where a perfect prince among gardeners—William Grant—presided. He could answer all my garden questions and answer them *accurately*. He was learned in bush-flowers and he arranged all flowers like an artist. Besides his professional opinions he held good sound views on a hundred subjects, and combined an absolute loyalty to the country of his birth, which he had left at the age of seventeen, with an unbounded belief in the country of his adoption. . . . But I must stop or I shall write a whole book about Grant, and that is not what I set out to do. I have said enough to convince all garden-lovers that I was a lucky woman in having the services of such a man. The garden owed to Lady Fanshawe, who left Admiralty House about two and a half years before we arrived there, one of the most beautiful mixed borders I have ever seen. Of this I possess two water-colour sketches, one made in November and the other in May, by that clever artist and good gardener, Miss Alice Norton, of Sydney. They have been a source of much comfort to me during the long dark months of our English winter.

CHAPTER X

PUBLIC DUTIES

I FOUND myself *ex-officio* president of various ladies' committees, notably that of the Seamen's Institute. The Institute was at that time quite inadequate to fulfil the demands made upon its resources, and funds had to be raised as quickly as possible if Sydney was to escape the reproach of lukewarmness towards the merchant-seamen who were maintaining her great position among the world's seaports. To Mrs. Napier, wife of the Captain-in-Charge, belongs the credit of conceiving the idea of holding a so-called *Café Chantant* at the Town Hall, and though it turned out to be nothing but an act of unblushing robbery when money paid and value received were weighed in the balance, it resulted in an accession of £450 to our funds. Her beauty and widespread popularity had enabled her to gather at her house beforehand all the most important ladies in Sydney, and, with practically no preparation to discount my newcomer's ignorance, I found myself presiding at a drawing-room meeting at Tresco, where we discussed details and solicited help. I tremble now to think what a poor figure I should have cut had I not had at my elbow a lady of the committee who became later such a friend as few people are fortunate enough to possess. This was Mrs. Gordon Wesché, wife of the Sydney agent of the P. and O. Company, now agent for Australasia. Money and suggestions poured in, my infallible prompter posting me up *chemin faisant* in names and facts undreamt of till that moment, and the enterprise was launched.

The Governor was specially interested in the Seamen's Institute and delivered himself of several home truths on the inadequate support it had been receiving—expressions of opinion which only his great popularity rendered endurable. Of course further efforts had to be made, and in the next two years I wrote myself blind and talked myself hoarse on behalf of the new Institute which was finally opened by Lord Chelmsford and named " The Rawson Institute for Seamen," a fitting memorial to the much-loved Sailor-Governor who had just then himself " crossed the bar."

But the raising of money, by whatever means,

seems to me harder in England than in Australia, where the slow-growing qualities of caution and reserve so characteristic of our race have not yet smothered the enthusiasm and checked the natural impulse to be promptly generous which mark the dwellers in the dominions beyond the seas.

Though a considerable number of public duties fell to me as the third lady in the official world of New South Wales, many of them were only disguised pleasures. Each of my predecessors at Admiralty House had had her pet charity and her particular interests and enthusiasms, and I soon found it would be impossible to follow in all the tracks left by at least half a dozen ladies bent on being useful. That not a few of these efforts had never reached to solid achievement was not the fault of their originators. Three years, at the outside, is not always a long enough period in which to establish a strong-growing perennial, and the Governor's advice to me, offered very early in our acquaintance, was, " *Don't spread yourself.*" So I tried to pick out those objects which seemed to me most useful and did what I could to advance them.

After the first six months I had to give up opening bazaars. They were too numerous, and a conscientious habit acquired in Plymouth some years before of carefully preparing the best speech I could devise for each occasion caused a greater expenditure of time and mental effort than I could afford. But the bazaars I did open were more entertaining than those at home. The people who worked for them, and bought or sold at them, took genuine interest in, and derived amusement from these sometimes desperate undertakings. Their good spirits were infectious, and once I had achieved my opening speech I was free to enjoy myself. One bazaar in particular deserves honourable mention. An Ode of Welcome to my unworthy self had been written and very cleverly set to music for the occasion, and this was sung by about thirty young girls with deliciously fresh voices—those happy Australian voices which never stick in the throats of the singers. The Ode began

> " O, Lady Poore, we all rejoice
> To give you hearty greeting——"

and the first three verses referred in flattering terms to myself, so I considered it proper to sit down in the comfortable chair provided for me. But presently the music of the Old Hundredth brought me to my feet, only to collapse a second time when the opening *motif* repeated itself at the close. It was pleasing, certainly, but it was also embarrassing to fill the *rôle* of subsidiary heroine in a partially sacred Cantata.

Later in the proceedings, when I had nearly achieved the round of the stalls, I found myself face to face with a beautiful sugar-covered cake bearing the words " Lady Poore " in bold pink characters upon its much decorated superstructure. And I had only three and sixpence left ! Feeling very hot and very mean I hurriedly bought some sweets for eighteenpence and passed on to the Fishpond, whose waters I troubled with four three-penny dips. At the last stall of all I begged plaintively for " something that only costs a shilling, please," and got it from the smiling and sympathetic stallholder. It was a narrow squeak, but my collection of miscellanies made a fine show as they were conveyed to the carriage, and comprised a bunch of carrots for our dear big horses and a pincushion like a prize tomato which I presented later to the flag-lieutenant. As I never invited him to accompany me on these occasions—unloved by young men—he humoured me by accepting the monstrous fruit with many expressions of gratitude.

I found it impossible to give away the prizes at all the various schools whose headmasters and mistresses invited me to perform this pleasing ceremony, but each spring I drove up to Abbotsleigh at Wahroonga, where Miss Marian Clarke—an old friend and coadjutor of my brother Charley—had a most successful school. The " bodyguard " of white-clad girls who received me represented so much beauty in bud and showed such welcoming faces that the ceremony was far from being a *corvée*. Schoolgirls as a rule have such pitilessly sharp eyes that it is not the most comfortable thing in the world to find oneself—a most imperfect elderly woman—exposed upon a platform to the gaze of a hundred pairs of well-opened optics, and the first time I went to Miss Clarke's I owed much of the kindness of my reception to the gentleman—Mr. Vane—who introduced me to my audience. His really witty speech was good all through, but when he said, " We are lucky to get Lady Poore here to-day so far inland, for we must remember that she belongs, properly speaking, to the Navy ; but the race is not always to the *Fleet*, nor the battle to the *Powerful*," I forgot I was going to make a speech and laughed with great comfort. Miss Clarke now enjoys the freedom and leisure she so well deserves, but Abbotsleigh goes on prospering, and I go on hoping to meet once more the charming girls— prize-winners or not—who were pupils there in 1908—11. And yet I might find them unrecognisable !

The Girls' Realm Guild has a branch in New South Wales so well organised and run by the secretary at Sydney that I felt proud to be its Vice-President. The work those girls did, the money they made, the help they gave simply amazed me. And it was the same with the " Harbour Lights," a society of girls affiliated to the Seamen's Institute Ladies' Committee. Practical, prompt, and persevering were their efforts to help the parent committee, whose members had, for the most part, worked year in and year out for the benefit of the seamen till many were nearly exhausted. When the " Harbour Lights " were instituted in imitation of the Melbourne Society a new era began. As these youthful helpers grow

older it will be possible to recruit the Ladies'
Committee of the Institute from their numbers,
releasing the old stagers and bringing experience as
well as new blood into the executive.

It would be hard to exaggerate the value of
women's and girls' unpaid work in Australia. They
seem to possess a genius for organisation and they
do not take their duties sadly.

CHAPTER XI

CHIEFLY CONCERNING WOMEN

DINNERS, small garden-parties, tea-parties and
dances at Admiralty House punctuated our first
four months at Sydney, and I enjoyed them all.
A husband who never shirked, a competent and
experienced flag-lieutenant, a friendly and helpful
flagship, and a staff of servants all willing to do
their best, reduced my responsibility to *nil*. I
pressed the button and the machinery worked. The
guests themselves did the rest. I will not say we
had no failures, but Australians are rarely bored,
and the ugly habit of posing as superior beings is
practically unknown among them, so they are
easy to entertain.

Of course there were cliques and circles outside which our official position placed us. Social divisions and sub-divisions must obviously exist in the life of every great city, but our guests rarely made us suffer for the ignorance which sometimes assembled incongruous and hostile elements under our roof, or in our garden. Australians are refreshingly adaptable and accommodating and their hearts are not cased in armour-plated or asbestosised envelopes that one must spend years in penetrating. Some writers reproach them with being sadly wanting in reserve. They certainly possess the gift of spontaneous and uncalculating friendliness, which is also to be met with in Irish people, and they are frank to a fault ; but they do not habitually, and without reference to their surroundings, discuss the diseases and divorces of their acquaintances, topics of conversation so common in England as to be almost unavoidable. On the other hand, I regretted the laxity, common also in England, which permitted too many of their girls under years of discretion to see *any* play which chanced to be presented at the theatres. I do not like to think it is my evil mind that causes me to find such a play as the " Merry Widow " objectionable. If it is so I must share the imputation of evil-mindedness with several other women—not old—who almost contemplated forming a " Society of Prim Wives " when the " Merry Widow's " popularity was at its height !

Australians are not specially interested in grand

or smart folk unless these possess attractions beyond grandeur or smartness. If a really nice and interesting duke happened to visit Sydney, his presence there would arouse a considerable amount of friendly curiosity and he would be given every opportunity for enjoying himself. But a dissolute or disagreeable nobleman would be left to himself and to the tender mercies of a few people who instinctively and unswervingly rate coronets higher than either hearts or heads. Any visitor with the slightest claim to distinction, from the chorus-girl of comic opera to a great explorer like the ever-lamented Captain Scott, is welcomed, *fêted*, helped and sped upon his way by Australians.

In Australian society nobody is more popular, no one more freely entertained, than the girl or woman who earns her own living, whether as an artist, a nurse, a masseuse, a teacher or a tradeswoman. But here I must observe that the working lady of Australia possesses the gift of putting off her business face along with her business gown the moment she " downs tools," and that she plays as hard as she works ; hence her social acceptability— and it is not because she is ashamed of her trade or profession that she so swiftly lays aside its insignia, including such traces of fatigue and worry as are effaceable. She possesses the capacity, rare among women, for doing one thing at a time and doing it thoroughly.

Real intellect, as distinct from intelligence, seems to me quite as uncommon among Australian women as English in proportion to the population. In intelligence, meaning common sense and quickness of communication between brain and hand, they strike me as being greatly our superiors. They are poor conversational linguists for the simple reason that there are but few educated foreigners in Australia—a country without neighbours—and I very soon found that foreign words, used perhaps too commonly by us at home, were better eliminated from my vocabulary. I made a bad mistake one day while talking to a dear old lady whose daughter I had known in England. In answer to my question, " Where is your daughter now ? " I received the disconcerting reply, " Oh, she is spending the summer at *Cayenne*." She meant *Caen*, but I did not realise her intention before I had blunderingly rejoined, " What a terrible place and climate for her ! I didn't know *any* English people went there."

The superior practicalness of the Australian woman is, no doubt, greatly due to inherited powers, as well as the conditions of her life, for her mother and grandmother had to use both brain and fingers to provide substitutes for such articles as were in their time unpurchasable or unattainable for her house and her wardrobe, and even now in the great cities good servants are hard to get and keep, while the standard of wages is so high that people of comfortable means have only three maids where five would be considered necessary by an English family of equal position. In the Bush it is almost impossible to get trained servants. Ladies' maids are few and far between even in such places as Sydney, and the capacity of Australian women for cutting-out, sewing and contriving, and for turning themselves out fresh and smart from the top of their shining heads to the toes of their small and well-shod feet never failed to excite my admiration and envy. This talent is shared by all classes, and there is nothing of the " outside of the cup and platter " about it, for their standard in *lingerie*—as I understand it is discreet to call it—is higher than ours, and in nine cases out of ten the invisible garments are made by the wearers' own clever hands. Thus it will be readily understood that Australian women have less leisure for the cultivation and petting of the intellectual ego of which one has heard so much in recent years in England. Perhaps some of them read Ibsen and Nietzsche. If they have never done so I am reactionary enough to think this a subject for congratulation rather than condolence. In my opinion, which I offer knowing full well my temerity, they have still a good deal to learn as regards the decoration and furnishing of their houses. Better colour-schemes and more unencumbered floor-space would make their rooms more attractive ; but as practical housekeepers, not directors of a corps of well-drilled servants, they are far ahead of us.

The perfection of domestic service, as it is to be found in the great houses of England, cannot be looked for in Australia of the Australians, because this is the growth of centuries, like the velvet turf of English lawns; and the independent spirit in Australia of that class from which our best servants are drawn forbids one to suppose that domestic service will ever appeal to its representatives as an honourable and desirable calling. But Australian ladies are house-proud. They cherish the antique, and even elderly, furniture brought out from home by their fathers and grandfathers, many of whom would charter a small ship and carry with them all their household gods; and beautiful china, old-fashioned glass and plate and valuable books and pictures are to be found in many Australian homes as well as in the salerooms of the great cities. Their houses are usually smaller in proportion to their income than ours, but there are fine specimens of the old " colonial " style among the villas on the shores of Sydney harbour, and their colonnaded verandahs, spacious four-cornered rooms and tall French windows are beautiful as well as suitable to the climate; far more attractive, in short, than the fantastic, many-bowed irregularities which can render a perfectly well-meaning house grotesque. The very high prices and taxation of building-lots crowning the rocky heights and commanding the lovely bays of Sydney harbour constrain the inhabitants to build up many-storeyed structures consisting of smallish rooms so as to leave space around them for lawns and gardens. Some are picturesque enough, but no one who has ever lived in a tower will contend that this kind of dwelling is either convenient or roomy. Of the " colonial " type *Redleaf* on Double Bay, and *Carrara* on Rose Bay are charming examples.

There are excellent girls' schools in Australia, and women's colleges are attached to the universities ; the standard of hospital nursing is extremely high,* and women doctors with good practices abound. Not once among Australians did I come across the woman who makes a guy of herself in the strange belief that to be well shod and gloved, *bien coiffée*, and, in fact, *bien mise* altogether, is unnecessary, and even unbecoming, in a person of " culture "— thrice odious word. Never shall I forget the hair of certain ladies—all presumably learned—whom I saw at a Greek play at Cambridge shortly before I left England for Australia. No brains could atone for the ill-brushed, ill-dressed hair that covered the skulls containing them. In front of me sat a lady whose very short and scanty grey locks were tied at the back on a level with the tops of her ears with a piece of whiteish tape and stuck out at right angles to her head. I do not understand Greek, so I had time to wonder why Mr. Genius wears his hair long and Mrs. Genius wears hers short, and concluded that, among men, great scholars are too deeply immersed in study to visit the barber, while

* Australian women possess a natural aptitude for nursing, and they must not only obtain the usual certificate after passing an examination at the hospital where they are trained, but satisfy the Australian Trained Nurses Association controlling the entire body of nurses. This A.T.N.A., which is the ultimate referee in nursing matters, is in reality a sort of trade union exercising, on the whole, a very salutary influence.

their womenfolk are too importantly employed in digging up Greek Roots or soaring amongst the very Highest Mathematics to brush or dress theirs properly.

I once heard an English girl, both clever and original, who was travelling in New South Wales find fault with Australian women living in the Bush because they were beautifully dressed for dinner every evening! To me it seemed only a very admirable evidence of self-respect. Their critic dressed abominably herself, and as she spoke in disparagement of the " too smart " Australians, I could not help taking a mental inventory of her own apparel. She wore a shabby, shapeless, old straw hat ; a coat both stained and frayed ; her gloves had holes in them and her hair hung about her ears in little lustreless wisps. It is fair to say we were out on the harbour in the barge and the weather was showery. Still she might have looked fresh and tidy.

I had a painful experience when presiding at an annual meeting of women-workers in Sydney. Just before I spoke I became aware that a short-haired woman (too obviously not Australian) who needed only trousers and the removal of her hat-elastic to be dressed precisely like a man, was one of the party on the platform. As I had carefully prepared what I had to say, and had neither the courage nor the inventive power to improvise, I was inevitably committed to go through with my speech, a speech in which I specially commended the professional girls and women of New South Wales for remaining feminine and showing proper self-respect by adequately caring for their appearance, no matter what their daily work and surroundings. I had actually sketched, as one to be avoided, the very type of woman-worker represented by the English-woman behind me !

When Woman Suffrage was painlessly introduced into New South Wales very few beyond working-class women took the trouble to vote. Now their responsibilities as voters have become apparent to all classes, but so far only a handful of extremists desire seriously *to occupy seats in Parliament.* I once read in a Sydney paper the report of a short and pointed speech made on this subject by the wife of a Labour member at a political gathering. Another lady had just expressed the opinion that women should be permitted to sit in Parliament, and this, as far as I can recollect, was Mrs. X.'s rejoinder :

" I can hardly suppose that Miss Y., who has just spoken, desires that young unmarried women should have seats in Parliament, as their unsuitability for such a position is obvious. Married women like myself have plenty of other things to do. There remain, therefore, only the unmarried women of a certain age, and they, in my opinion, are disqualified since they are, and have always been, *notoriously unfair .o men.*"

The Women Suffragists of this country, when they hold up (as they love to do) the legislators of Australia as a pattern to our own, forget, or ignore, the fact that in that continent which possesses universal suffrage, the men voters still far outnumber the women.

CHAPTER XII

ENJOYMENT AND ENTHUSIASM

AUGUST, 1908, found Sydney in all the excitement preceding and accompanying a " monster " visit of American battleships. That our own squadron in Australian waters consisted only of one 1st-class, three 2nd-class, and five 3rd-class cruisers did not deter the Prime Minister, Mr. Deakin—unversed, no doubt, in the etiquette of international courtesy—from inviting this vastly preponderating fleet of sixteen American battleships to come and be *fêted* in Australian ports. Enthusiasm was boundless. Everyone was agog to see battleships, which were popularly supposed to be as far superior to cruisers as are Archangels to men. So Sydney Harbour was dotted with large white ships picked out with what is known in the navy as " dockyard yellow " and adorned with the " spar-tangled banner "—a bibulous sounding variant for the "star-spangled banner " coined by someone who had been celebrating its arrival. American steamboats dashed hither and thither, knowing, or acknowledging, no speed limit.

Triumphal arches were erected ; reviews, banquets, gala performances at the theatres, illuminations, balls and receptions filled the days and nights, and visitors from the shore swarmed on board Uncle Sam's ships and sang all the national anthems they happened to know as they " tripped " about the harbour.

The following extracts from the papers will give some idea of the wave of hospitable delirium which invaded the country at this time. A Melbourne man had proposed that " eagles be captured if possible and liberated as the fleet " (American) " approaches Port Melbourne, or eagles made of a large size in rubber properly ballasted, sent up like balloons, carrying in their beaks American flags." But a writer to a Sydney paper actually improved upon this idea :

" It would be even better " (he wrote) " to obtain a number of eagles and, bringing them to some suitable spot, when the ships have taken up their positions in Sydney Harbour, liberate the birds ; but before doing so to attach to the leg of each bird a light rope long enough to allow freedom of flight for wings and tail, and to this rope attach a bannerette of Stars and Stripes. This would be no inconvenience to the bird owing to its size, great carrying power, and having a wing-spread of anything up to about nine feet, and of which it could easily free itself on the first tree on which it alights. Not only would my suggestion be most pleasing to our visitors, but souvenirs of their arrival will be found by others—perhaps by those who had not the great pleasure of witnessing the arrival of the fleet, these souvenirs being carried by the birds probably to even remote parts of the Bush, and certainly treasured by the finders. If eagles are not obtainable I would suggest white cockatoos, which are not at all difficult to procure, and of course reducing bannerettes in size and proportion to the bird. As the white cockatoo is a typical Australian bird, and when carrying the Stars and Stripes would form a combination that may be the more pleasing to many individually, I would favour both birds being used on the occasion."

The syntax of the above paragraph is not more involved than the unlucky eagles or cockatoos would have been had these birds been actually employed as " bannerette "-wavers and souvenir-shedders.

Still, when all is said and done, this almost childish enthusiasm for the unknown and untried is one of the great charms of the Australian character. It causes Australians to welcome strangers with a heartiness unknown in old and overcrowded countries. It offers a chance for reformation to the dog which has elsewhere got a bad name, and it encourages experiments which in England we are too cautious, or too self-satisfied, to countenance. Australians, thank Heaven, are not *blasés*.

And how they enjoy the present! When I arrived in Australia I was inclined to agree with many English critics that all classes spent too much money on amusement and were entirely indisposed to lay up for a drought (not a rainy day) or for the advantage of the next generation. But I came to see that strong common sense was a factor in their expenditure on pleasure and variety.

If an Australian has a windfall he will, as likely as not, invest it, not in shares, but in a trip to Europe, and I was particularly struck by the spirit and enterprise of two elderly ladies of small means who, having unexpectedly sold a bit of land, promptly took their passages for England, which they had never visited. Taking with them a young niece, they gave themselves a delightful wander-year, and the recollections of their time at home, where they were most cordially welcomed, are, I am certain, worth more to them now than the consciousness of *possessing*, but not *enjoying*, a few hundreds of invested pounds.

The absence of rights of primogeniture is responsible for the fact that there are not many " men of leisure " in Australia. There are few of those eldest sons who have no incentive to work because their inheritance is secure. Fathers do not stint themselves so that their heirs shall cut a fine figure in the world after they themselves are gone, and great estates which have degenerated into burdens, as they so frequently do in England, are practically non-existent.

CHAPTER XIII

RACES, BALLS—AND " BIRTH-STAINS "

IN solemn state all available Excellencies attend the Spring and Autumn Race-meetings at Randwick —the beautiful course outside Sydney—and, whenever possible, the flagship repairs to Melbourne for " Cup-week " in November. The enormous gatherings of well-behaved citizens and their families at these great race-meetings are among the sights of Australia, or indeed the world. Any racegoer can vouch for the excellence of the arrangements in every particular as well as for the high standard of the horses run. The police reports answer for the good conduct and the sobriety of the crowd. On Cup-day at Melbourne in 1910 there were between 120,000 and 130,000 people at Flemington, and not one single case of drunkenness or theft was reported ! I, alas ! never succeeded in going to Melbourne for Cup-week, being by the end of October in each year absolutely exhausted by the work and play of the preceding six or seven months of a Sydney season. Though I am far from intelligent in racing matters I should have liked to see so famous a sight as Flemington on Cup-day. At the Randwick (Sydney) meetings I used to watch the steeplechases with a fearful joy and put a couple of half sovereigns on horses fancied by some connoisseur, but I was always ready to go home before the proper moment arrived, and I regretfully admit that my impressions of Australian racing are absolutely without value.

The big public balls at Sydney were admirably done, and those at Government House in Lord Northcote's time had both charm and dignity, but at all these balls the anxiety as to whether we should pull through the lancers, or quadrille, in which the big-wigs took part, without disgracing ourselves sat heavily upon our minds until these solemn exercises were over and we were freed from the burden of our official importance. On such evenings we dined rather hastily and then practised our steps—my husband, Mr. Fisher and myself, with an unsympathetic chair for second lady—in the hall at Admiralty House. I wonder if the crowds that watched the *quadrille d'honneur* from the gallery of the Town Hall realised how hard we tried to dance correctly. No matter how carefully we were drilled it happened occasionally that we were paired off with ignorant or obstinate partners, or confronted with untrained *vis-à-vis*, and then all was lost.

In some inexplicable fashion the fact that the Commander-in-Chief of the Australian station is, *pro. tem.*, " His Excellency " had encouraged the fantastic idea that he was to be treated like a minor vice-royalty, and my poor husband was aghast to find ladies actually inviting him to pass through doors before them and standing up when he was on his feet ! While abating none of the claims to precedence which were admittedly his as

Naval Commander-in-Chief (and Excellency) he speedily and successfully combated this curious heresy—or delusion—but not before it had caused him considerable embarrassment.

Unlike Lord Beauchamp, who had, one must suppose, left England to take up his appointment as Governor of New South Wales without realising that one does not allude to " birth-stains " in Australia, I never spoke of the old penal settlement days until the topic was introduced in the course of conversation by one of our friends at Sydney. It was he who told me the following stories :—

One of my predecessors at Admiralty House through nervousness, or possibly temporary insanity, remarked one evening at her own table to the man who had taken her in, " I think, you know, it is *so* interesting when one remembers that so many of the people one meets here are actually the descendants of convicts." Mr. Z., whose ancestors were quite as free from reproach as were those of his hostess, drew his heavy brows together and glared fiercely at the poor lady. Just then general conversation suddenly collapsed and the entire party heard her say, " Oh, I beg your pardon ; of course I should not have mentioned convicts to *you*. Suppose we change the subject."

An old Australian lady who had just inherited a nice little legacy " got a bit of her own back " rather neatly when she replied to the question of a travelling Englishwoman calling to congratulate her : " And now, of course, you'll be making a trip to England ? "

" England ! No, *thank* you. Why, that's where all the convicts came from."

The narrator of these two stories had a theory that there were distinct advantages to be derived from convict ancestry. " Taking it all round," he said, " I am not sure that I would not prefer to have just one convict great-grandparent rather than be, as I am, the descendant of eight perfectly blameless ones. It gives a nice wild flavour to the mixture ; and, when another hundred years or so have gone by, plenty of people in this country will be ready enough to admit to the possession of a drop of *Red Rover* * blood, because it will prove they are not mere mushrooms, but twigs of a well-grown family tree."

We in England are far too apt to forget that people used to be transported for sheep-stealing— a crime rated at one time in Scotland as more commendable than certain virtues—and for political offences. What turned a large proportion of the convicts transported to Australia into brutes or devils was the inhuman treatment they were subjected to, and their close association with the worst class of criminal, on board some of the convict ships which, of course, took many months to accomplish the voyage.

* A ship " freighted " with female convicts.

CHAPTER XIV

EMPIRE DAY

NOTHING opened our eyes to the meaning of the bonds of Empire which unite the dominions overseas with little far-away England as did the celebration of Empire Day in Australia. It was a tremendous day—something like Christmas, and one's wedding day and one's last breaking-up day at school combined—as far as sensations went. I cannot now give the whole programme of events which filled the hours of May 24th, 1909, at Sydney, but the two scenes in which we ourselves took a prominent part can never be forgotten by us. The Royal Exchange was crowded to overflowing; speeches, both appropriate and sensible, were made by the President, my husband and others, and to me fell the proud privilege of breaking the flag at noon from the high steps outside the building, amid cheers for the King that might have penetrated the intelligence of the deafest socialist that ever stopped his ears to all but his own eloquence. Later in the day there was a stupendous gathering on the great cricket ground at Moore Park, where ten thousand school children, massed and drilled to form the giant letters of the words

ONE FLAG
ONE FLEET,

were assembled. Ranks of Scouts (2,500 of them)

formed the border of the brilliantly-coloured legend, and when this great army of young people sang " Rule, Britannia "—every run and grace-note as clear and even as one always wishes to hear them, but never does—the volume and purity of sound would have awakened in the most Keir-Hardened heart a thrill of patriotism. Then again I broke the flag (one given by Lord Roberts himself to the best shot among the Scouts) and while " God Save the King " was being sung by children and spectators together—perhaps fifty thousand in all—I shed tears behind my veil which must have left glazed patches on my cheeks since I was in too conspicuous a position to use a pocket-handkerchief unobserved.

Certain " advanced " newspapers would describe this display of enthusiasm for King and Empire as nothing but sentimental rubbish. It is matter for regret that there is not more of such rubbish in the heart of the Empire.

As my husband's speech on Empire Day, 1909, was in some degree prophetic, I append it here.

From *The Daily Telegraph*, Sydney, May 25th, 1909.

NOW'S THE DAY.

AUSTRALIA'S TRUE DEFENCE.

THE DREADNOUGHT MOVEMENT.

EXPLICIT SPEECH BY ADMIRAL POORE.

At the Empire Day celebrations, at the Royal Exchange, yesterday, Vice-Admiral Sir Richard Poore, Bart., delivered an important speech on the naval crisis, and Australia's relation thereto. His Excellency, who was very warmly received, said :—

I see in this morning's paper a speech of great Imperial importance made by Lord Charles Beresford. He is an officer who enjoys the confidence and affection of the Service, and under whom I had the honour of serving, both in peace time and on active service, and should be proud to do so again. If my views, in part, disagree with his, it is because I have been out here for fifteen months, and have had exceptional opportunities of studying the question.

A year has passed over our heads since I last had the honour of being present at the Royal Exchange on Empire Day. A year ago we held the unchallenged right to the proud title of mistress of the seas ; we hold that title still, but it is not un-challenged. (Hear, hear.) Personally, I consider that the near approach of danger may be of intense value to us. It forms an additional bond between the different parts of our Empire ; it links us closer together, and brings us nearer to a realisation of the true meaning of the term " Imperial unity," without which we shall cease to be an Empire. (Applause.) For an Empire such as ours I object to the oft-repeated phrase " separated by oceans," and in its place would substitute the words " linked together by our ocean highways." It is an absolute necessity for our very existence that we should be so strong on the seas that our right of peaceful passage along these ocean highways should never be seriously threatened. We are now brought face to face with the fact that, under certain conditions, our peaceful command of the sea may be endangered, and that, during the next four or five years, we must strain every nerve, and gladly make any sacrifice to the end that this command of the sea shall be recognised as being absolute, and in so doing we shall make for a world-wide peace. (Cheers.)

The Facts of the Case.

The facts of the case are briefly these :—That Germany has reached the point of being able to build her men-of-war as speedily as Great Britain. That she can turn out armour-plating, guns, and their mountings as speedily as Great Britain. That her docking accommodation is equal to ours. That in 1912, three years from now, she will have an equal, if not a superior, force of the latest type of battleship ready for sea. That there still exists the Triple Alliance of Germany, Austria and Italy. That Germany is a Power in the Northern Seas, and Austria and Italy in the Mediterranean. That both of these two latter Powers are also building Dreadnoughts. That any disaster to our fleet in the North Sea or English Channel imperils the safety of the Empire ; and that this fact holds equally good in the Mediterranean. That in either case the main routes to the East and to Australia are cut. I beg of you not to consider that I speak either as an alarmist or as a pessimist. I simply put my opinions as a naval officer, speaking absolutely on his own responsibility, before the members of this Royal

Exchange. If such an emergency as I have spoken of were to make us despondent in the least degree, we should no longer deserve to hold our Empire. (Hear, hear.) Our responsibilities compel us occasionally to look some grave crisis in the face. We have done so in the past; we do so now; and if my forty-three years' experience in the service of my country have taught me anything, it is this—that our race is never at its best until it is face to face with an emergency. (Cheers.) Why a state of things which threatens our existence as an Empire should have been suddenly brought to pass is a matter which is difficult to understand. If there are two races in the world which should march side by side they are the British and Teutonic races. (Applause.) Both are mercantile in their instinct; both have a world-wide experience, and both aim for the distribution and settlement of a great population whose instincts and feelings are almost identical. Consider the capital invested in the world's affairs by the British and Teutonic races. Should either fail there would be a world-wide financial catastrophe which would shake each quarter of the globe to its very foundations. Consider what power for good would ensue from the two races meeting in commercial rivalry only. Instead of this peaceful competition there unfortunately exists at present an extraordinary and acute military antagonism, for which I cannot but think there have been excuses on both sides.

We Must Hold Our Inheritance.

It is idle and illogical to blame any country for competing with us. We have a great inheritance handed down to us, and we have a right to hold it just so long as we can show a united resolve to defend our inheritance, and no longer. (Hear, hear.) There is to-day in Sydney Harbour a man-of-war of the Navy of H.I.M. the German Emperor, and I take this opportunity of saying that there is no thought in my mind of discourtesy in speaking of the rivalry between our respective countries, in their presence. There exists, and I feel there always will exist, between our two great naval services, a cordiality and a respect for each other's patriotism and devotion to duty which is one of the characteristics of a great brotherhood, the brotherhood of the sea. (Applause.) Those of whom I am now speaking are our guests, and with no one am I more glad to grip hands than my brother sailors of the German Navy. The means which we must adopt to meet the present crisis are those which will give the greatest advantage to the Empire as a whole, and this can only be arrived at by co-operation between the mother-country and the colonies.

The Three Schemes Suggested.

In speaking of this as regards Australia, I think there is some confusion existing in the minds of many people with regard to the different schemes suggested. These I may note as being : First, the Dreadnought movement ; secondly, the establishment of an Australian torpedo flotilla ; thirdly, the formation of an Australian navy. All these schemes show a resolve on the part of Australia to meet a danger which is common to all parts of the Empire, and I trust that one result of the proposed Imperial Naval and Military Conference will be to turn men's thoughts from political and personal motives, and to direct them towards the main issue—what action is best for the security of the Empire. (Applause.)

FIRST AND FOREMOST NECESSITY.

The fitly-named Dreadnought movement shows a keen appreciation of the fact that our first and foremost necessity as an Empire is the command of the sea. That command lies in the strength of our main fleets. If ever war comes, the sea fight which will determine the fate of the British Empire will, without doubt, be fought many thousand of miles away from these shores. Then, as regards our commerce, look where you will, you will find thousands of miles of sea routes, which can only be secured by ships of high speed, great radius of action and gun-power ; trained, officered, and manned from the greatest naval school in the world, the British Navy. On the upkeep and superiority of our Imperial Fleet in being depends the command of the sea and our very existence. The Dreadnought movement fully realises these principles as regards our present position. (Cheers.)

A TORPEDO FLOTILLA.

To come to the second scheme : The establishment of a torpedo flotilla. Such a force would be a great advantage as the floating part of the defences of ports in Australia, or as an auxiliary to the main fleets, if they were ever engaged in these waters. Or, if the Imperial naval forces were withdrawn from Australasian waters to a more efficient strategical ground for the defence of Australia, the presence of an efficient flotilla would have a great moral effect in Australia, and a practical one in case of possible raids. But in considering this point, the fact must be remembered that the true defence of Australia lies in the capacity of the main fleets of the Empire to overpower the main fleets of a possible enemy. If the Imperial main fleets fail in their object, no flotilla, however strong, can beat back a determined naval attack in force, and that attack need never be made directly ; Australia could be cut off and isolated by operations at points far distant from these shores on the main ocean routes. (Hear, hear.) Also, in my opinion, whatever form of floating defence may be adopted for local purposes in Australia, it must be under Imperial control ; the *personnel* must be trained by Imperial officers and men ; and there must be a constant flow of officers and men, Australian or otherwise, passing through the force from our great naval manœuvre grounds. I lay great stress on this last point ; they must pass through our great manœuvring fleets. Only in this way can stagnation be avoided and efficiency secured. There can be no divided control in the naval defence of the Empire ; there can only be one fleet and one flag. (Cheers.)

A QUESTION OUTSIDE THE RANGE.

The third scheme is the establishment of an Australian navy, which I hardly think this is the time to discuss. If Australia can build fifteen Dreadnoughts, or the equivalent, in the next five years, for duty in the Pacific, equip them, man them, and train the *personnel*, well and good ; but otherwise I ask you to remember that we must not at this crisis in Imperial affairs look too far into the future. The period with which we are concerned is that which is comprised in the next five years, and we have got to act NOW (and that word " now " must be spelt in capital letters). We cannot allow ourselves to be led into speculation as to what may happen in twenty years' time. It is a question of ships, officers and men to man them, and the thousand and one considerations which are necessary for fighting ships of the present day. These questions mean money, and that fact brings us face to face with a term which is looked upon with scant favour, but which, I am confident, is the only solution of the case, and that term is " contribution," which you may look upon as being an insurance on Imperial security. The present emergency contains a lesson in Imperial unity. If we are united, and if we realise that there is danger, we shall, in the end, hold our own. If we are not united, and let matters drift, or run into wrong channels, then we are each of us here to-day more or less responsible, should disaster occur. That disaster will come to us is very far from my thoughts ; shoulder to shoulder we will keep the old flag flying over the Empire on which the sun never sets, and on which, please God, the sun never will set. (Cheers.)

CHAPTER XV

NOTABLE VISITORS

WE had the opportunity of becoming acquainted with such travellers of note as visited Sydney during our time there, whether Governors from other States, people with missions, authors, explorers, or stars of the musical and theatrical world. This was extremely pleasant and interesting. Some of them were old friends or acquaintances, such as Lord Kitchener and Sir Frederick Bedford ; others we might never have met had we not fortunately occupied an official position at the Antipodes.

When Lord Kitchener was invited to visit Australia with the object of advising its military authorities, H.M.S. *Encounter* fetched him from Port Darwin. Luckily for one who so dislikes the blowing of trumpets, the plaudits of the crowd and ceremonial banquets, it was in the hot month of January, 1910, when nearly everyone was away, that " K." arrived at Sydney, and so successful was he in evading those who came to gaze upon him that an insober person who had spent long hours in endeavouring to catch sight of him was heard complaining to his fellow-passengers in a tram that he wasn't going to trouble any more about it. " I call him," said the disappointed hero-worshipper thickly, " I call him an ill-ill-lusive p-p-pimpernel. That's what he is."

My husband and " K." had been close friends in the campaigning years of 1882–1884 in Egypt, and among the former's wedding presents in 1885 was a cigarette-case bearing the inscription, " R. P. from H. H. K., Alexandria, The Nile," followed by the dates. This case, a valued token of friendship, has now become a historical treasure. It was within an ace of failing in the first instance to reach its owner thirty years ago, as it lay for months *perdu* behind the skirting board of the porter's box at his club, and was found there in its torn and defaced covering when some repairs were being carried out.

I also had met Major Kitchener in Egypt in 1883 and remembered him well, but he was too truthful to pretend he remembered me when he came to dine with us at Sydney. He certainly reminded me but little of the slim and strenuous young officer in the Egyptian Army which he helped so materially to create, and, though I tried to be brave, I confess there was something distinctly intimidating about him. Knowing his tastes, we had a very small party to meet him, but amongst our guests was as pretty and intelligent a girl as one could find in a long day's journey, and she had come three hundred miles to meet the Hero of Khartoum and Paardeberg ! But at dinner he remarked with annihilating emphasis that he had heard so much of the beauty of Australian girls and *so far he had not seen a single decent-looking one.* V. le P. smiled disarmingly at this damaging assertion but it made the rest of us feel crushed and out of curl, and so, hurriedly switching the conversation off to the traditional beauty of " Limerick lasses," I dashed into a story about a young gunner with whom both " K." and I had been acquainted, —and " K." *laughed.* It was as though Jove himself had accepted the humble offering of some trembling votary, and I breathed more freely. This was the story—it shall serve again—that made " K." laugh :

A subaltern of Artillery with a weakness for great folks was quartered at Limerick many years ago and went down one summer with other young soldiers to the Cork Park Races and Ball. He danced a great many times with a girl who was neither well dressed nor a good dancer, and we in Limerick should have called her plain. Later on his friends chaffed him about this inexplicable assiduity. " She is a very nice girl," he protested, " and *very* well-connected. She is a sister of the Countess of Ayr." His friends were surprised, but a local man in the group roared with laughter. " Not the *Countess of Ayr*, you fool," he explained ; " the *County Surveyor*." (The official in charge of the roads.) I cannot remember whether I was encouraged to recount the pendant to this little true story, but perhaps I may be forgiven for wedging it in here : An elderly and gouty colonel was sent to Homburg by his doctor, and as he was strolling about after his first morning glass feeling lonely and depressed in the midst of a crowd he espied a well-known face. He almost ran to meet its owner and shook him warmly by both hands, crying, " How are you, old fellow ? I can tell you I'm d—d glad to meet a friend in this beastly place. But, God bless my soul, I declare I've forgotten your name ! " " Made your breeches, sir," faltered the other man, who was indeed a hunting-tailor in London. " Of course, of course—*Major Bridges*—I've such a head for names, you must excuse me."

After dinner " K." sat out on the verandah and smoked with my husband, and it cost me an effort to ask him to write his name in V. le P.'s autograph-book. It is so hard to believe that a man who belongs to us as a nation—a man of whom we are so intensely proud—is actually shy.

Some time ago at Malta I heard a rather silly woman ask her neighbour at dinner, who was a friend of " K.'s," " Do you really *know* Lord Kitchener ? Is he *nice ?* " The ludicrous ineptitude of the adjective combined with the child-like lisp which caused the speaker to pronounce the words " *Ith he nithe ?* " made her hearers smile involuntarily.

Admiral Sir Frederick Bedford was as much beloved by the people of West Australia, where he was Governor for several years, as was his brother-admiral, Sir Harry Rawson, in New South Wales. His direct and, I am told, sometimes unconstitutional methods gained the affection and respect of the less cultivated and more shifting population of the younger State. We had known him since 1883 when he commanded the *Monarch* at Alexandria and was a dancing partner of mine in those merry days. I loved curtseying to him when he came to Sydney as a visiting Governor.

Sir Ernest (then Mr.) Shackleton was at Sydney when the little *Nimrod* was in dock in 1909 after her return from the Antarctic, and we saw something of him. He was more fluent as a lecturer than Captain Scott, but he possessed the same direct and convincing style which must hold any audience however careless or prejudiced. He gave me a Samoyede puppy born on board the *Nimrod* on her voyage back to Sydney. She was a little round ball of white velvet at ten days old, and, as the public were allowed on board the ship and Samoyede puppies were then so rare as to be a temptation to dog-stealers, " Shacky," as she came to be called, was handed over to me at this tender age as a necessary precaution. The flag-lieutenant volunteered to take charge of her at night and used to feed her with warm milk at frequent intervals until she was grown-up enough to sleep the night through. As she grew bigger her fur became thicker and thicker, and its silvery points stood out round her dear little fat person like a halo. She was the gentlest dog I ever knew, but she had no more notion of town geography than a blind beetle, and once outside the garden gate she was immediately and totally lost. This was a trial to herself and her mistress, but she was quite satisfied to stay in the garden and was beloved by all the household, so hers was not an unhappy life. When she was fifteen months old she caught influenza and, though her many friends did their best, she grew weaker and weaker and died after a short and blameless career, regretted by us all. She never gnawed boots or gloves, straw hats or chairs ; she was never known to snap at anyone, even in play, and her dark eyes with their black lids and thick white eyelashes expressed nothing but trust and affection. I had meant to bequeath her when we should leave Sydney to Professor David, whose own beautiful Samoyede " Ambrose " had recently died ; but it was not to be.

Madame Melba paid a long visit to her native land while we were there and I had several opportunities of hearing her. Her singing of English ballads left me feeling vaguely irritated, but I can hardly, even now, *think* of the " Salce ! " in *Otello* as I heard her give it in 1909 without a tightening of the heart.

She lunched with us one day at Admiralty House and made herself most agreeable, and it was amusing to see her afterwards trying to get music out of a great conch-shell which Captain Glossop had brought me from the Islands. It would not respond to treatment, so she just sang a big note into the blow-hole and I imagined that the pink lining of the conch-shell blushed a deeper rose with pride.

One afternoon I was asked to tea on board the *Planet*, a small German man-of-war lying in Farm Cove, and Madame Melba, who had come with Lord Dudley's party, shared a little table on deck with myself, an Austrian resident civilian and the first lieutenant of the ship. This officer spoke English beautifully and was in every respect a " good type " ; and, even now, relations with Germany being what they are, I think Madame Melba provoked him wantonly. The *Planet* was shortly recommissioning, and " You must be sorry to be going back so soon to ugly old Germany," was hardly an ingratiating remark. " Madame ? " said the young officer, feeling he could not have heard aright. Madame Melba repeated the *injure* more loudly. " But, Madame . . . " he protested. Then, turning to me, the aggressor observed in a distinct aside, " These Germans have no sense of humour."

Mr. and Mrs. Oscar Asche (Miss Lily Brayton) also lunched with us one day. As the actress sat beside my husband I had little opportunity of conversation with her, but she looked very handsome in a big black hat with a drooping " vallance " of lace which shaded her face. I found Mr. Asche a most interesting neighbour, a really good talker on a wide range of subjects and rather grave than otherwise.

Of Captain Scott's expressive face I have several pictures in my mind. It was gay and pleasant when he and his wife and I were photographed by Mr. Arthur Allen in the latter's car outside Admiralty House one day after they had lunched with me ; it was desperately courageous as he battled with the intolerable acoustic conditions of the Sydney

Glaciarium when lecturing to a vast audience ; steady, true and devoted when he met his wife's beautiful eyes.

CHAPTER XVI

OTHER NOTABILITIES

VERY soon after arriving in Sydney I had to consult Dr. Scot Skirving, to whose care Dr. Purves Stuart had commended my troublesome head. Then and during the three years which followed, I found the man himself so original and interesting, his wit so keen, his whole personality so vivid, that it was very hard to talk to him of *migraines*, and more than once I only remembered as an afterthought that I had come to him to be advised and patched up.

Two of his many stories I must tell :

A Scottish immigrant maid-servant had been remonstrated with by her mistress for having far more than the usual number of " followers." " Weel, mem," protested the accused, " a'buddy hes their hobbies ; minc's men."

A young English doctor who, as a very " new chum " in the " back-blocks," had been sent for to attend a man badly bitten by a poisonous snake, arrived at his destination stiff and sore after a long ride in the dark. Local remedies had already been

98

applied, and a square-cut black hole in the patient's leg was exhibited for the doctor's inspection. "My God ! man," said the horrified doctor, " what an enormous *serpent* it must have been ! "   The rough surgery of the man's mate had consisted in cutting away a considerable portion of the sufferer's calf and filling up the gap with a mixture of tar and other Bush condiments.

Mr. A. B. Paterson, the author of " The Man from Snowy River," and many other truly Australian poems, dined with us one night. Face, voice and manner—all had a special charm, and though I daresay he was not anxious to talk, being a most modest man, he was the very best of company. He proved a good friend to the Bush Book Club of New South Wales, of the usefulness of which he was not fully convinced until he chanced in a very " outback " spot to meet a decidedly illiterate little " cocky " (*cockatoo* = a very small settler) hugging a parcel of books under his arm. Mr. Paterson, unable to believe his eyes, inquired what he had got there. " Books," was the answer, " an' mighty good books too. You get 'em from a place called the Bush Book Club at Sydney."

We had the pleasure of making the acquaintance of Sir Kenneth Anderson, who visited Sydney while we were there. A scholar and an artist such as he might be thought out of place as the head of a great steamship company like the *Orient*, but his accession to that post has brought nothing but good with it, and the beautiful decorations, fittings and furniture

of the newer ships of his line—some, alas ! ripped
out and swept away when the ships were taken up
for war purposes—were chosen by him. There was
not one ugly thing on board the *Otway* when I visited
her at Sydney in 1910. From the settees and chairs
in the music-room to the very sponge-baskets in
the sleeping-cabins, everything was good, attractive
and appropriate. That Captain Symonds, who
commanded this beautiful ship, was the *Omrah's*
old skipper added to the *Otway's* advantages in my
eyes, and I wished we could have managed to return
with him when the time came.

Colonel Forster, Professor of Military History at
Sydney University, was lunching with us on the
same day as Sir Kenneth, and I wish I could
remember half the delightful stories the two of
them told. Colonel Forster contributed the yarn
—new at that time certainly—about the small
candidate for Osborne who was asked by the
President of the Board of Nomination, "What
animals eat grass ? " The boy appeared so confused
and embarrassed that the Admiral helped him by
saying, " Well, my boy, you know *cows* eat grass.
Can't you think of any other animal that does the
same ? " " Oh-h-h ! " gasped the little fellow, " I
thought you said ' What *Admirals* eat grass ? ' "

The examination question, "Write down what you
know of the fauna of Australia," was once answered
—so Sir Kenneth assured us—by another scholar of
tender years, " There are emus, kangaroos and
peccadilloes in Australia."

The Bishop of Goulburn, Doctor Christopher Barlow, is as good a story-teller as he is a bishop. He is responsible for the following :

A very old clergyman in the diocese of Goulburn had outlived his usefulness and decided to resign his post. His congregation, remorseful for having found him something of a bore and anxious to show their gratitude for past good work, presented him with a handsome testimonial in money and kind. The parishioner who acted as spokesman on the occasion was so eloquent and referred in such touching terms to the long and valued services of the recipient that the old man started up and cried in broken accents, " My friends, my dear, kind friends, had I known how much you loved me, I should never have resigned ! " And he forthwith *withdrew his resignation*, to the great disappointment and embarrassment of his well-wishers, who, on their side, were unable to withdraw the testimonial.

An " out-back " parson in another State who had had the misfortune to lose his wife, telegraphed to his Diocesan as follows :—" My dear wife passed away this morning. Will your Lordship kindly send a substitute before next Sunday."

Sir George Reid, late High Commissioner for the Commonwealth of Australia, was at Sydney during the greater part of our time and was always genial, clever and amusing. I have heard that whenever he can he goes to sleep ; in fact, at " any old time " by day or night he has the happy knack of snatching forty winks or more. And yet it is almost impossible to " catch him napping," for his wit is of the rare order which flashes out like lightning, and the more he was heckled at political meetings the more brilliant were his rejoinders. Indeed, he complained once in my hearing that he found it very hard to make a speech to which there were no interruptions.

It is told of Sir George that, on being accused by someone in the gallery at a political meeting of " having two faces," he retorted, " It is very evident my interrupter has only one, for if he possessed two he would certainly have left the one he is using at home."

On another occasion his audience booed and hissed so vigorously the very moment he began to speak that it was some time before he could get a hearing. Then he wailed in his curiously high, nasal tones, "I don't see what I have done to deserve this treatment. *I had only addressed you as ' Gentlemen.' "*

When a woman in the audience cried out, " If you were *my* husband I'd give you poison ! " Sir George remarked, " Madam, if you were my wife I'd take it."

Some critical hearer asked him after the departure of the Australian contingent for South Africa in 1900 why he had not volunteered. (Sir George was a big, stout man and already middle-aged.) " Well, you see," he answered, " you would miss me here, but *they would not miss me there.*"

He was, as far as I know, only once entirely

nonplussed. He had been very ill, and when he reappeared and spoke again for the first time in public he was most warmly received. One speaker had just said, " We thought not so long ago that we were going to lose Mr. Reid, and I hardly dare to think what would have been the result," when a ribald voice from the back of the hall interjected, " The fat would have been in the fire then, eh, Georgie ? "

It would not be fair to give the name of the Minister who made in speaking to me the following delightful malaprops, since he has lately shown how much greater is the importance of deeds than words, but for the benefit of those who collect such curiosities I feel constrained to record them here. This gentleman had attained Cabinet rank at the early age of forty—about twenty years after his arrival in Australia as an emigrant—and I said to him, " How little you dreamt when you landed in Australia what the future held for you ! " " Yes, indeed," he rejoined, " for, curiously enough, I was actually on my way to New Zealand when a mere chance decided me to disembark at Brisbane ; but," he concluded, " how true it is that we are unable to control our own *destinations*." Later on he said he had heard English people complain that Australian children were not so *venerable* to their parents as English children.

After meeting a considerable number of distinguished Australians it seems to me a pity that, though at home peerages are so lavishly distributed among persons mainly famous for possessing great fortunes amassed in trade, or for performing services to their party, " honours " of this nature are so rarely bestowed upon the most honourable and useful gentlemen of our overseas dominions. Knighthoods are given commonly enough, and very occasionally a baronetcy, but I fail to see why picked men of long and clean record, benefactors, to, and ornaments of their country—whether Australia, Canada, or New Zealand—are not chosen by the authorities at home when the ranks of the peerage are being filled up or augmented. Perhaps peerages have been offered to such men and refused by them. It would be interesting to know.

CHAPTER XVII

SIR HARRY RAWSON

MY story of our life in Australia would be incomplete without something more than a few casual references to Sir Harry Rawson. His personality cannot soon be forgotten by those who knew him, and his Life, written by a member of the family, will have brought his services and his character to the notice of many who never had that privilege. I do not lay claim to a very long or a very intimate acquaintance with him, but I can speak from my own knowledge of what he stood for to Australians at the close of the seven years spent by him in New South Wales. Five years is the customary limit of Governors' appointments, but New South Wales would not let Sir Harry go when his time had elapsed, so the period was extended, and I believe that only advancing years and the accumulated fatigues of a life devoted to his country prevented his continuing, as he was invited to do, still longer at his post.

The lameness contracted in the campaign of 1897 in West Africa had become not only a serious inconvenience to him but a cause of actual pain while he was in New South Wales, though he never grumbled. And yet I know he would lie awake for many hours after such public functions as necessitated long standing, solaced only by the smoking of innumerable cigars.

He never scamped his work, never considered himself, and commanded such a full measure of respect for his office as has rarely fallen to the lot of a Governor or Governor-General in Australia. His capacity for suggesting improvements or modifications to the State Government without any appearance of high-handedness or interference in what was not actually his concern was most remarkable. But he was prompt and straightforward to the verge of bluntness, never missing the psychological moment through an overstrained diplomacy, or an unwise regard either for the feelings of his hearers or the security of his personal popularity.

As an orator he was not famous, but his extraordinary capacity for holding statistics in his mind and using them with the fullest effect in his speeches would often make his hearers marvel. Generous he was to a fault. There was no lurking thought in his mind of saving a penny of his pay, nor yet of his private income, so long as he could be of use to the people of New South Wales. He was as simple in his manner of life as was compatible with the position he held, and his dignity was never impaired by his benevolence nor his benevolence by his dignity. A visiting Governor once said to me with a sigh, " I don't know how Sir Harry manages it, but no matter where he goes there is never a covered head in the crowd when the National Anthem is sung. I wish I could say the same."

His own loyalty to the Governor-General was a solid thing, and he never spared himself when it was a question of adding to the weight and importance of his superior, though I am very sure his superiors learnt much from him privately, since his knowledge of men, gained in the long years of constant employment in the Navy, had been supplemented by an acquaintance with the customs and conditions of the State he governed which few, if any, of his predecessors could rival.

His thoughtfulness for others and his carelessness of his own comfort were illustrated in a hundred ways. I still possess the little silver chain with a clip at the end of it which he devised for preventing one's table napkin from slipping off one's knee at dinner-parties—a constantly recurring annoyance to anyone wearing slippery gowns of silk or satin. Once I sat beside him on the daïs at a great ball at the Governor-General's under a marquee through which the rain had forced an entrance; little puddles were collecting close to our chairs, and an occasional fat drop of rain would fall on our heads or slide down the back of our necks, but he bore it with such a pleasant patience that I could only try to imitate him and laugh when he said that in a dry country like Australia one could not complain of being situated in the "catchment area" (the area whence water is drawn for supplying public reservoirs).

The devotion felt for Sir Harry in New South Wales included his daughter, who was officially recognised as the chief lady of the State and had put aside all the ordinary pleasures and pursuits of a girl to shoulder her burden after the death of her mother. That Lady Rawson, whom alas! I never met, literally lost her life in the fulfilment of her duty is well known. Regardless of pain and exhaustion, she worked till she could work no longer, went home for a holiday and died at sea on the return voyage to Sydney. Her goodness was of the quality which shines from the eyes of such a brave and selfless woman, and her memory is revered and loved in New South Wales, not only by those who knew her, but by countless others of whose very existence she was ignorant.

People who have never lived in one of the far-distant dominions can hardly be expected to understand what a woman of Lady Rawson's temperament and ability can effect for the solidarity of the Empire. Some Governors' wives have been noble examples of sweetness, courage and helpfulness; others have been merely useless; the conduct of a few has been actively prejudicial to the prestige of the Crown their husbands represented. Lady Rawson was what I once heard described as " a piece of Empire-cement."

I went to say farewell to the Governor at his office in Macquarie Street early in January, 1909, before we left for Hobart, whence we returned only after his final departure from Australia. Sir Harry and I were alone, and as I could not find words in which to tell him how I hated to bid him good-bye, I took his kind old hand and kissed it. He made no protest, which was like him, for even if he thought me silly he would not embarrass me by implying it. Perhaps he understood how I felt and did not wish to protest.

CHAPTER XVIII

HOLIDAYS AND VISITS

My husband was away in the flag-ship for about seven months in each year, and during his absence, though I spent the greater part of my time at

Sydney, I paid a few visits and each spring took a short holiday before the rush and racket of the race-week. On these holiday trips I was lucky enough to secure Mrs. Wesché (hereinafter known as Phœbe) for my companion, and the first of them was to the Blue Mountains. Commander H. W. Bowring, of the *Powerful*, who had been left behind in Sydney with a broken knee-cap when the ship went south in August, 1908, was just well enough to join us, and we went up together to Medlow Bath (about 3,500 feet) to find it snowing hard. He, of course, could not take vigorous exercise other than that supplied vicariously by the hands of a fierce but effectual Swedish masseur, but Phœbe and I set out at once, and almost ran along the road for miles to come back glowing. The nights were very cold, but a kind Irish chambermaid made up a fire of logs in the little windowless vestibule off which our rooms opened, and there we sat and toasted ourselves in an atmosphere which just stopped short of suffocating us. The snow was succeeded by days of cloudless sunshine, and we walked on the flat ridge-top, or scrambled about among the clefts and ravines of the mountain-side, drinking in the wonderful air and feeling younger and stronger with every draught. After weeks of enforced inaction in hospital our lame escort performed feats of mountaineering which considerably impressed and alarmed us, and we were all three in the gayest spirits when we returned to Sydney.

And yet there was something uncanny about the

great dark chasms, the huge trees and the silence of those blue mountains. The hoarse drawn-out cawing—like the cry of a sick child—of carrion crows, ever on the look-out for some dead or dying animal as they hovered high overhead, seemed only to emphasise the stillness around us, and when the gorgeous roses of the sunset faded and the intense blue of the sky turned to a star-pierced black we repaired gladly to our log fire to play foolish games or spin yarns with two young lieutenants who had come up to Medlow, like ourselves, for a breath of mountain air.

Next spring Phœbe and I went by ourselves to the quiet little hotel at Stanwell Park, about forty miles south of Sydney. It was set in the shadow of a thickly-wooded hill and overlooked green glades that merged into the yellow sands of the Pacific shore. Here we performed no feats of pedestrianism, but paddled happily along the beach, picked shells, read and slept till it was time to go back to our work and play at Sydney. This we did refreshed and restored by the contact with unspoilt nature and the complete release from responsibility which such a holiday affords.

For our last spring outing we chose Austinmeer, a little further along the south coast than Stanwell Park. Here, between the mountains and the sea, we passed a week of peace and simple comfort in the boarding-house kept by an English lady, not too proud to be a good cook. The late Judge Louis Russell, of the Bombay Courts, who in Australian air had miraculously recovered from a severe illness, came with us, as gay as a lark just out of a cage ; and Professor Barraclough, of Sydney University, Lieutenant Harrison * of the *Powerful*, and Mr. C. Bundock, a man of Devon, long and well known in New South Wales, joined us later. Our table-talk is not worth recording, for all our appetites were good, and we spent our days in the fresh air and sunshine, poked about on the long beaches and among the tumbled masses of dark rock, boiled the " billy " for tea and watched the red-heads flitting among the bushes. We made but one expedition, and that was to the top of the Bulli Pass. The Bush flowers, which were then at their best, scented the pure air as we climbed the road leading to the plateau which was our goal. Thence we looked down over primeval forest and past the blue foot-hills to the long curves of the Pacific shore where white-plumed ocean rollers were moulding into crescents the edges of the golden sand.

Besides these little recreative pauses every spring I allowed myself a delightful week at Tuggeranong (Mr. J. Cunningham's) in November, 1909, and stayed a few days at Bishop's Court with the Bishop of Goulburn, at Pomeroy with Mr. and Mrs. A. Dalglish, and at Cunningham Plains with Mr. Bundock in the following summer.

My husband and I together visited Baroona, the home of the late Mr. Albert Dangar, genial sportsman and generous capitalist, in 1910. There was never

* Drowned in H.M.S. *Natal*.

any question of roughing it on any of these visits, so my experiences were only those of a perfectly ordered hospitality—a hospitality seasoned, however, with a peculiar cordiality and consideration which raised it above the ordinary level. It had, too, a Bush flavour, warm and aromatic, like the atmosphere created by a fire of myall-wood or the scent of fresh gum-leaves in the sun.

My first acquaintance with the Bush was made at Tuggeranong, near Queanbeyan, and as first impressions have a certain value owing to their freshness I will record them here.

The impression above all others which the Englishman new to the Bush receives is one of stillness and space. The stillness is such that he can hear, or thinks he can hear, every revolution and pulsation of his own internal machinery; the space makes him feel as insignificant as a solitary midge in St. Paul's Cathedral. The Bushman's heritage is one of wide horizons; of far-stretching landscapes uncut by macadamised roads, unscored by walls and hedges, unspoilt by cities; and over his head a high dome of clear air, unsullied by coal-smoke and untainted by the exhalations and emanations too common in the well-thumbed, dog's-eared little Mother-country.

Such conditions as these create in the Bushman born and bred a sense over and above the number usually allotted to human beings, a sense which he shares with the Red Indian, the sense we are busily, and very properly, attempting to cultivate in the

Boy Scout. It is the compendium of all the senses; the essence and apotheosis of seeing, hearing, smelling, tasting, and touching; in a word, the sense of observation. Can we wonder if the Bushman, possessing this sense, pitched and focussed for use in the wilderness, feels cramped and baffled almost anywhere in the Old Country? There he is deafened by the multiplicity of noises, bothered by the whirling and vibrating zoetrope, choked and blinded by fog and smoke, and exasperated by "cross-trails." A, to him, short ride in any direction would bring him to the sea, an element which he regards rather as a barrier than a way of escape and expansion. He is a quiet and law-abiding person as a rule, but the geographical limitations, the narrow conventions, the regulations and discipline necessary in a country where air is measured by the cubic foot, make him long to break things, to trespass and to poach. The nostalgia felt by a Swiss peasant serving as a waiter in a London restaurant is nothing in comparison with the craving of a Bushman visiting England for the first time for the fresh and sunlit spaciousness of his own great continent. Even a five-year-old Australian-bred boy driving with his grandmother in Hyde Park has been heard to remark contemptuously, "Why, you could hardly turn a buggy here!"

At Tuggeranong the sensation of aloofness is almost disconcerting. We might have been dropped from an airship on to a spare planet among a folk so little given to speech that they might well be of another race than ours. Shearing is in full swing, and fifty men and boys—shearers, musterers, and rouseabouts—work, eat, and rest within a hundred yards of the homestead, and yet neither by day nor by night does any noise of shouting, singing, or angry voices reach our ears. The lonely stillness of the Bush engenders in its sons an astonishing power, habit—call it what you will—of silence. Messengers ride into the yard, do their business and go about their business, and we look on as though at a cinematographic display. In the shearing-shed only the whirring of the sixteen machines is to be heard. The sheep before their shearers are dumb; and but for the occasional call of " Tar ! " from a shearer who has drawn blood and summons the " tar-boy " with his pot of antiseptic, the eight-hours day might pass undisturbed by the sound of a human voice.

The very children at the homestead are quieter than ours. Barefooted and bareheaded they steal about the garden and orchard, and never seem to shout and quarrel at their play. Half the day they spend among the gnarled branches of the big almond-trees that shade the flower-filled courtyard from the morning sun, as much at home there as the red and blue parrots who share the fruit with them. And then, when the lamps are lighted, they creep into the central hall, to bury their small persons in armchairs and sofas and their minds in books.

Tuggeranong is a sheep station pure and simple,

and the month is November. Miles and miles of fairly green grass, broken by groups and patches of gum-trees—eternally varied as individuals, eternally monotonous as forest—surround us on every side, rising to the knees of the bluest of blue mountains in the west. A river, not unlike a Highland stream in summer, lies between us and the foothills, and close to the homestead there is a willow-fringed creek where precious water flows perennially, burrowing and reappearing like a silver bodkin as it threads its difficult way over and under the golden sand.

In one of the hurdled yards the sheep for to-morrow's shearing are already collected, and from the shearing-shed into the pens outside trickles a stream of freshly-shorn ewes, bewildered and ghostlike, with ears unnaturally prominent now that no ruff of wool makes a background for them, and eyes red and blinking ; pinkish-striped where the shearer has grazed them, and spotted here and there with the black compound smeared upon their cuts. They are all merinos, the breed which above all others has proved profitable in this country. Fold upon fold of loose skin drapes the merino's body, so that the fleece, when skilfully gathered up by a " rouseabout " and spread out upon the wool-roller's table, looks as though it had been worn by some beast as large as a lion. From the pens the ewes (with two pet lambs, now elderly but still coquettish, leading the procession as decoys) are driven to the yards where the famishing lambs await them, and there a piteous scene ensues. The mothers, dazed and unnerved by the terrors of the shearing-shed, and hungry after the fast of twenty-four hours, are hustled in among their woolly, wailing babies who may well be pardoned for not recognising in them the comfortable and indulgent parents of yesterday. The poor ewes on their side seem to have lost what little wits they had, and make no effort to sort themselves. . Pushing and thrusting, the seething mob of shorn and unshorn sways hither and thither, and long hours will pass before each of the twelve hundred ewes of this day's shearing will be reunited with her own particular lamb. The babel of bleating and baa-ing will go on, now rising to a frenzied chorus of tenors and altos, now dropping to a single distracted cry. The sound is more like the cheering during a Royal procession through the streets of London than anything else, and far into the night we who are unused to the noise and un-hardened to its pathos will hear it, thankful when it ceases and we know that at last all is well, and that the one great event in the sheep's calendar is safely over for at any rate twelve hundred merino ewes and their innocent progeny on this station of Tuggeranong, N.S.W.

At daybreak there is silence in the sheepyards, and the musical jangle of the magpies down at the creek first wakes, and then lulls us back to sleep until such time as the bare feet of Bolton, Unity, and Pax, pattering on the boards of the long verandah, announce that another day has fairly begun.

CHAPTER XIX

VICE-ROYALTY IN VILLEGGIATURA

WE were the guests of both Sir Harry Rawson and Lord Chelmsford, his successor in office, at Hill View, some fifty miles from Sydney, where the Governors of New South Wales have a country house, and both these visits had an informal character very pleasant to recall. Hill View is not a large or imposing house ; rather, indeed, what used to be called a *cottage orné*, and there is nothing specially beautiful in the surrounding country of sparsely-wooded, round-topped hills. It was therefore due to Sir Harry himself and to his daughter that my visit to them has left an abiding record on my mind. To Captain Leslie Wilson, R.M.L.I., A.D.C.,* I owe gratitude for the ready kindness and the cheerfulness which so marked this, in every sense, distinguished officer. It is true that his parrot bit me without provocation, and to my pained surprise (for I am always humbly polite to parrots), but for this I could not hold him responsible.

It was on Christmas Eve of the following year that my husband and I arrived at Hill View to visit Lord Chelmsford. We had said good-bye to our hostesses, the late Mrs. Onslow and her daughter, at Camden Park a couple of hours earlier, when the thermometer stood at 105° in the shade, Bush-fires

* Unionist Member for Reading, and serving as Lieutenant-Colonel in the Naval Division.

were blazing on both sides of the railway-line, and we were limp and jaded from airless nights and scorching days. But before we reached Hill View rain fell in torrents, and when Lord Chelmsford greeted us on the door-step with the words " I've got three tons of coal " (a coal-strike of long duration was then in process) we were glad and thankful to know fires could be lighted. That night the temperature dropped to 45° and I rejoiced beneath a pair of blankets. It seemed incredible that we had sat out in the garden at Camden Park only the night before—sat, too, in the almost total silence of despair, for, after a most disastrous drought, each one of us was anxiously watching the sky and literally praying for rain.

We all wore fancy-dress that Christmas night, a time-honoured custom dear to the four clever and high-spirited children of the house, and Lord Chelmsford as a sleek, meek, bleating curate was so excruciatingly and unexpectedly lifelike that I was truly relieved to find him restored to his own attractive personality next morning.

Miss Meriel Talbot was our fellow-guest at Hill View during this visit, and I have written in verse what I should scarcely dare to say of her in cold prose.

At this time Lady Chelmsford was in England, but she had earlier in the year been my hostess at State Government House, Sydney, and then, and ever since, my good friend. Her little daughter Margaret, born in 1911, is my god-child—one to be pioud of—and in addition to my name she bears that of Sydney, the beautiful capital of the State which will never forget the three and a half years of valuable work (1909—1913) and sympathetic, yet conscientious, friendship given to it by Lord Chelmsford and his wife.

When Sir Harry Rawson, after a period just twice as long in the same office, bade good-bye to New South Wales it seemed impossible that his successor —or any successor, in fact—should earn and hold the respect and warm affection he had continuously enjoyed. But, fortunately perhaps, Lord Chelmsford was so complete a contrast to Sir Harry in all but the essentials of straight dealing and hard work that comparison was out of the question.

In the hot months of February and March, 1910, I gradually drifted down through New South Wales to Victoria, and spent a very pleasant fortnight up at Macedon, forty miles from Melbourne, where Sir Thomas Carmichael (now Lord Carmichael and Governor of Bengal) and Lady Carmichael were passing the summer. The many-sidedness of Lord Carmichael and his remarkable fund of knowledge, ranging from the origin and value of gems to the breeding of horses and cattle, made him a valuable as well as a popular Governor of Victoria, and it would be impossible to say too much of Lady Carmichael's suitability for the position she then held. She not only inspired such of the people of Victoria as needed inspiration ; when she started an enterprise she piloted it to success.

It was cool to chilliness on Mount Macedon in March, and I used to go for a quick scramble up the steep wooded slopes to warm myself every morning after breakfast. We motored about the charming neighbourhood in the afternoons and sometimes paid a surprise visit to a school, which I always found interesting. On the walls of these country schools there were displayed pictures of snakes, so many of which are poisonous in Australia, with detailed descriptions and rules for the treatment of snake-bite underneath, and I have no doubt that the information so given was of great service. The ignorance of our own country folk, generally speaking, about snakes strikes me as remarkable, and to get a clear description of a grass-snake, a slow-worm, an adder (or viper) in Wiltshire has taken me a very long time. Only once did I have any dealings with a poisonous reptile in Australia, for I suppose the tarantula which sat above the door of my bedroom at Hill View cannot be called anything but an insect. At Cunningham Plains I discovered what is known as a wood-adder tucked up in my mosquito net one morning. Luckily I had braved the mosquitoes on the previous very hot night rather than lose any air by pulling the net round me, for it would have been highly unpleasant to bring the wood-adder down upon my head. The housemaid would have no dealings with it, so I begged Mr. Bundock to come to the rescue, and with due precautions he secured and then despatched it. It had a nasty three-cornered head, but no tail more important than a lizard's, and it certainly had legs.

But to return to Lady Carmichael. No day, even while she was supposed to be having a holiday at Macedon, was free from work requiring thought and care. It would be only too easy for the thoughtless or careless wife of a Governor to embarrass his position and handicap his usefulness by her blunders, and, though of course her husband's staff are her advisers and " scouts," she has great responsibilities which cannot be delegated to anyone. Indeed the amount of real hard work done by the wife of a State Governor in Australia—such a one as Lady Carmichael—would surprise the amateur-philanthropist at home who is at liberty to choose her line and resign her post when she feels so disposed.

From Macedon I went west to Marble Hill to stay with Sir Day Bosanquet, Governor of South Australia, and Lady Bosanquet. This was far the most attractive and convenient of the country houses allotted to State Governors which I had an opportunity of seeing. It is perched on a spur of the Bush-clad hills above Adelaide, and from it one has a wide view of the sea and the plain below. The climate is delicious, and at that season—early autumn—we enjoyed a succession of perfect days, none of which were overcrowded with visiting or sight-seeing, and it was most refreshing to sit on the wide verandahs or motor along the winding roads which gave access to valleys and gorges of great and varied beauty.

The garden at Marble Hill was then sadly handicapped by want of a good water supply, which grieved Lady Bosanquet, a practical and devoted gardener ; but at Government House, Adelaide, she had all that could be demanded by the most exacting horticulturist. There one found masses of dazzling colour in flowers and foliage, and in the Botanical Gardens hard by there were stretches of rose-coloured water-lilies and other aquatic beauties which positively took my breath away.

As I recall those sunny days in South Australia the kind thoughtfulness of the Governor's two A.D.C.'s throughout my visit comes back to me. Captain Nigel Baines, who retrieved my wandering luggage mis-sent to Adelaide, was one, and Captain Edwin Wright the other. Since then both have given their lives for their country, and each has left a widow to mourn his loss. It was during my visit to Marble Hill that Captain Wright announced his engagement to Miss Barr-Smith, of South Australia ; it is less than two years since Captain Baines wrote to tell me he was married.

CHAPTER XX

SOME ASPECTS OF BUSH-LIFE

THE distinction between the Australian of the towns and the Australian of the Bush is one so marked that the most casual visitor cannot fail to notice it. A far wider gulf separates the man bred and employed in an Australian city from the Bushman than that which lies between our cockney and his bucolic brother, for nowhere in these islands can one find the utter isolation which characterises the Australian " back-blocks." It produces splendid men, silent, self-reliant and thoughtful ; possessed of a natural dignity, and showing a quite peculiar courtesy and gentleness towards women and children. Few men afraid of their own thoughts could long survive such an utter severance from the means to stifle them as long solitary months in the Bush entail, just as few sailors who can live for weeks with no more than a plank between themselves and eternity can be wholly bad.

Nearly every real man, however, has something tough and insensitive in his fibre which enables him to enjoy a solitude not unmixed with danger ; few women do more than endure these conditions. The wives of Australian pioneers were for the most part heroines born or made, since in their day to the fear of bushrangers and the discipline of exile was added the oft-recurring trial of bearing children where no skilled woman, much less a doctor, was within reach. And can anything be more harrowing than the spectacle of a mother whose baby had died while its father had gone two hundred miles to fetch a doctor, nailing down the coffin of that baby *with her own hands* because the carpenter who had fashioned the rough box was so drunk that he was driving the nails in at random and piercing the little body inside ?   This is a thing that really happened.

Only faith in God, the purity of the air they breathed, and the constant occupation their home duties afforded could have produced and maintained the level-headed courage and the constitutional hardiness that marked the mothers and grand-mothers of the present generation of Australians.

Nowadays the tendency to hand over the management of " out-back " stations to paid deputies while the owners live in or near the great cities is on the increase, and, though the conditions of life in the Bush are far more civilised than heretofore, one can understand that men do not as a rule desire to expose their wives and children to the hardships and the unutterable loneliness inseparable from it. And the women themselves shrink from such an existence, and cling to the comforts and the society to be found in towns.   It is a perfectly comprehensible reaction.

Here and there will be found a woman of stiffer mould who actually enjoys the glorious freedom of the Bush oblivious of its loneliness and risk.   With the use of her head and hands and the society of her husband and children she can make as fine a thing —perhaps a finer—of her life than many of her sisters in Melbourne or Sydney.   She is the " mistress " of the station, a little community numbering from ten to fifty souls, for whom she provides and by whom she is looked up to.   I have been on one such station, not " out-back," but poor in neighbours and many miles from an unimportant railway station, and if one dare apply such an adjective as patriarchal to the atmosphere of any spot in Australia that of X. was patriarchal ; but in the best sense. Every soul on the station was to the mistress a friend as well as an employé, for every soul was befriended as well as employed. The maid-servants married the boundary-riders, or other station hands, and their children when old enough found employment about the place. When the first of the great bullock-wagons piled high with bales of wool started for the railway station (I was there at shearing time) young Mahony was in charge of the leading team. With the second wagon came old Mahony, blue-eyed and white-haired, with a tie to match his eyes and an incongruous band of rusty crape round his battered billy-cock ; and little Mahony of the third generation brought up the rear on a half-broken pony. The shearers— transitory hands—the shearers' cook (a most important functionary), the casual " sundowner " in search of a night's lodging, all saluted the mistress, not because she expected or exacted the tribute, but because she was well known and well liked. It was an unconscious acceptance of the patriarchal system ; the result of wise and kind management, not by a manager but by a master.

Managers, however good, are hampered in their relations with their men by the fact that they are deputies. It is not theirs to make allowances, remit debts or lay out money in such improvements as do not pay but merely increase the comfort and happiness of employés. They may be admirable in every relation of life, but they are only middlemen after all, and the most untamed of " native-born " Australians appreciates the difference between the owner and the best possible agent.

The absence of companionship for both children and their parents in the less accessible parts of the Bush is an evil and a hardship which only closer settlement can mitigate, but the difficulty of educating isolated children has been courageously met by the responsible authorities. There are now travelling schoolmasters who go their long rounds among the scattered settlers, taking care that no child, however remotely placed, can grow up without education. This opportunity is frequently taken advantage of by the parents to the great improvement of their own characters and of their usefulness as citizens. I have good authority for quoting as true the following story which illustrates the almost incredible loneliness of the back-blocks. A little boy, on seeing a man approach the solitary cottage where he had been brought up, called out to his mother, " See, mum ; here's a thing like father coming ! " The *thing* was the first man other than his father the child had set eyes on !

The desire of successive Australian Governments that every child in the great continent shall have equality of educational opportunity has already had magnificent results, but in quite recent years an even greater effort has been made to render

State education more perfectly adapted to the needs of each individual child and to give it that continuity which alone leads to success. School examinations are not now held to suit the ambition of teachers and foster the pride of foolish parents by the production of prodigies. The education offered is carefully designed and graded to fit the needs of the country which produces the pupils, who, in return, will become its worthier citizens.

If Australia is underpopulated, if she suffers from the various ills, social and economic, which arise from her inadequate population, she can at least lay claim to the credit of making the best possible provision for every one of her children from the first moment of his life. Adequate wages for the breadwinners, sound education for their children, Children's Courts for juvenile offenders, a system of State Children's Relief which it would seem impossible to better—all these are secured to the working class in the Australia of to-day, with National Service, as a guarantee for discipline and patriotism, to top up with. One can see that the Statesmen who devise, and the public departments which carry out, such measures as affect the mental and bodily welfare of the working class aim at making of each unit a valuable national asset.

Immigration is very necessary since great spaces are still uninhabited, great resources still untapped, but I can understand now, as never before, the passionate desire of Australians for the best immigrants only and their equally passionate hostility to the introduction of inferior human material. Immigration is slow, but it is being encouraged with increasing liberality. The " landless man " is being welcomed to the " manless land."

After the war, who knows whether an influx of men from these shores, flatly refusing to resume conditions of office or domestic life grown intolerable, may not be the best gift England can make to the Australia which has given so freely to England ?

CHAPTER XXI

VARIOUS REFLECTIONS

I WAS very much struck by the superior education of the class in Australia corresponding to that which attends the Board Schools at home. That the Public Schools, as their free schools are called, provide a far better education than do ours, is apparent from the better grammar used among Australian working people and the superiority which is very noticeable in their handwriting and epistolary style. Their correctness of speech often surprised me. They have their own slang, of course, and very quaint and pointed it is, but the dropping of the *h* and a general slovenliness as regards both grammar and articulation are far from being as common as they are in England.

This may arise from the fact that what may be called self-respecting people are the rule—people with the wish, the opportunity, and the space to rise in the world, whereas in this overcrowded country the conditions of life are apt to crush ambition even in its most modest forms.

As for the Australian accent, it remains a mystery, and why it attacks some members of one family and not others, like a capricious epidemic, I have no idea. It is simply a cockney accent, more or less virulent, which may affect to some degree the best educated and most carefully brought up of Australians. At first it offends one's ear, and in very severe cases it will always do so, but in a general way one becomes used to it, so much so, indeed, that if one were asked " Has So-and-so an Australian accent ? " it would be hard to answer the question with certainty without having a fresh opportunity of listening to the person under discussion. On the other hand, if one chanced in some public place to hear an English voice, known or unknown, among a babel of Australian voices its different *timbre* and accent struck one immediately.

The *Sydney Bulletin* loves to gibe at the English accent, and it was quite true that most of us pronounced the flagship's name as though it were spelt *Pah-fle*, for which there can be no valid excuse. But when all is said and done the standard accent for Britons is presumably that of the best-educated *and* best-bred persons in the capital of the British Empire. One can no more maintain that Cornishmen, Glaswegians or Corkovians speak with the " right " accent than that Canadians, or Australasians, or Barbadians alone possess the secret of doing so. Individuals anywhere may possess it, but if there is a standard it must be looked for at the hub of the Empire just as certainly as one looks for longitude 0° at Greenwich.

We were both much impressed by the great superiority in physique and intelligence observable in the dock-labourers of Australia when compared with those at home. The drink-soaked, bulbous-nosed horror who may be described as a " casual "— for he alternates between casual employment and the casual-ward of a workhouse—was not to be seen. During a strike in Sydney we had a good opportunity of seeing the stevedores who crowded round the ships alongside to watch the amateur volunteers loading up, and a pleasanter, healthier-looking set of men it would be hard to find. Intelligent faces, with square brows and the beautiful thick-lashed grey, or hazel, eyes of the New South Walesmen, predominated, and the personal cleanliness of the men, accounted for by the universal habit of the bath in Australia, particularly struck us. At Admiralty House itself there were four bathrooms in the house ; one at the barracks, where the boats' crews lived ; one in the men-servants' quarters ; and one in the *chef's* cottage. In shame and confusion over our own shortcomings in this department we had a second bathroom installed in our little house in Wiltshire before we returned there.

We had been warned that the offer of higher wages would tempt our English servants to desert us in Australia, so it was, we thought, something of an achievement to bring back every one of those who went out with us—eleven, counting the flag-lieutenant's and secretary's servants who lived at Admiralty House. Of the men-servants who came home with us, no less than three have found their way back again to Australia, where they are—unless they have enlisted—in civil employ but not in domestic service. Thus strongly does that big new country appeal to those who have once known it.

There is no doubt that the conditions of life at Sydney proved extremely pleasant to all our servants, and the two maids who went out with us readily adapted themselves to their surroundings, and were so kindly and cordially welcomed by hitherto unknown relations, and the friends of those relations, that their outings were made very enjoyable. In addition to this the excellent steamer-service on the harbour made it possible for them to get plenty of fresh air in the hottest weather at a negligible cost. But they had no desire to remain in Australia. There women-servants can rarely confine their duties to the exact limits laid down in an English household. With us a carefully-trained cook or housemaid is a specialist, and does not easily expand into the *bonne à tout faire* who will wash, or wait at table, or act as maid without considering whether it is " her place " to do so or not. It is the *bonne à tout faire*, the " cook-general " of the advertisement sheet, who is chiefly needed in those parts of the Empire where wages are almost double those given in England. Such a servant welcomes the help of her mistress in the kitchen and elsewhere, whereas the specialist resents or suspects it. One hears it said that Australian mistresses expect too much of their servants and give them only indifferent accommodation. There may well be mistresses answering to this description, since there are everywhere careless or exacting employers, but in Australia, where the demand so greatly exceeds the supply, a mistress would be extraordinarily short-sighted were she to overdrive or underfeed her servants. But the State, which leaves very little to chance in these matters, has recently ordered an investigation respecting the housing of servants.

CHAPTER XXII

PICKETT

HE was a Blue Marine and only second orderly when I took up my abode at Admiralty House, but, though the chief orderly weighed more, Pickett, who was spare to leanness, overtopped him by a couple of inches. Dark-eyed, straight-featured, with the most symmetrical of black moustaches, drilled to perfection and as neat as a new pin, he was certainly a fine figure of a man. I might never have come to know him well had he not been left behind as office messenger when the flagship was cruising in the winter of 1909. Very soon I looked upon him as my chief adviser and prop. Our telephones in North Sydney, which were atrociously bad, always yielded to his treatment, though they reduced me to despair or imbecility, and often I descended to the empty and echoing office to beg Pickett's help in getting my messages through. While we waited till the " cross-talking " (always more distinctly audible than the answers we elicited) had subsided we discoursed of many things, and once Pickett produced a very old magazine containing a short story— unsigned—of mine. It was not a very good story, but he found it interesting because I was the author. How he knew that it was mine I cannot now remember.

That winter the white barge—later dedicated to my service in the *Powerful's* absences—was away, and when one of the carriage horses developed a corn on its foot which required rest and " fermenting " (in the language of the stable) my mobility was so seriously interfered with that I was compelled to use the steam-ferries and electric trams when I wished to shop in Sydney proper. I did not mind the ferries, but I hated the trams, because I did not know the geography of the city, and the conductors were unsympathetic, not to say curt, in their replies to my simple inquiries.

So it came about that I asked Pickett to convoy

me on a round of shopping one sunny morning, and he accepted the responsibility with all the promptness and dignity which were so admirably united in his speech and manner. He took charge of the pennies and walked close behind me to the Kirribilli landing stage, whence we crossed to the busy vortex of Circular Quay. Both in the steamer and the tram he sat where he could keep an eye upon me, but as far away as possible, and when we embarked and disembarked he watched to see I was safe, but refrained from helping me. He led the way straight as a die to the right tram and showed me when it was time to leave it by rising from his seat. So far so good ; and my first errand was accomplished at my own pace because I happened to know the way. But later, when he had to be my guide through the intricacies of street traffic, he strode on ahead of me, and I had to scurry panting behind lest I should have to traverse a crossing without his protection. I was a long time in one shop, but when I emerged I found him considering the spring hats in the window with unruffled calm He never made me feel that there was anything odd in the " job " he had undertaken to oblige me. *Per mare, per terram* he was, like a true marine, quite equal to any situation.

When the establishment of an Australian branch of the Royal Navy was under consideration I asked Pickett if he would like to join it, hinting that under a democratic government he would have the chance of getting a commission. The gravity of his demeanour combined with the twinkle in his eye as he said, " No, thank you, m' lady. I find it *quite* hard enough to be an acting-bombardier," was something to remember.

Pickett became chief orderly in the same year, and never was there a better, for if he did not know anything about a place or a person he made it his business to inform himself without loss of time. It was distressing to leave him behind when we came home, but there was no vacancy for him at Chatham, where the messengers were pensioners and the orderlies Red Marines. However, when he finally returned from Australia we were still at Chatham, and " though not partial to the place *as a rule*," he spent two week-ends at Admiralty House, or rather in the coxswain's quarters over the garage, and he was upright and grave as ever, very smart in plain clothes, with the same twinkle in his dark eyes and the same interest in the big affairs of the Empire on which we used to converse in the telephone room at Sydney.

I have Pickett's portrait in my room and beneath it a coloured photograph of the *Powerful* as she looked leaving Sydney Harbour on the day of my departure in 1911. These he sent me from Australia. At present he is " somewhere in the North Sea," pining to have a go at the Germans.

CHAPTER XXIII

SUMMER AT SYDNEY

SOCIAL duties are, to a great extent, remitted at Sydney in the hot weather, and social intercourse is, if more restricted, more easy in its character, since there is less of the official element at this season.

In November, 1909, my husband and I took to bathing in a swimming enclosure about four miles down the harbour at Clifton Gardens (formerly called Chowder Bay), whither we used to go by barge, and we got a great deal of healthful pleasure out of this exercise, one we had always loved wherever and whenever the sea was warm enough to suit our ideas of comfort. There was never any crowd of swimmers at Clifton Gardens, because surf-bathing is far more popular in Australia than the tamer delight of plain swimming in smooth water. I confess that neither of us was daring enough to face the risk of meeting a shark, and though it may be humiliating to swim in a circle of some fifty yards diameter, like a goldfish in a big bowl, the sense of security we enjoyed was worth the hazard to our reputation as persons of courage. All the same, I know there is a special fascination in the wild game of surf-bathing, for those who take to it find little pleasure in smooth-water swimming and seem to derive some peculiar benefit from dashing about among the buffeting breakers.

Nothing could have been more attractive than the setting of the bathing-place in the bay at Clifton Gardens. The greensward touched the sand, and behind it rose steep hills, wooded and boulder-strewn. None of the banalities of a popular French *plage* or English beach were there, and the fact that we went and returned by water added greatly to our enjoyment, and spared us all the fatigue which so easily neutralises the pleasure and benefit of bathing for " those no longer young."

We spent the greater part of the hot weather of 1909—10 at Sydney, as the *Powerful* had gone to Colombo to recommission, and the usual summer cruise was delayed until February in consequence. We said good-bye with much regret to those of the old commission who were not returning, and by way of a farewell entertainment for their special benefit we decided to give an evening garden-party at Admiralty House. Of course we had counted on moonlight, and Captain (then Commander) Wilfrid Nunn, navigating-commander of the flagship, in whose charge were all those things connected with the solar system in so far as they affect ships, had faithfully promised me a moon which should be large and brilliant by nine o'clock. For no good reason, or reason good enough in the eyes of a hostess, the disobliging satellite hid herself, or played a game of bo-peep, perverse and fugitive throughout the party. We received ironical congratulations on having provided our younger guests with so adequate an opportunity for unobserved leave-taking—and some of them may indeed have had cause to bless us—but it was extremely awkward for guests and hosts alike to be unable to see each other's faces at the moment of arrival or departure, and hunting for missing members of the party when it was time to leave must have given the chaperons a lot of trouble. We had meant well, for daylight garden-parties at Sydney in the month of December can be extremely hot and uncomfortable; it was therefore entirely the moon's fault that things went wrong. There were Chinese lanterns, certainly, but they were far more ornamental than useful.

As a rule a spell of three days of hot and searing westerly wind is followed at Sydney by a cold and boisterous " southerly buster," which sweeps the cobwebs from every brain and procures for over-strung nerves and aching eyes the luxury of a long night of refreshing sleep. My husband and I had adopted the Australian practice of sleeping out on the verandah—a practice so pleasant and healthful that we regretted it should be impossible of continuance when we returned to England to confront the memorable heat of the summer of 1911. But verandahs in this country are such thieves of the light and sunshine we cannot afford to waste, that our houses are better without them, even though at first I thought our windows looked like lidless eyes, flat and fishy, unshaded by these picturesque additions.

Admiralty House had wide verandahs on the south and east fronts which looked over a garden full of colour and well shaded by trees of various beautiful and interesting species, from the cypress that would have felt at home on the Pincian Hill to the big-leaved, wide-spreading Moreton Bay fig. Steep grassy slopes, bounded by hedges of scarlet-flowered hibiscus and grey salt-bush, lay between the house and the brown rocks of Kirribilli Point against which the rippling waters of the harbour broke in sapphire splinters, advancing and retreating with the soft, long " hush-sh and drawl " that of all monotonous noises is the most delightful.

Even in a mean street, narrow and densely populated, the outer air is preferable to that inside its houses, but where a garden of any size surrounds a house and the garden is in turn bounded by the sea, sleeping out is a positive delight, and a delight incomparable, since it provides a sensation unlike any other. To camp out tentless in the Bush is all very well in superlatively fine weather, and to sleep out at a sanatorium for consumptives is in accordance with modern ideas on the treatment of tuberculosis ; but to go to bed voluntarily on the verandah of one's own home night after night, and wake to the full freshness of dawn with lungs, heart and brain all joyfully receptive, is quite another matter. In the height of summer the heat of the corrugated iron roof makes the first part of the night much less perfect, but a patient immobility will be rewarded in the small hours by light and refreshing slumber, and when the busy sun arouses the sleeper he can creep indoors to find between the smooth, cool sheets of his second bed a resting-place where sleep will quickly reinvade his only half-awakened senses.

The sound and doubly invigorating sleep which winter nights bring lasts till the tardy dawn breaks, and then the thought of relinquishing his well-warmed nest for a cold one indoors is fraught with such terror that its occupant pulls the sheet over his head to shut out the light and dozes on till his cup of morning tea nerves him for a hasty return to the shelter of four walls. It is in spring and autumn that the full delight of sleeping out is tasted, for then the sun allows the sleeper a reasonable term of actual oblivion. The roof of his verandah is cool by bedtime, and the dawn is delayed till he is ready to admire its pale pink or amber glories and gently to exercise his awakening faculties as he rejoices upon his bed with the conscience-free rejoicing of the justifiable sluggard.

Close to the verandah where my bed was placed stands a Norfolk pine some seventy feet in height, which possesses about fifteen neatly arranged tiers of branches, ten of which were visible to me as I lay at my ease watching the birds whose playground I commanded. From the tiny silver-eye to the plump, bottle-shouldered ground-dove, with its queer little collar of black spotted with white, all the birds of the garden visit that tree in the morning sunshine, chattering, laughing, piping, whistling, or cooing as they discuss their plans for the day or the season. The branches of the Norfolk pine (which is no pine at all in reality, but an araucaria, and a near relative of the monkey-puzzler, but far more hospitable in character) are set almost at right angles to its straight trunk, with only the slight curve upwards and outwards of an Oriental eyebrow, finishing with a second and far slighter upward curve. This particular tree is not a very good specimen, and nearly every branch ends in a rat tail, or at best a tail like the heraldic lion's, with one little tuft at its extremity. But these bare terminals suit the smaller birds very well as perches, and show their little forms silhouetted against the clear southern sky, or the glassy, lavender-blue water of the harbour. Flights of silver-eyes, whose wing-spread is no wider than that of the ordinary cabbage butterfly, dart in and out of the upper branches, and so swift are their movements that the watcher can scarcely distinguish the soft olive-green of their plumage, or catch the gleam of the white circlets round their eyes. *Whistle* is too windy and boisterous a word to describe their short, sweet note ; *siffler* is nearer the mark.

Starlings, big-headed and yellow-billed as at home, sit whistling and " clicking " on the next storey or two, and pairs of dowdy doves nod and coo and wave their tails like mechanical toys on the more stable parts of the platforms.* Occasionally a *kookooburra* (unkindly called a laughing-jackass by those who

* These doves do not say, " Tak' *two* coos, Taffy," but reiterate the advice to " Tak' a *r-rough* towel " with the *r* strongly *grasseyé.*

have never heard its pretty native name) comes in from the Bush and honours the verandah-tree with a visit, and, perched on one of its lower boughs, bursts into full-throated laughter, prolonged, infectious, and inimitable. Or a pair of magpies may spend a week in this seaside garden and make their curious music—the music of " sweet bells jangled out of tune "—in the early morning and late afternoon. *Peewees* (not pewits, but cousins of the jay) commonly resort thither—smartly dressed, " tailor-made "-looking birds with blue-black hoods and mantles, spotless white faces and waistcoats, pied wings, and the long and slender legs of the swift runner. Of seagulls there are hundreds, mewing and scolding as they swoop and circle close inshore ; and though they never poise on tree or lawn, the flash of their white wings against the blue sky and bluer sea adds still one more charm to the morning landscape.

But of all the birds that frequent the tree the most dear to me are the " Willie Wagtails," as they are called in Australia. They are the handsomest, the friendliest and the most entertaining in this aviary of volunteers. The glossy black head, large bright eye, creamy white breast, and coal-black wings and tail belong to a beautifully proportioned bird, strong and graceful, and not quite like anything in the old country, either in marking or shape. He wags his tail, not up and down, but from side to side like a dog, and this is long and full enough to embarrass him seriously on a windy day as he runs about, an unconscious weathercock, picking up grubs on lawn or midden. These wagtails have more power of expressing themselves in song than most Australian birds, for not only can they screech like a parakeet, but they can whistle a pretty appoggiatura of three notes, execute variations on the theme of " sweet pretty creature " in a most engagingly melodious chuckle, and in early spring warble a short song not unlike that of a thrush.

It had been raining heavily one night, and the drops still drummed softly on the iron roof when the sleeper on the verandah was suddenly aroused by a loud, gay " Cweacha ! " proceeding apparently from under her bed. Very cautiously she raised herself and peeped over the foot-rail to see a happy wagtail standing on the shore of a nice new pond of rain-water which had drifted in on to the floor of the verandah during the night. Undismayed by the gaze of a human being, " Willie " went on making his morning toilet, sipping his bath-water at intervals and prattling blithely of " cweachas," " pwetty cweachas," and " sweet pwetty cweachas " (for he is a perfect Dundreary where " *r*'s " are concerned) as he adjusted his feathers above the shining mirror. The forelegs of the bed were literally in the pond, but a canvas screen had kept the " business part " of the bed, and therefore its occupant, out of the actual " catchment area." Some people prefer to use a wooden stretcher, for when rain invades their sleeping-place they can easily drag so light a bed indoors. But for the more luxurious a spring mattress has greater charms, even though they are sometimes forced to snatch the bedding off the bedstead with what haste they may and put it out of reach of a deluge so intrusive that it cannot be slept through. Everything depends on the width and the aspect of the verandah, and in Sydney a southerly exposure is not to be recommended, since the coldest and wettest gales come from the Antarctic Circle, and drive even the most inveterate sleeper-out into the tame security of a bedroom. But he feels humiliated and indignant, for he who has once proved the joy of nights out of doors can never again accept with proper gratitude, or even common patience, the indoor bed. Some unenterprising persons will assure one that it is just as good to sleep with all one's doors and windows open, but this is an ignorant mistake. There is all the difference in the world between draughts and the circumambient air.

Night on that verandah is very beautiful. The mile-long illumination of the opposite shore—from the quay lights of the city to the brilliant electric lamps glowing like balls of fire on the wooded slopes of the Domain—is plainly, but not too plainly, visible from it. Long, low ferry steamers glide hither and thither through the night. The radiance streaming from their myriad windows paints a golden fringe upon the dark water, and the red and green of port and starboard lights break and blur the fringe with patches of vivid colour. Ships' lights gleam from rigging or portholes, and the restless signal-lamp at the mast-head of each man-of-war flashes and winks its messages from ship to ship, or ship to dockyard, until with returning daylight it gives way to flag and semaphore.

There are some disadvantages connected with sleeping out on the shores of this great harbour. In thick weather steam-whistles, foghorns, ships' bells, and blood-curdling sirens effectually prevent sleep at both ends of the eight hours devoted to it ; in the summer belated excursion steamers, filled with festive singers of " Auld Lang Syne " or " God Save the King " (the most popular barcarolle on the harbour), pass close inshore, and cargo-boats, with shrieking winches and derricks, load or unload early and late when time presses. But there is no such thing as a *nuit blanche* for the sleeper-out. A peace, serene and benignant, pervading mind and body alike, descends upon him in the small and quiet hours. The soft wash of the water against the rocks below, the sighing of the light breeze in pines and gum trees, lull him to rest, and as he drifts into the haven of unconsciousness he feels himself specially and supremely blest—blest with the triple benison of earth and sky and sea.

CHAPTER XXIV

THE FOURTH ESTATE

ON reaching Australia I at once found all the newspapers interesting because they introduced me to the various interests—pastoral, agricultural, military, social and political — of that, to me, undiscovered continent, but as my home was at Sydney it naturally fell out that the Sydney Press particularly engaged my attention. In 1908—11 I should have said that the principal Sydney papers ranked with the best of our English provincial ones. But nowadays I should rate the *Sydney Morning Herald, Daily Telegraph* and *Evening News* far above the group of metropolitan productions of which the *Daily Mail* was the pioneer, both as literature and as channels of accurate information. Among Australian papers of smaller circulation which I had an opportunity of reading, the *Mercury* of Hobart had a special place in my esteem owing to the remarkable ability, good sense and good scholarship of its editorials. The Australian picture-papers contain a more interesting and varied letterpress generally speaking than ours, but the serious reviews and monthly magazines are not yet full-grown. These will come to maturity later.

Obituary notices in the advertisement pages of the daily papers containing rhymed tributes to the departed were sometimes curious and often pathetic in spite of their halting numbers. Of these rhymes the best, or so it appeared to me, was the following :

" God takes the good—too good on earth to stay—
And leaves the bad—too bad to take away."

The most matter-of-fact (it might have been written by Max Adeler's country editor in " Out of the Hurly Burly ") was, to the best of my recollection, this verse :

" I heard my mother she was ill ; I flew to ease her
   pain ;
I left my home in Ballarat by the one-thirty train.
But when I got to Melbourne just after half-past
   four,
I found she was already dead ; dear mother was
   no more."

A third ran :

" Pale death could scarcely find another
So good a husband and kind a father ;
In all his actions he was kind,
He left his loved ones all behind."

The last two lines seem to imply that the departed might, had he been less indulgent, have taken his family with him.

In the country newspapers I sometimes found such journalistic gems as are collected by Mr. Punch, but quite the best example of local talent was given me by the Bishop of Goulburn. It is from the *Morpeth Want* of New South Wales. " Mrs. B. has just passed away at the age of eighty-five. For some months she had been in failing health but during the last few days *she approached the grave in leaps and bounds.*"   The announcement was headed "Death of an Old Identity."   This curious use of the word " identity " is very common in Australia. It is not a malaprop exactly, but I take it to mean a person who has been long identified with a particular locality.

For a genuine malaprop it would be hard to beat the following, overheard by a lieutenant of the *Powerful* in a crowded Melbourne tram : A polite man got up and offered his place to a lady. " Oh, thank you very much, but I don't like to deprive you of your seat," said the lady. " Don't mention it, madam ; no *depravity* intended, I assure you," was the polite man's rejoinder.

But I must return to the Fourth Estate at Sydney. Its members were as generous to my small successes as they were blind to my blunders. The redoubtable *Bulletin* (whose cover is the only thing about it that ever blushes) wrote up the Bush Book Club when it most needed judicious advertisement, and Mr. Lionel Lindsay's sketch of a typical Bushman enjoying one of the Club's books added immensely to the success of our initial effort to obtain funds. Of the ladies of the Sydney Press I have nothing but kindly and grateful recollections. When I say that they invented fresh descriptions for my elderly gowns it would seem I could have no greater cause for gratitude ; but they did far more than this, and especially to the editor of the Woman's Page of the *Sydney Morning Herald* do

I owe much pleasure and much profit. Would that our "Aunt Jemimas" and "Lady Esmeraldas," who advise their readers on every topic purporting to interest women—from how to stop blushing to how to receive Royalty — might model their pages on those of Miss Amy Mack (Mrs. Launcelot Harrison) !

Five years have passed since I said good-bye to Sydney, but friends often send me a *Town and Country Journal* or a copy of the *Herald*, and I never fail to find in their pages reminders of the people and the places I love to think of.

Now, as it may, not unnaturally, occur to English readers of these recollections of my life in Australia that I have described my relations with the Press of Sydney with a pen dipped in rose-coloured ink, I must add that certain fortuitous circumstances predisposed many people in my favour.

My eldest brother, Alfred Perceval Graves, is the author of "Father O'Flynn," a lyric secure of immortality wherever Irish men and women shall be found, and towards me as the author's sister, and to all my doings and dealings, the Irish Roman Catholic element, very strong in New South Wales, showed a vicarious indulgence. Another, and smaller, section of society recognised in me the sister of C. L. G., whose verses, satires and absurdities are dear to connoisseurs. Yet others knew me to be the daughter of an Irish bishop whose scholarly sanity and remarkable freedom from prejudice (in a country where hot-headed prejudice runs mad) endeared him to persons of all creeds and parties.

In addition to possessing these recommendations, valuable assets with the public, I had had the good luck to meet in England a number of Australian ladies, wives of naval officers ; and it was, therefore, not as a complete stranger that I made my first steps in Sydney society. I had friends among the Allens, the Lambs and the Macarthurs ; I was indirectly connected with Mrs. Massie (*née* Browne, and sister of " Rolf Boldrewood ") ; and I had cousins—Cheynes, Macartneys and Graveses—settled in Australia. These circumstances must make it apparent that I had not myself to thank for the kindness I experienced.

CHAPTER XXV

RECIPROCITY

My Australian critics are bound to object that, situated as we were, it was impossible for us to become acquainted with anyone in Sydney or elsewhere beyond the three or four thousand who wrote their names in our book at Admiralty House or on board the flagship during her cruises to other ports. They will also say that there are great numbers of interesting and delightful people who find neither time nor inclination to call on the Admiral and his wife. Both these objections appear quite justifiable. But, as a matter of fact, we did, in less conventional ways, become acquainted with a good number of these agreeable " nonconformists," and whenever the flagship was cruising I had leave to consider myself semi-official, free to go where I liked, and to accept and offer hospitality of an informal sort. The general rules laid down by our various predecessors were the outcome of experience, and we carefully adhered to them when my husband was at Admiralty House. These rules provided that the Admiral and his wife should dine only at certain official houses and return only certain official calls. But there were many months in each year when I did as I liked, and greatly did I enjoy making the acquaintance of those whom under ordinary circumstances I might never have met. There remained numbers still unknown whom I should have found both interesting and congenial, but I did what I could to add to my circle of acquaintance when I had both leisure and opportunity, and on this " supplementary list " were the names of some specially qualified to help me in understanding Australian conditions and Australian character. That I succeeded in doing so with any completeness would be an absurd assumption, but some of the rocks upon which English visitors are wrecked in Australian waters were pointed out to me before I encountered them, and over and over again I had reason to bless the advice given to me before I left

England : "Don't be in a hurry to criticise Australian ways. Praise what you can honestly praise at first, and wait as long as you can without criticising." As the result of following this counsel I found that there was very little to criticise, and I soon became so warm a friend and admirer of Australians that I had little inclination to do so. I do think that Australians are ultra-sensitive, but it is, in my opinion at least, the step-motherliness of England which is mainly to blame for this. Australia was the Cinderella of the British Dominions for many years. Her earliest colonists were starved during the long and exhausting European wars at the end of the eighteenth and beginning of the nineteenth centuries—starved both literally and metaphorically. In the eyes of the British statesmen of the day Australia was an expensive and inconvenient reformatory for erring Britons. The good and honourable man who presided over her early years—Governor Phillip—was cruelly handicapped through lack of practical sympathy from those in authority at home who were unwilling to sanction a reasonable outlay on the infant colony of New South Wales. They little dreamt that Sydney Harbour was the main-gate of a continent teeming with rich surprises ; had they done so, greed of gain alone would have induced them to listen to the well-grounded complaints of Governors Phillip and King.

Until comparatively recent times the step-motherly attitude has been persisted in. The South African

War awakened England to a semi-consciousness of Australia's strong claim on her affection, gratitude and respect. The war to-day must surely establish that claim as never before. What right have we now, divided and subdivided as we are in our own islands into friends and foes, pacifists and fighters, workers and slackers, to sit in judgment on this young and warm-hearted people who are giving, out of all proportion to their population, blood and treasure that the integrity and the honour of the Empire may remain inviolable ? At this time, if ever, we are not in a position to criticise a nation which is showing us the way. Their lamp is burning bright ; ours, though alight, is obscured by the thick cloud of personal and party interest.

It must not be inferred that, with the opportunities vouchsafed me in Australia, I never ventured in those years to make fair comment on the wide difference in character and customs which undoubtedly exists between Australians and " Great Britons." The following address delivered in 1910 to the girls of a large and important school near Sydney will show my desire to establish a better understanding, and if these words, of which I have not altered a single one, should help to interpret even one Australian to one Englishwoman, and *vice versâ*, I shall have been of some use.

" I want you to-day to have patience with me while I prose for a little about the difference in characteristics and temperament between English people and Australians, for after two and a half years out here (and I dare not disclose how many at home) I think I can formulate my ideas on the subject sufficiently to be of some slight service to young and inexperienced folk. You will very often hear it asserted that the English are cold and unresponsive, suspicious, narrow-minded and close-fisted, and perhaps come to believe that such is actually the case, so that when you go to England this will be with you an article of faith. If you are thrown at first among reserved and sober-minded people your faith will become conviction, and you will brand us all as uncongenial and unsympathetic, and thank your stars privately (and perhaps publicly) that you are Australians. Well, there are plenty of such unsympathetic and un-compromising people in England, and I do not like them better than you would ; but England is not peopled exclusively in so unsatisfactory a manner, any more than Australia is exclusively inhabited by pleasure-worshipping, duty-neglecting beings. The sweeping and inaccurate judgments of many of us on both sides of the globe are no doubt founded on individual cases, and I fear I must admit that it is persons of the female sex who are peculiarly prone to generalise from in-sufficient data. The notion that the most salient points of any race or nation are its defects leads to disastrous misunderstandings. Still, it should always be re-membered that virtues run to seed become faults. The open-handedness of Australians not infrequently de-generates into extravagance ; their hospitality towards, and interest in, strangers sometimes—I only say some-times—leads them to admit undesirable people into their circle of acquaintances, and their natural gaiety of temperament tempts them now and again to overlook the duties and responsibilities of life. With us, on the other hand, reasonable economy may, and does, easily degenerate into stinginess ; caution in making friends as easily becomes coldness to strangers, and a certain seriousness of temperament can quickly solidify into dullness. We have a bad habit of expecting the worst instead of hoping for the best. There are good reasons for the differences between us, and if we know the reasons we can make allowances. You may have heard the French proverb, *Tout comprendre c'est tout pardonner.* To understand all is to forgive all.

" Now at home we are so closely packed together in our little island that newcomers are less welcome, and we take less interest in them than you do in strangers here, mainly because we have such a multiplicity of other interests ; indeed, we look upon them rather as interruptions, interlopers or poachers, than as possible friends. We are more conventional than you because our ways and manners are, generally speaking, the product of centuries of unbroken conventionality in a country always less democratic than this. Your ancestors came out here to fight and tame nature, and life for them was too hard and circumstances too exacting to permit of their maintaining all the rules and regulations (many of them, no doubt, meaningless enough) which governed society in the old country.

" You see, I admit that many conventions *are* unmeaning, but without reasonable conventions and rules for the conduct of society it would be impossible to maintain any social standard worthy of acceptance in the centres of civilisation. I have heard girls say, ' I do not mind what people think of me so long as I know I have done nothing wrong.' That sounds a very noble sentiment, but the truth is that there are lots of things not actually wrong which are unwise, inexpedient and indiscreet ; and as a governess of mine once said to me, ' Remember that the very people who will applaud your unconventionality to your face are those who will make fun of it behind your back.' Public opinion is a very useful check on society, and Mrs. Grundy is a most valuable bogey. Do not bow down to her, but do not fly in her face. There are men, and women too, who will take advantage of your youth and inexperience and encourage you to overstep the limits of decorum ; and a girl so encouraged who is simply full of crazy spirits may find herself talked about as ' that noisy ' or ' hoydenish ' Miss Brown, or described by some not very nice man as being ' very good sport,' which, in English slang, does not mean a good rider or tennis-player, but a girl who is wanting in the refinement and the wise reticence which are desirable and beautiful things in a woman.

" This is rather a long sermon on the subject of conventionality, but what I want to point out to you is this : that Australians who are merely light-hearted and full of spirits are sometimes misunderstood by English people—people whom they themselves would call dull and straitlaced, but who are in reality only sober-minded stay-at-homes, wanting in insight and lamentably deficient in animal spirits.

" There is one particular matter in which we are equally culpable and equally obstinate, and that is that we both cherish a rooted conviction that our way is the right way. We English people will lay down the law on a hundred points to Australians as though we actually possessed and set the only standard of etiquette, fashion and morals ; as though, in fact, the meridian in all those matters passed through English atmosphere like the meridian of Greenwich on the map. This is extremely annoying to people who hail from distant portions of the Empire, and awakens in them a spirit of opposition, at once natural and pardonable. But the fact remains that in England was found the one standard of British thought and sentiment up to less than a hundred years ago, and we are tenacious people. The fault is not so much in the standard itself as in our dogmatic use of it. I am not sure but that an Imperial Conference on Manners and Customs might not be a good thing. I honestly think that it is our unfortunate climate that makes us less ready to be amused, less joyfully responsive than you (I have yet to meet a bored or *blasée* Australian girl), and, as you are strong in the possession of an almost perfect climate, you can afford . to be merciful in your judgments of us who live under far less brilliant skies. Your almost constant sunshine and clear atmosphere, which enable you to spend half your lives out of doors, undoubtedly help you to be light-hearted, and the spaciousness of a great continent must affect your character and habits. Our hedges and ditches and high stone walls, our ' No Thoroughfares ' and ' Trespassers will be Prosecuted,' combined with a preponderance of rainy days, limit our sphere of outdoor operations and throw us back upon the circumscribed shelter of our homes in a way unknown to you ; and there is obviously a greater sense of freedom about the Australian Bush than there can possibly be in a country where nearly every square inch of nature belongs to some one whose great object it is to ensure what peace and privacy he may in the midst of a vibrating, fresh-air-consuming crowd. Life for all classes is much more of a struggle with us, and a densely populated country presents problems that you have not yet had to deal with out here. We have competition more severe and poverty more terrible than any you can dream of, and the machinery and motive power of an older social or-ganisation than yours is proportionately more com-plicated. We are apt to use our intellects more, and our senses and instincts less, than you, puzzling our poor brains, often fruitlessly, over problems, social and economic, to the exclusion of such necessary and practical matters as the cutting out of a skirt that will hang properly, or the making of an eatable cake or pudding. Is it any wonder that—class for class—we are less high-spirited, less expansive, and more con-ventional than you ? I wonder if you know how much you owe to the difficulty your mothers often experience in getting and keeping good servants. It is this very difficulty which serves to encourage practical usefulness in Australian girls, and effectually prevents their indulging in enervating day-dreams and profitless speculations, or in the adoption of some fad or pose which wastes time, energy and opportunity and leads to nothing admirable or useful. I hope the day is very far distant when the worship of the Toy Pomeranian or the Japanese Spaniel will become as common among you as it is now at home. I would have you make friends of your dogs, but never exalt them above human beings nor squander upon them the care and love which should be given to your fellow-creatures.

"Notwithstanding the keen affection and admiration I feel for Australian girls, I cannot conceal from myself nor from them that there is need among them for a more exhaustive study of art in all its branches, and for a deeper and more general interest in literature and history ; and if you realise this now you will be all the more appreciative of what you see and hear when you go to Europe, and all the better able then to store up in your memory much that you did not and could not possess before. This is not a criticism, but a statement of fact. Europe contains what Australia does not and cannot—the accumulation of past centuries of art and science, from A for Architecture to Z for Zoology. And you Australians are such intrepid travellers, making so little of the 11,000 or 12,000 miles which inspired, and still inspire, me with dread, and so wise in spending money in seeing the world, that there is good hope that every one of you girls will one day visit the great treasure-houses of Europe. Would that all English girls and women could come out here, as I have come, and appreciate *without effort,* as I have done, the wonders and the beauty of Australia, and the goodness, capacity and charm of Australians. When you do go home let me beg of you to lay aside all preconceived prejudices against

English people. By doing so you will disarm criticism and effectually dispel from English minds any counter-prejudices that may linger there with regard to Australians. Be at your best yourselves and try to see the best in others. I have been told that there is some fruit in Australia which carries its kernel outside. English fruits *always* have theirs inside, and it is quite worth while to open the fruit. Remember that your surroundings and those of English people have been widely different and have made you both what you are. And remember also that you are of one race and blood with them, actually sharing grand or great-grand-parents, and inheriting the same traditions, and that, however much and rightly you love Australia, England is your country too, and has given you to Australia—a great gift to a great continent."

CHAPTER XXVI

ENGLAND'S ANTIPODES

THE small cruisers of the Australian Squadron had (among many others) the duty of visiting the outlying islands in that part of the South Pacific where violent storms and a savagely inhospitable climate render the position of shipwrecked mariners one of peculiar peril and embarrassment.

We speak carelessly of going " to the Antipodes," but, short of the rarely met geographical expert, which of us realises that an inhabitant of, say, the

Isle of Wight would, if he had bored a hole under his feet right through the globe, actually drop out in the neighbourhood of the Antipodes Islands ? Before starting for Australia I had a mistaken idea that if such a scheme of perterraneous tunnelling were practicable it would save me a vast amount of time and discomfort, but since I discovered that I should have regained the outer air in the middle of a group of islands among the most forlorn and inhospitable on the face of the waters, and situated hundreds of miles from the mainland of either Australia or New Zealand, I have changed my opinion.   Round these islands the sea is unceasingly rough—rough to a degree peculiar to the Antarctic Ocean and its immediate neighbourhood.   There is no port, no safe anchorage, and scarcely a spot in the whole group where a small boat may effect a landing.   The islands are uninhabited for the excellent reason that no human being could sustain life upon what the soil and climate would produce at the cost of the hardest possible labour.   Even fishing is out of the question, for the shores are surrounded by stretches of thick kelp, and no ordinary boat could live among the mountainous seas or face the breakers by which its beaches are guarded.   Though this group is as nearly as possible the Antipodes of Greenwich there are others lying, roughly speaking, within a radius of six hundred miles, all more or less ill favoured and all well qualified to gather a pitiful harvest of shipwrecked sailors.   These are the Aucklands, the Campbells, and the Bounties, the first two being inhabited, and the last uninhabitable to a pitch even higher than that reached by the Antipodes Islands. Yet the Antipodes and Bounties are from time to time tenanted by the survivors of crews wrecked upon their shores. In bygone years these luckless beings less happy than their drowned comrades, starved slowly to death in the scant shelter of some hollow amidst the stony hills. At Terror Cove, in the Aucklands, memorials raised to the memory of such victims of the combined cruelty of land and sea may be seen. A wooden board bears the inscription : " Erected to the crew of the ss. *Scotland*, over the remains of a man who had apparently died of starvation, and was found by the crew of the *Flying Scud*, 3rd Sept., 1865 " ; beside it stands a round-topped stone, " Sacred to the memory of John Mahony, master-mariner, second mate of the ship *Invercauld*, wrecked on this island 18th May, 1864. Died from starvation " ; and a third—a rough slab of wood, fastened horizontally to a tall post— carries the single word, " Unknown." But this is ancient history. For many years the Government of New Zealand has supplied for the use of castaways on each of these four groups of islands a roughly constructed depôt for provisions and a boat. These depôts are visited and replenished twice a year by Government schooners, and some ship of the Imperial Navy on the Australian station used always to inspect the islands every six months, re- turning now and then with the gaunt remnants of

some South Sea trader's crew. Not many years ago
H.M.S. *Lizard* found a company of poor Norwegians
encamped actually upon the beach and afraid to
move even as far as the provision depôt " because
the lions roared so loud."   The lions were, of course,
sea-lions, which abound in Enderby Island in the
Auckland group.   Their size and weight make them
appear formidable, but the four ridiculous flippers
which successfully propel their huge carcases through
the water are so inadequate to support them when
they wish to take exercise ashore that any active
child of five could literally walk away from them.
If the reader can imagine an incredibly fat cow
mounted on four finny feet sprouting directly from
its shoulders and hind-quarters, he can form some
faint idea of the appearance and anatomy of the
sea-lion.   It might perfectly well be a mythological
animal, invented, along with the Quangle-Wangle
and the Pobble who had no toes, by Edward Lear.
That it is a very tame beast is certain, and unless it
fell upon a man and crushed him by sheer weight
it should be harmless, for a pair about the size of
large Clydesdale cart-horses permitted the gunner
of the *Lizard* to place his camera ten feet from their
starboard quarters as they reclined side by side
upon the sand.

In the Campbell Islands an enterprising Scot
feeds his flocks, but neither this nor any other
evidence of civilisation would seem to scare the
monarch of sea-birds, the royal albatross, from its
home in that group, since the hen-bird will sit

imperturbably upon her nest (and, incidentally, for her portrait) with a sporting blue-jacket, gun in hand, beside her. If the sea-lion is ill-equipped as a pedestrian, so is the albatross, whose wings are so inconveniently long that when their owner would walk among the thick tussocky grass he frequently trips and falls upon his head, only recovering his feet after much floundering in one of the sandy hollows which occur between the grass tufts. Of penguins, which positively crowd these islands at certain seasons, so much has been delightfully written by Captain Scott in his " Voyage of the *Discovery* " that little remains to be said of their ways, but the pictures I have seen of them assembled in tens, perhaps hundreds, of thousands on the rocks of the Bounties suggest more than anything the legend " Standing room only," and provide a reason for the shortness of their wings and the erectness of their habitual pose. A common seagull must occupy twice as much space when he perches.

A company of castaways was rescued from the Antipodes Islands in 1909. They were the captain and crew of the four-masted French barque *Président Félix Faure*, of 3,500 tons, laden with ore, and had been sixty days hoping to be picked off, when H.M.S. *Pegasus* hove in sight. There were twenty-two of them and they had not fared sumptuously. A cow which had been placed on the island by the New Zealand Government they killed and ate, but the skeleton only of her consort was discovered. The sheep which they had believed to exist were, alas ! not forthcoming, but a small ration of biscuit was served out daily from the depôt, whence fifteen tins of beef were also drawn for Sunday dinners. The penguins, for some obscure reason of their own, deserted the island on Good Friday, and this was a serious loss to the commissariat. But the Frenchmen were resourceful fellows. They caught and ate albatrosses ; they built cabins of turf and sticks, and thatched them with tussock grass ; a needle was fashioned from the blade of a penknife, and a fish-hook from a nail out of a biscuit barrel—but it caught no fish !— limpet shells were used as spoons and knives were manufactured from barrel-hoops. Never once did the castaways see the sun during their imprisonment ; leaden skies, chill mists and raging gales were their portion for sixty long days. The last message to the world of the despairing crew had, they thought, been penned before the *Pegasus* was sighted. Every day they had sent an albatross adrift with a paper enclosed in a hollow quill tied round its neck, and the last of the series consisted of a small photograph of the mother of the youngest of the crew, on the back of which was written : " *Président F. Faure*, four-masted barque, wrecked on Antipodes Islands." It was while trying to trap the bird destined to carry this forlorn hope that the Frenchmen descried the smoke from the funnels of the *Pegasus*. It was a day of wild squalls, and a capricious wind whisked flurries of icy sleet over the top of the cliff under whose lee the ship lay while her boats went ashore to pick up the sea-waifs. They were soon safely on board, and rescued and rescuers were alike thankful to quit a shore of such evil repute. But, alas! poor " Sara," the French captain's dog, was missing. It appears that she had jumped overboard from the boat in which the Frenchmen left the wreck, and made her way to a cove surrounded on three sides by inaccessible cliffs. The boat went to pieces on the beach, leaving the dog's master without any means of reaching her. No calls or entreaties could coax her from her ill-chosen asylum, where she subsisted at first upon the penguins she killed, and later Heaven knows how. " She seemed to have gone wild," the men said. But she was still alive when they left the island. At that moment delay was not possible, for darkness was coming on and the wind was rising. And thus it happened that poor " Sara " was abandoned, a lonely, famishing derelict, a figure than which nothing more pathetic in the history of dogs can be conceived.

CHAPTER XXVII

MY LETTER-BAG

APPEALS for pecuniary help were so frequent during our time at Sydney that we were glad to enlist the services of the local secretary of the Charity Organisation Society in dealing with them. Even he was taken in by one of my correspondents whom I will call Mrs. Q., and for nearly two years I had this ingenious and unscrupulous person " on my back." Her tale was tragic. She had lost her only child, and her husband had committed suicide the same week. These awful griefs had unhinged her mind, and when she emerged from the lunatic asylum she was broken in health and dependent on the work of her hands. She sent me a parcel of knitted ties which she entreated me to sell for her, and, touched by her misfortunes, for the genuineness of which the secretary vouched, I victimised every man of any age who came to Admiralty House. The ties were cheap and some were not ugly, so I easily got rid of them. Then she sent some silk socks, also purporting to be the work of her own hands. They were so evenly knitted that any woman wider awake than myself would have known them to be machine-made. These socks had a great vogue until half a dozen pairs ordered by the flag-captain arrived with such extraordinarily badly-worked clocks that these had to be unpicked. I remonstrated, and the lady explained with every sign of abasement that the person who had been in the habit of working the clocks for her was dead and she had done her poor best to finish the socks ordered by Captain Prowse.

Custom slackened and I was at my wits' end to keep the poor creature going, for want of occupation was certain to upset her rickety brain, and I blush now to think of the number of Mrs. Q.'s ties and socks I palmed off upon uncomplaining young men at this critical period.   One only had his suspicions —Commander Bowring—and he resolutely refused to buy.

Then came the news conveyed in rapturous terms that Mrs. Q. had been given a knitting-machine and was now secure from want could she but find " some little premises " where she might show and sell her work.   A generous lady found the premises, had them attractively decorated and Mrs. Q. installed. She sold writing-paper and various other commodities, as well as the produce of her industry, at her little shop and wept large tears of embarrassing gratitude over my hand when I visited her there.

Then she became a Christian Scientist, and, suddenly convicted of error, she confessed to her spiritual adviser that she had *never knitted a stitch in her life.*   Everything I had sold for her had been bought in Sydney shops and was cheap machine-made stuff !

I was not more disgusted with the crookedness of my *protégée* than I was with myself for having tricked so many people out of half-crowns and even sovereigns.   It was the spiritual adviser who got rid of the shop and its stock-in-trade and planted Mrs. Q. in a single room as a plain needleworker, and for this I was deeply grateful, since the poor creature had to earn her living somehow.   Not long ago I heard of her death.   How much of her story was true neither the secretary nor I could determine, but I daresay she was even more sad and mad than she was bad.

The secretary was not often deceived. Once he was sent for to a miserable house where a weeping widow and several children were gathered round the dead body of the breadwinner. The secretary had quitted the house after taking notes of the case with a view to immediate investigation and relief, but, finding he had forgotten his umbrella, returned, and, without knocking, re-entered the living-room. He was confronted by the corpse, who, surrounded by his family, was sitting up and drinking stout out of a bottle !

On another occasion the secretary had to visit a poor woman afflicted with triplets. Again for some reason he went back after taking leave of the family and found the third baby—a temporary loan—being conveyed home by its authentic mother.

The following extraordinary letter was written to me by a very sadly " decayed " gentleman employed on a Salvation Army farm. He turned out on inquiry to be an incorrigible.

" To Lady Poore.

" May it please your Ladyship to peruse carefully the following statements, and if you can assist me I shall be most grateful, if no other way than a few kind words of sympathy which I shall most dearly appreciate to my dying day. I am an aged (80) Priest of the Ch. of Engd. having held high appointments and been on visiting terms with the élite of society all over Gt. Brit. and Europe. My first wife was the Hon. Evylyn (*sic*) ——, was presented at Court by the Duchess of ——, was taken ill, attended by Sir B. B., went to the S. of France and died there."

The next paragraph is full of the financial operations of his second wife, which were complicated and generally unfortunate.   The letter proceeds :

" In short we were ruined—the darling wife died broken-hearted, age 75 years and I left desolate and a beggar. By the help and influence of M.P.'s for whom I had voted and other friends I managed with Dr.'s certificates for ' extreme nervous debility and senile decay' to obtain the Govt. pension of 10/- p. w. paid monthly and was brought down here 18 months ago hardly responsible for my words or actions" (this is but too true) "where I have been ever since partially recovered though exceedingly and excruciatingly effected (*sic*) by surroundings, men, farm-labourers and pensioners, who use not forks for their food nor pocket hkfs. when required.

" Oh ! how I would bless you both to my dying day could you deign to honor me by the appointment of domestic chaplain, with just sufficient income to keep me in necessary and proper clothing, upper and under, I would bless you to my last breath.

" Now will you dear lady understand that my object in writing is to ask and beg of you not to send me money but that you will in the nobleness of a generous heart forward £1 or 30/- to —— on my behalf that I may obtain a pair of dark-blue serge trousers, a light clerical coat, pair of shoes (I cannot wear boots) 4 prs. cheap socks 6d. each and two (2) shirts, and words fail to express my thanks for I am ashamed to be seen even by the day laborers much more by visitors. I may just say, *en passant*, that I saw, providentially, that a lady who I believe is first cousin of my late precious wife is a millionairess and I having obtained her private address in America have written a long and explanatory epistle reminding her of our childhood's happy days spent on our adjoining estates adjuring her to do all she can for me, so I am making my will in anticipation of a few thousands but perhaps not until after · my death, as one of the young farm-laborers states that he saw her name mentioned as travelling over Gt. Brit. and the Continent, so that she may not receive my letter for many months.

" I would like to ask if either you or the Admiral were acquainted with another cousin of my wife's, Captain B., R.N. He died I think in the year '74, but unfortunately all her diaries—6 or 8 vols.—written in French were destroyed. I have written to many ladies including the Mayoress but most people will not do anything unless their names and gifts appear in Subs. Lists ! ! !

" I am, yr. Ladyship's
faithful and obedient Servant.
—— —— —— D.D., LL.D.
" Formerly Rector, Surrogate and Archdeacon
Gt. B. and Austr."

To this I replied that we were not entitled to a private chaplain and that I had referred his letter to the Secretary of the Charity Organisation Society who investigated such appeals. I regretted that we had never met Captain B.

The D.D., LL.D., etc., promptly wrote the following fanciful letter to the secretary :

" MY DEAR SIR,

" Having written to Lady Poore hoping that they would take me to England as Chaplain on Board the Flag Ship I this morning received a most kind courteous and sympathetic reply stating that the Rules of the Service did not allow such an appointment and in regard

170

to my application for assistance the claims upon her were too numerous to enable her to help me, but that if I applied to you you would be able to send me some clothing. I therefore enclose a list of what I urgently need, and should you be able to enclose 10/- or 20/- my gratitude would be unbounded. I thank you most sincerely for all you have done for me in the past which I mentioned to Lady Poore (!) and am only waiting to hear from you to tell her Ladyship what you have sent me. I may just state *en passant* that she and the Admiral knew my late wife's first cousin, Capt. B., R.N. I may also say that a first cousin is a millionaire in America and have written a long letter stating my sad condition and reminding her of our childhood's happy days when we were playmates almost daily as our parents' Estates adjoined, and I am firmly trusting that she may forward me a cheque for a few thousands.

" Yours faithfully and gratefully

—— —— —— D.D., D.C.L. (Yet another degree !)

" 1 pr strong but soft leather shoes. Socks, under-vests —under-pants, Shirts, Braces. Trousers of dark Blue Serge. Clerical Black alpaca Coat, Long. Collars, Pkthkfs, Writing Pads and Envelopes and if possible 3 plain studs with spring opening ends—and *above all* 10/- or 20/-."

Comment is needless. The poor old wreck was not even an ingenious beggar.

Very soon after my arrival at Sydney I received the following anonymous advice as to my social duties :

" MADAM,

"I am so glad you are doing something to get to know Sydney Society better. The best people really never get invited to Government or Admiralty House ; but only the vulgar parvenus with money made anyhow who generally by their marriage settlements are bartered for by the lieutenants and have the audacity to call themselves the upper ten. Surely this state of things could be remedied by the Aide-de-Camp making inquiries as to the mental endowments and social position of those invited—not how much *old brass* they have made in their second-hand shops Darling Point way."

I invited the flag-lieutenant to inquire into the mental endowments and social position of the three thousand-odd people who had written their names in our book, but he confessed himself as unable as he was unwilling to undertake this colossal and embarrassing task !

Not long after receiving this communication I heard from a lady who offered me her daughter of eighteen as a companion on the grounds that " she would like to enter into good society." The writer added : " my great granmother (*sic*) was the Duchess of ——."

It was difficult to decline the offer of the great-great-granddaughter of a Duke gracefully and gratefully, but I pointed out that " so young and inexperienced a girl could hardly fill the post of useful companion to a very busy woman."

Three closely-written sheets of severe reproof, interlarded with texts, were launched at me by a total stranger because in the only interview I ever granted to a newspaper correspondent I had been represented as speaking slightingly of the district-visitor type of English girl who out of her own inexperience lectures the poor of the parish. I have not preserved this reprimand because the flag-lieutenant—my only confidant in the matter—was so annoyed by it that he promptly flung it into the fire without asking my leave. I daresay the epistle was in the nature of a wholesome corrective, but I cannot say I had any wish to kiss the hand that penned it.

I had also anonymous friends; Christian Scientists anxious to convince me of " error," and truly kind people who recommended remedies for neuralgia.

One very hot day an old lady well over ninety, who had already written to me about my health, dropped in upon me in the middle of a small afternoon party and urged me to drink camomile tea, to which specific (combined with *two cold baths* daily) she attributed her longevity. I have reason to believe she had eluded the vigilance of her devoted family in order to perform this kind act, for the gentleman who accompanied her was a total stranger to her. The spirited old lady was very nearly blind, and I gathered that she had accepted, perhaps asked for, his guidance to our door.*

Though I am loth to publish pretty sentiments referring to myself, I am impelled to quote the concluding phrase of a letter written to a friend of mine by " a red-hot Irish rebel," simply because it is the only testimonial I have ever received from one of this desperate band. He said: " Lady

* My friend is now in her hundredth year.

Poore is a Royal woman. I shall take off my hat every time I pass Kirribilli Point." (Admiralty House is situated at this Point, round which the harbour-steamers to and from Neutral Bay pass.)

CHAPTER XXVIII

NEW ZEALAND—VISIT TO THE GOVERNOR-GENERAL AND LADY PLUNKET

In December, 1908, I crossed that very uneasy piece of ocean which lies between Sydney and Wellington, and spent a month in New Zealand. The flagship was cruising up north at the time I left Australia, and, before joining up at Auckland, where we were all to be for Christmas, I paid a visit of ten days to Lord and Lady Plunket, who were then living at Palmerston North. Theirs was quite a makeshift establishment, for the new Government House at Wellington was not then completed, and the Government had accepted Lord Plunket's offer of the old one as a temporary Parliament House in place of that which had been recently destroyed by fire.

As was usual with me after a sea-voyage, I disembarked in the faint yet rejoicing spirit of one escaping from the torture chamber, and the consciousness that I was setting foot on a land where no

174

snakes were (I never, as a matter of fact, saw a live one in Australia, but never ceased anticipating this horror) added to my feeling of complacency. As I stepped ashore I was handed a pass good for all railway travel in the Dominion, and as I already possessed a document presented to me by Sir James Mills, of " All-Red-Route " fame, available for three years over all his steamer lines, I was provided with transport by land and sea. There was a " handsomeness " in the dealings of overseas people in these matters which never failed to stir my gratitude, and now that I squeeze myself into crowded corridor carriages and am thankful when my train does not miss its connection I can scarcely believe that those dignified days of free travelling in reserved compartments ever existed for me.

After lunching with Mrs. Charles Johnston at Karori outside Wellington and hearing such stories of the former earthquakiness of this part of New Zealand as made my newly-restored equilibrium totter, I went on to Palmerston North, where Captain Lyon, A.D.C. to, and later brother-in-law of, Lord Plunket, met me. It was dark and very wet, and my train was late, so I pitied him in my heart for the *corvée* he had been told off to perform. In answer to his polite inquiries about my voyage from Sydney, I told him I had not been sea-sick, but that my brains felt rather out of joint ; to which he returned sympathetically, " Ah, yes ; I quite understand. You probably have the same delicate mechanism that clocks *made about fifty years ago* possess." That I also had been manufactured about half a century before, when " Bee " clocks were unknown, was the last thing he wished to convey, but it was within so very little of being an accurate estimate that I could not leave the joke unnoticed, and, skipping preliminaries, we laughed ourselves into comfortable relations on the spot.

There was no specially distinctive characteristic about Palmerston North—a small town, or large village, on a grassy plain from which rose modest undulations—and the house which sheltered the Governor-General and Lady Plunket was merely a moderate-sized villa. The simplicity and homeliness of my host and hostess did not prevent their appearing out of place in such surroundings, and I know that the close proximity of the kitchen to the Governor-General's office caused Lord Plunket considerable discomfort as meal-times approached.

Though he was acquainted with my relations in Ireland I had never met Lord Plunket before, and in the days of my girlhood in Egypt, where Lord Dufferin was Minister Plenipotentiary in 1883, Lady Plunket (then Lady Victoria Blackwood) was in the nursery. Still, I had known her father and Lord Plunket had known mine, so we were not complete strangers starting from " scratch," and I shall always preserve a happy recollection of their hospitality and of the many entertaining Irish stories Lord Plunket told so well. Of these, two about Father Healy were new to me, although with many of the sayings and experiences of that witty priest I had long been familiar.

It seems that Father Healy was on one occasion invited to dine to meet Mr. Gladstone, who asked him pointedly at the dinner-table how the Roman Catholic Church could defend such a practice as the sale of facsimiles of the footprints of a saint at some well-known church in Spain for half-a-crown apiece —each facsimile *carrying with it a dispensation of five hundred years of purgatory.*

" Did you buy one, sir ? " asked Father Healy.

" Yes, I did," Mr. Gladstone replied.

" Then all I can say is that you got it dirt-cheap, sir."

Father Healy was once walking along the seashore in Wicklow and came upon a man lying actually at the point of death where the waves had washed him up when the ship he belonged to was wrecked. He was conscious when the priest stooped over him offering spiritual consolation, and, seeing the abhorred dress of the priest, he raised himself with an effort, shouted " Till (to) Hell with the Pope ! " and fell back dead.

A less tragic tale, which also shows the intense antagonism felt by the Orangeman for the Catholic priesthood, was also told me by Lord Plunket. There had been " fighting as usual " between opposing parties of Orangemen and Ribbonmen in one of the northern counties, and late at night one of the combatants, being very tipsy, fell into a deep ditch by the roadside on his way home. He howled for help, and a priest who was passing that way heard him and pulled him out of the ditch.

" Who ar-re you ? " asked the still fuddled Orangeman.

" Parish priest of Kilboy," was the answer.

" Then putt me back, I say ; putt me back ! "

The dry and quiet manner in which Lord Plunket told stories of this sort added to their value. I believe his modesty, and the simple domesticity and entire absence of pomp and circumstance which was so noticeable in both Lord and Lady Plunket were a stone of stumbling and rock of offence to many New Zealanders. It must be very hard to give satisfaction all round in a position such as theirs.

From Palmerston I went north to Auckland as soon as the flagship arrived there. My journey was a curious one, though uneventful. The line through the North Island from Wellington to Auckland, although just completed, was not then trustworthy enough in one section to be negotiated at night, so we drew up at Ohakune when darkness fell, and I confess I was glad that Lord Plunket had lent us one of his private cars and an orderly to take charge of us, for there were no locks on the doors, and the navvies who were camped at each side of the line did not appear to be the sort of neighbours one would choose, though I may have done them an injustice. No one except myself, my maid and the orderly was allowed to pass the night in the train, and the other passengers had a most uncomfortable time seeking for beds at a township .some miles away whence they had to rejoin the train at daylight.

Through a volcanic region of black soil that gave off a fine and penetrating dust, climbing up and down a corkscrew route among the inhospitable mountains, our train slowly pursued its way ; then, passing through pretty country, wooded or pastoral, it trotted more quickly on to Auckland, where we arrived, very hot, tired and dirty, thirty hours after leaving Palmerston. My husband, who " looked to see me dead," generously disregarded my travel-stained appearance, and we were soon sitting comfortably in a big, airy room at a good hotel, talking up the two months' interval which had elapsed since we parted at Sydney.

CHAPTER XXIX

CHRISTMAS, 1908

IT was now near Christmas, and after a couple of days at the hotel I shifted my quarters to the *Powerful*. The usual solemnities and absurdities of the day on board a man-of-war were duly observed, but the elements provided an unrehearsed item which frightened me nearly out of my wits. My husband

and I, accompanied by a number of the officers, were going the rounds of the mess-deck after church, and the large dish borne behind us by my husband's coxswain was being piled high with cakes, slices of plum-pudding, apples, nuts and what not—a friendly tribute from each mess—when a truly terrific explosion occurred. Nobody turned a hair, and, so infectious is a good example, that I continued to say " Merry Christmas " and " Thank you ; the same to you," adding a piece of richly-plummed pudding or a macaroon to Ward's burden as I proceeded on my way, but wondering *when* we should go to the bottom, or *if* we should go to the bottom. However, the fleet-footed flag-lieutenant had been despatched on deck to find out what had occurred and returned very soon with the news that a flash of lightning had come out of a clear blue sky, simultaneously with the crash of thunder we had heard, and struck the main wireless mast. My husband himself thought at first there had been an explosion on board one of the ships of the squadron lying close by, and of course from the lower-deck we had been able to see nothing. Much relieved, we continued our rounds with St. George and the Dragon and the Clown gambolling about us, and after a final rampage of the mummers on the poop our Christmas was over and the men's began.

A couple of days later my husband and I went up to Rotorua, that wonderful place whose name and fame have been made by earthquakes and volcanic eruptions. The next chapter is called " Hara," since it was Hara, with her funny English and friendly ways, who introduced me to the queer sights and sounds and smells of Whakarewarewa, although my husband had become acquainted with them on a previous visit.

CHAPTER XXX

" HARA "

SHE was a Maori girl of, possibly, sixteen, and by profession a guide in the thermal district of Rotorua, and we yielded ourselves without a struggle to her guardianship when she stepped forward on the bridge at Whakarewarewa, wreathed in smiles and flourishing a silver-topped walking-stick with one hand while she bestowed vigorous handshakes upon us with the other. The village to which she welcomed us contained a few men, numbers of amphibious children, and a pack of undenominational dogs. Ereti,* the chief guide, was mourning in the village meeting-house (*wharehui*), for her old mother had died the night before ; but Hara was her cousin and accredited substitute, and, after waving her stick towards the river, which bounds Whakarewarewa on two sides, to indicate the miscellaneous

* The celebrated Maggie Papakura, called *Ereti*—a Maori abbreviation of *Margaret*—by Hara.

crowd of bathers in its chilly waters as an object worthy of a tourist's interest, she led us, all unconscious of her design, straight to the *wharehui* and firmly pushed us inside. It was an embarrassing introduction to the women of Hara's tribe, but resistance was out of the question. The floor was covered with mourners crouching round the bier, over which feathered quilts were thickly spread, and only the dark face of the dead woman, surmounted by heavy coils of iron-grey hair in which a couple of black-tipped *huia* quills were stuck, was visible. From the mass of mourners a small but dignified figure detached itself. This was Ereti, who silently clasped our hands in a grip that was painful, and then resumed her place. Never have I seen a face expressive of such intense sorrow. The still features might have been cast in bronze for a bust of Grief itself. Another mourner arose and pressed our hands—Pera,* Ereti's half-sister—but not one of us uttered a word. Hara's black eyes were full of tears when we turned to leave the *wharehui*, but, once outside, she permitted herself the " comic relief " of poking a stout Maori in the waistcoat with her wand of office, an overture which was kindly received and provoked no reprisals.

Brown imps were bathing out in the sunshine in little tanks of warm water and stretching out wet claws for the pennies we did not give them. Our guide led us to a round pool brimming with boiling water, blue as a solution of sapphires, that swirled

* Bella ; but there is neither *B* nor *L* in the Maori language.

and danced in its deep basin. "Here," she said,
"we used to wash our clothes. But two years ago
my uncle fell in and we *could* not get him out. He
is here still; but of course he is all to pieces now.
Government will not let us wash here any more,
and this railing has been put up to keep other people
from falling in." This was said in the gentle, level
English of the educated Maori, and appropriate
comment, such as "How shocking!" died upon our
lips. Hara wore a sailor-hat with a black ribbon
(into which was tucked the inevitable *huia* quill), a
black-and-white striped cotton blouse and skirt,
black stockings, and laced shoes. A more inoffen-
sively commonplace costume could not be imagined.
Even her pigtail of stiff, crinkly black hair was tied
with the conventional wide white ribbon bow just
as the pigtail of an English high-school girl is tied.
But the boiling of an uncle would have surely been
alluded to in terms more moving by the English
high-school girl. Hara's uncle was as likely as not
a cannibal at heart, if not in fact—opportunity being
denied him by a paternal Government—and the
words "we *could* not get him out," conveyed to our
minds, warped by dwelling on the horrors of Maori
history, the idea of a good housekeeper's regret for
so much unavoidable waste. Do vegetarians realise
that New Zealand produced no animal food except
rats and birds when the Maoris drifted thither in their
war-canoes from the North, and that cannibalism
was the natural result of this dearth? If there
should ever be formed a community of "convinced"

vegetarians ready to exile themselves to some far island supplied only with the provender they affect, they would do well to read up the early history of New Zealand before embarking.

From the blue pool we climbed to Ereti's *whare*, where a piano and a bookcase full of standard works proclaimed its owner's high degree of intelligence and civilisation. Photographs of Governors and Admirals once guided by Ereti were there in plenty, and the closely-packed neatness of her little abode was that of the captain's cabin on board a mail-steamer. As we made our way between high *ti*-tree-hedges and across a wooden bridge to the mud-geysers, I asked Hara if there were any very old Maoris in Whakarewarewa who remembered the long war with the English. " Yes, there are some very old," she answered cheerfully, " but now we die very young ; many between twenty and thirty." This, alas ! is sadly true. The civilisation which has dressed Hara in a black-and-white cotton frock, and tied up her pigtail with a white ribbon, has brought with it the seeds of consumption. The feather-covered " mats " worn by the uncivilised Maori were thrown aside altogether when damp, in the days before imported propriety exacted the habitual wearing of a complete costume ; but European garments composed mainly of cotton are not healthy when worn wringing wet, and the modern Maori has not yet learnt that they should be changed.

The old Maoris killed one another in fierce and

never-ending tribal warfare ; their descendants fall a ready prey to alcohol and to the germs of diseases undreamt of a century ago. In physique they are much inferior to their forefathers, and it was the passion for firearms that began the mischief. As long as they were spear-throwers and lived on high ground in fortified and almost inaccessible positions, whither they had to retire when attacked, the Maoris were a robust people ; but with the advent of the musket they descended to the lowlands in the centre of areas fit for cultivation, and there erected dwellings adapted to the scope of their new weapons. Enormous quantities of flax (scraped by hand with a shell) were given in exchange for a single musket and a small supply of ammunition, and the strain of incessant hard work in the flax swamps, combined with the semi-starvation caused by the inevitable neglect of their food crops, sapped their vitality. What a text is here for the peace-preservationist ! But he must use it gingerly, for with spear, tomahawk, and *mere* (club) the untutored Maoris had gone a long way towards mutual extermination before ever the use of the musket was known in their land. It is interesting to reflect that, although the peace-preservationist and the Little Englander think we should be a much happier and holier race if we had never founded any colonies, they themselves, as a matter of fact, would have fared badly in the over-populated, under-victualled, and dependent England of their dreams. They might, indeed, have been eaten.

In spite of national defects and imported vices and failings, the Maori, of all coloured men, stands highest in one respect in the white man's estimation. A white man does not lose caste by marrying a Maori girl, and no New Zealander is ashamed of having Maori blood in his veins. Hara, who is waiting to show us a tiny boiling pool actually no more than a hand's-breadth from the cool reed-fringed waters of the rushing brown river, may marry a white man one day and be welcomed and respected by his people. She is very brown, it is true, and her lips are undeniably thick ; but the Maori head is as superior to the head of a West African negro as a nugget of gold is to a cake of soap or a cheap football.

The walking-stick now calls our attention to a group of mud-geysers, dirty grey, like much-handled semi-liquid putty, which bubble and squirt and cluck almost unceasingly. One of them grunts like a pig in a well of its own, and some achieve the most grotesque and kaleidoscopic contortions as they chuckle and writhe. A gargoyle face with three ever-shifting eyes and pouting lips is the worst of all, and we stand and watch it till we can contemplate its peculiarly offensive ugliness no longer. Then Hara leads us on very carefully (for a false step or a slight deviation from the narrow track might plunge us into a bottomless pit of boiling nastiness), and halts before the brush-concealed mouth of a rocky cave. " Here a chief was hidden for three years," she says. " His friends used to bring him food ;

but at last his enemies found him, and cut off his head and boiled his brains in the brain-pot over there." The " brain-pot," a round cauldron of petrified mud, has run dry of late, but, like most of the pools and geysers in this district, it is probably intermittent in its activity. One important geyser, *Waikiti*, stopped spouting the very day, fourteen years ago, that the railway to Rotorua was opened, but woke up again eighteen months back. Another spouts every quarter of an hour, and a third every three minutes, so if the passer-by does not know their idiosyncrasies, and forgets to consider how the wind sits, douches of hot sulphur-scented water, worse far than those of the practically-joking fountains of the Pallavicini Gardens at Genoa, may surprise him on his way.

Hara resolutely refuses a tip, and we part from her with much handshaking upon the bridge where we met. Looking back from the corner where the road bends away towards Rotorua, we see our little guide standing where we left her. She waves the cherrywood stick frantically. " Good luck, Atmirahl ! " she cries ; and " *Kia Ora* (Good luck), Hara ! " we reply.

CHAPTER XXXI

THE WILLIAMS FAMILY IN NEW ZEALAND

AFTER I had put in ten hot days at Rotorua, my husband, who had been fishing at Lake Taupo, rejoined me there and we returned together to Auckland, employing ourselves on the journey by learning Maori words and phrases out of a manual of conversation.

It strikes me as a beautiful language *written*, for it abounds in vowels, but harsh and guttural as one hears it spoken by the average Maori. The missionaries, who committed the spoken language to writing, established its grammar and translated into it the Bible and prayer-book, did a great work under great difficulties in a thoroughly scholarly manner. They used the Italian vowel sounds, thereby avoiding the clumsy doubling of vowels which in Australian native nomenclature produces such ungainly words as *Woolloomooloo*, or stumbling-blocks like *Bulli* and *Bondi*, which I naturally, but most incorrectly, pronounced as though they were Italian words instead of calling them *Bull-eye* and *Bond-eye*. This difference in fixing the spelling of native words is in a great measure due to the fact that sailors were the pioneers in Australia, and sailors are not scholars ; whereas the early missionaries in New Zealand were for the most part learned men who had received a classical education.

THE WILLIAMS FAMILY IN NEW ZEALAND

We made the acquaintance at Auckland of several members of the Williams family—a family greatly renowned for courage and ability, as well as for their magnificent physique, in those early days of missionary work when cannibalism among Maoris was the rule, and loneliness and hardship sorely tried even the most intrepid and single-minded of the pioneers of Christianity in New Zealand.

Mrs. Thomas Williams, a beautiful lady whom I hesitate to call old, gave my husband a copy of a book, now rare, written by Hugh Carleton and published in 1874 at Auckland, entitled " The Life of Henry Williams, Archdeacon of Waimate," and the story which it tells of the early missionary settlers, their dangers and trials between 1823 and 1867 (the year of Archdeacon Williams' death) is extraordinarily interesting. Mrs. Henry Williams was fully as heroic as her husband. They had been five years married before leaving England, and she had the care of young children for many years in addition to the work of civilising and teaching the Maori women and girls who attached themselves to the Mission.

Mrs. Thomas Williams was the wife of Archdeacon Williams' fourth son whom we saw as an old man at Auckland. She told me that, as a child of four, he had run off without leave from his parents' house and been actually present—though an unseen and most unwilling spectator—at a cannibal feast with all its horrors, returning home to receive a whipping for his truancy !

Missionaries on the whole were not ill-used in those days. What they had chiefly to apprehend was the chance of being stripped of all they possessed (not indeed recklessly or wantonly, but according to the strict letter of Maori law), for some offence committed against an etiquette of which they were ignorant.

Mrs. H. Williams tells in a letter to her family at home a story of " Tohitapu of the Koroa," whom the biographer describes as " a great chief *tapu*'ed an inch thick," a priest and a sorcerer. The Maori sorcerer's power was as real in its effect as is the Obeah of the African negro. " That the victims of this sorcery waste away and die is an undoubted fact, whether from fear or through mesmeric influence must remain a question." Tohitapu, however, endeavoured to bewitch Mr. Henry Williams, and, failing, lost his power from that time forward. " When the incantation was proceeding the house-servants were trembling with fear, expecting Mr. Williams to turn black in the face and fall from his seat, but as Tohitapu's failure became evident the bystanders concluded that the white man's divinity, or *atua*, had overpowered that of the Maori." It is interesting to learn that after being fairly worsted by Mr. Williams, Tohitapu became a staunch friend of the family until his death in 1830. Mr. Carleton observes that, " A Maori seldom bears malice. He respects and likes you better for having fairly beaten him. Revenge is with him not so much a matter of feeling, as of duty."

Mrs. Williams' account, somewhat abridged, of Tohitapu's strange behaviour at the Mission Station in the spring of 1824 gives a very good picture of the position of a missionary's wife and family among a population of cannibals who were extremely touchy and whose pastime was war.

" After dinner a most troublesome chief, named Tohitapu, who lives about a mile from us, put us all in confusion. Mr. Fairburn " (a coadjutor of Mr. Williams) " saw him coming and called to someone to fasten the gate. Instead of knocking in the usual manner for admittance Tohi sprang over the fence. Mr. F. told him he was a bad man for coming in like a thief and not like a gentleman. He immediately began to stamp and caper about like a madman, attracting all around by his vociferous gabble and flourishing his *mere* " (greenstone club) " which every chief carries concealed under his mat " (a short cloak of feathers) ; " then, brandishing his spear, he would spring like a cat and point it at Mr. Fairburn, apparently in earnest. Mr. Williams, upon joining them, told him his conduct was very bad, and refused to shake hands with him. The savage, for so in truth he now appeared, stripped for fighting, keeping on only a plain mat similar to those worn by girls. Mr. W. and Mr. F. beheld his capers with great appearance of indifference. At length they left him and he sat down to take breath, and, upon their going to the beach, he went out. Engaged with the children indoors, I did not hear all that passed : you will, therefore, have only part of the scene. When Mr. W. returned he saw some mats, apparently thrown down in haste, which he imagined to belong to Tohitapu, and, putting them outside, shut the door and went to the back of the house. Shortly after the furious man returned from the beach and, snatching up a long pole, made a stroke at the door, but it not yielding to his violence, he sprang over the fence, resumed all his old antics, and when Mr. W. appeared he couched and aimed his spear at him. Mr. W. advanced towards him, not heeding his threats and, though Tohi trembled with rage, he did not throw the spear. He said he had hurt his foot in jumping over the fence and demanded payment for it. Mr. W. said it was well for him to hurt his foot when he came in that manner, and that he should have no payment. He then walked to the store, and having snatched up an iron pot in which pitch had been boiled, was springing towards the fence, but then, retarded by his unwieldy burden, was making for the door when Mr. W. darted upon him, snatched the pot out of his hands and set his own back against the door to stop his retreat ; he then called to someone to take away the pot which Tohi made several attempts to seize, at the same time brandishing his spear over Mr. W.'s head with furious gestures, while the latter, coolly folding his arms, resisted his attack upon the contested pot, occasionally remarking ' *Kati, emara, heoi ano !* ' " (Gently, sir, that is enough !)

" As I looked through the window with no little trepidation, the scene reminded me of a man attacked by a furious bull who steadily eyes the monster and keeps him at bay. The blacksmith now came forward and shoved his shoulder against Tohi, who seemed to relax a little, though he still flourished about in a way I can hardly describe. He ran to and fro with his spear in his hand something like a boy playing at cricket, except that the Maori dances sideways slapping his sides and stamping with a measured pace and horrid gestures, every now and then squatting down and panting as if trying to excite his own rage to the utmost before he made a final spring. He continued to demand payment and said he should stay here to-day and to-morrow and five days more and make a great fight ; and to-morrow, ten and ten and ten men, holding up his fingers as he spoke, would come to set fire to the house. . . . When prayers were over he came to the window, and without any ceremony put his leg in, pointing to his foot, and demanded payment for the blood which was spilt. Mr. W. told him to go away and come again to-morrow like a gentleman and knock at the gate as Te Koki did, and then he would say ' How do you do ? Mr. Tohitapu,' and invite him to breakfast with us. . . . After talking some time Tohi again worked himself into a terrific passion and stripped for fighting. It was now eleven o'clock at night. Tohi had thrown off all his garments and by the imperfect light looked like some wild animal running

to and fro in furious rage. . . . Our friends "
(natives) " looking in at the window, one and
another called to me, ' Mother, you see a great fire
in the house. Oh yes, children dead, all dead, a
great fight, a great many men, plenty of muskets.'
. . . Tohitapu, who is a great priest, now began to
chant a horrible ditty which Mr. F. told us was
for the purpose of bewitching us. . . . The natives
said he had ' Karakia'd ' us—a term they apply to
our religious worship—and said he had killed a man
on board the *Active* schooner, in this way. We
were awakened early in the morning by the noise
of Tohi and others who were continually arriving
until our premises were surrounded." Mrs. Williams
sent Tohi out a pint-pot full of tea at breakfast time
" hoping it might prove a quieting draught ; but
before long he was again prancing about inside the
yard with many of his followers, all hideous figures
armed with spears and hatchets, and some few
with muskets. They looked the more formidable
to me knowing my husband was in the midst of
them. Our native girls were all out and I had to
remain close prisoner with my children, the windows
being blocked up the whole day by ranges of natives'
heads looking in. The poor children began to pine
for air and liberty, and at about five o'clock Mr. W.
came to the window and said things were more
tranquil now and the natives dispersing. I then
put the children through the window, but scarcely
had the feet of our little girl touched the ground
when a sudden noise was heard of loud strokes and

it seemed as if they were making a breach through the wooden walls of the store for the purpose of forcing an entrance. Mr. W. put back the children head foremost through the window and ran to the spot. The noise and clamour now became very great. A chief brought our little boy in his arms, screaming and looking pale. I asked where he was hurt. The poor child exclaimed, ' No, mamma, I am not hurt, but they are going to kill papa. We shall all be burnt, and they will kill poor papa : I saw the men, I saw the guns.' As I sat in the centre of the bedroom, the baby in my arms and the three others clinging around me I saw through the little back window the mob rushing past and a man pointing his gun at the house, and immediately Mr. W. stepped in between. My feelings were now excited to the utmost, yet I felt an elevation of soul it is worth much suffering to possess even for a few moments. . . . The dear children, sobbing and crying, fell on their knees and repeated after me a prayer prompted by what was passing. The noise continued. They repeatedly shook our slight walls, but the house remained unbroken and the children grew more calm. The younger ones soon began to be troublesome, trying to get to the windows to look out. The women outside kept coming to the window, exclaiming, ' *Emata, tena ra ko koe ?* ' " (Mother, how do you do ?)   " Po at last put up her goodnatured face, telling me there would be no more fight to-day, that all the men were gone away and that she had been making a great fight for us—

for women fight in New Zealand. I gladly unbolted the door for my husband to enter. He told me all was over and that the second disturbance was quite distinct from the first. Tohi had remained quiet during the whole affray and was rather inclined to take our part ; in compliance with the request of the friendly chiefs the iron pot had been given to him with which he had departed. It seems that in the course of the day the son of one of the chiefs who came as our friend had stolen a blanket from Mr. Fairburn. Some of our people charged him with this, unknown to us, and this second disturbance was made by him because he was annoyed at the exposure of his conduct."

No wonder that, some twenty years later, writing to a friend in England, Mr. Williams says, " My wife gets older every day," and hopes she will soon be able to give up her native school. Her first years were spent in household drudgery, for her native servants were not to be relied on. " The moment a boat arrives," she writes, " down scamper all the native servants, men, boys and girls, to the beach. If there is anything to be seen, or anything extraordinary occurs, in New Zealand the mistress must do the work while the servants gaze abroad. She must not scold them, for if they are *rangatiras* (of noble birth) they will run away in a pet and tell her she has ' too much of the mouth.' Having been forewarned of this I wait and work till they choose to come back, which they generally do at meal-times."

Archdeacon Williams had been a lieutenant in the Navy before taking Holy Orders, and his skill as the navigator of the little fifty-ton hooker (home-built on the slip at Paihia, the mission station) brought him and his crew through many tight places on a practically uncharted coast. It must have been hard for him to give up the use of all weapons, and even the exercise of physical force, in his dealings with the violent and excitable natives among whom he found himself, but his biographer gives three instances of his success in impromptu self-defence which occurred at long intervals during his ministry.

Very early commissariat difficulties arose. The missionaries in 1824, before the *Herald* was built, had been nearly driven to eating fern-root owing to the non-arrival of their stores, and native supplies were withheld in the hope of starving these men of peace into bartering gunpowder and muskets for food. One day Mr. Williams had " bought and paid for a basket of fuchsia berries ; but the seller, thinking to extort further payment, thrust himself in Mr. Williams' way, barring the road and hoping to be struck. Disappointed in this he seized Mr. Williams in wrestling form, striving to throw him, his confederates biding their time. He failed, but Mr. Williams called out to the rest, ' If you do not take this fellow away I shall give him something.' No notice was taken of the warning and, happening to have the key of his study in his hand with his thumb in the ring, Mr. Williams dealt his assailant such a tap on the temple with closed fist and key that the man dropped as if shot. Mr. Williams, though not feeling quite easy about the result of his work, put a good face upon it, saying, ' See now ; I told you what I would do.' The fellow recovered after a while and the whole party skulked away. Mr. Williams was afterwards known as the ' man with the iron thumb.' "

In March, 1845, at the sacking of Kororareka, in which H.M.S. *Hazard* was engaged, both Bishop Selwyn and Archdeacon Williams, completely regardless of danger, had been caring for the wounded and hastily burying the dead. " Te Harawira, with two others, put their muskets to the Archdeacon's breast upon his endeavouring to rescue a whale-boat taken by them from an Englishman and his wife," and the Archdeacon was seen " *brushing* the Maoris to right and left *with his umbrella* to make way for himself." That the word *brushing* is a peaceful synonym for *whacking* I feel convinced.

On yet another occasion the Archdeacon successfully defended himself against assault at close quarters by shoving his telescope against his assailant's chest. The telescoping of the telescope so alarmed the Maori that he was with difficulty persuaded that half of it had not entered his person.

At the time of this valiant missionary's death a fight between two tribes over a disputed boundary-line was actually in progress, and a large district was being rapidly drawn into the quarrel. The day for a pitched battle was fixed, but on the very eve the combatants were stayed. " Te Wirimu " (Archdeacon Williams) was dead. The natives were paralysed by the news. The patron chief of the district where the Archdeacon resided, Pakaraka, insisted upon being one of the pall-bearers, and after the funeral he said, " My hand has touched the pall. I cannot now go back to fight." Time was thus gained for angry passions to subside and peace was effected.

The late Mr. Thomas Williams, in the course of conversation, gave my husband two very curious instances of the strong sense of fairplay—one might, indeed, say chivalry—which characterised the Maori warrior. During the long fighting between the Chiefs Heke and Kawiti and the Government in 1844—1846, Mr. Williams, then quite a young man, fell in with a strong party of natives when he was in the act of driving some cattle to the English camp. It was no use trying to disguise that his object was to provide the soldiers with food, but the Maori leader, instead of molesting the passage of the beasts and their owner, turned to with his men and helped Mr. Williams to get his drove to the camp, only leaving him when at too close quarters for safety. His reason for this action was simply that " the fighting couldn't go on if the English were not fed " ; and fighting is the breath of life to the Maori. Shortly after this Mr. Williams overtook an ammunition-wagon guarded by English soldiers who had piled their muskets on the wagon in which many of their comrades were asleep. Just before he came up with the party an armed Maori suddenly appeared out of the Bush at his side. Unaided this man might have held up the wagon, unprotected as it was, but no; it would have been a pity to prevent the ammunition reaching camp, since without ammunition the English could not continue fighting! When the wagon was out of sight no less than a hundred Maori warriors appeared from their ambush, all quite contented that their enemy should have the means to keep up hostilities. What a contrast to " civilised " methods of warfare the attitude of these " savages " presents !

Of works of fiction of which the scene is laid in New Zealand I have read none, though a book of sketches entitled " Brown Bread from a Colonial Oven " has given me quite peculiar pleasure by its evident sincerity and great charm of local colour.

Far more amazing than any fiction are the true stories of New Zealand's wars, and, on their final cessation in 1871, her magically swift development into what she is now. It seems incredible that forty-five years ago she was racked with wars, and wasted and crippled by the internecine fighting, not of decades but of centuries. Forty-five years ago she beat her bayonets and muskets into reaping-hooks and plough-shares, and now thousands of her magnificent sons of British and Maori blood, born and reared between the thundering seas that gird her, are carrying new rifles and bayonets in the great fight for the life and freedom of the Empire of which she forms so important a part.

CHAPTER XXXII

A VOYAGE IN THE FLAGSHIP

As it behoves me to describe one of my voyages on board the *Powerful*, if only that my experiences may act as a deterrent to other Admirals' wives to whom the notion of making pleasure-trips with their husbands appears attractive, I will choose the first and longest I made—that from Auckland to Sydney. I may as well say that, in spite of the indulgence invariably shown me by all on board, my feeling that a woman is out of place as an " inmate " of a man-of-war was accentuated by my experiences, and I am glad I did not ask my husband to take me to Fiji and " The Islands " when he visited them —a petition he would quite certainly have refused. That I travelled with him from Auckland to Sydney in January, 1909, was due to the fact that there was at the moment fixed for the flagship's departure no steamer in which I should have been comfortable due to sail, so common humanity decided him to give me a passage. I went to Hobart and back in the *Powerful* the same summer, and again to

Hobart on my way home in 1911, because the steamers between Sydney and Hobart were somewhat small and, at that holiday season, overcrowded and inconvenient for people travelling patriarchally, as we did, with horses and carriages, menservants and maidservants.

On every trip I made, the fact that I was an unintentional and embarrassed eavesdropper and nuisance was brought home to me without any rubbing in. When I was in my sleeping cabin I could hear through the *jalousies* everything that was said in the fore-cabin, or in the lobby outside it. If I sat in the after-cabin I was in the way when officers came to see my husband, and the fore-cabin was only an open anteroom to the after-cabin. Strict privacy was impossible, for all the partitions, properly called bulkheads, were either very thin or merely *jalousies*, the doors were all hooked back and, as many naval men are deaf, lowered voices were not the rule. When it rained I could neither walk nor sit on deck, and when we had a head wind the hail of blacks (they have no Welsh coal to burn on the Australian station) made the poop equally untenable. It was, of course, possible to sit in my husband's little deck-cabin where he slept when I was on board, and thither I used to flee when I felt myself intolerably intrusive down below, but it was not a specially attractive retreat, holding as it did only the *stricte nécessaire* of a dressing-room.

When I embarked at Auckland I took possession

of my husband's sleeping cabin, and it reminded me but little of the ordinary sleeping " compartment " in a mail steamer. Indeed, it appeared palatial. Two port-holes, two capacious chests of drawers, a wardrobe, and a bunk (the springs of which did not leave dints on the backbone of the sleeper), raised it far above the level of most cabins, and there was a bath-room off it, where fresh water, hot and cold, flowed abundantly. From these details it will be seen that the *Powerful* was quite a " superior " ship, and myself a very fortunate person—as fortunate as a bad sailor can be. But the sea was so calm on the first day out that it could hardly have rocked a wicker cradle, much less the big ship that slid over its shining expanse at a speed so easy as to minimise vibration. The steering engine occasionally committed a breach of the peace, but for the most part profound stillness prevailed, and thankfulness for the blessing of a good start reigned in my heart. Such wind as there was carried the smoke well away from the ship and left the poop smutless, so, when my husband sent a message to say that he hoped his passenger would come up and enjoy the air and the prospect, I gladly emerged to gaze in comfort upon a picture of sea, sky, and coast that fairly took away my breath—a harmony in blues, from the silver and lavender of a diapered sea-surface through the clear azure of the sky to the deep indigo of mountain peaks and sides. A single brown-sailed schooner struck a pleasant note of life ; a strip of golden sand at the water's edge imparted a welcome sense of equilibrium to a mind clinging passionately to the firmly horizontal.

At four o'clock there was an evolution. Life-buoys were let go, engines reversed, and two cutters hoisted out and raced to pick up the lifebuoys, which floated astern, showing the pale flame of Holmes' light. The starboard cutter picked up the first lifebuoy, and was back alongside and hoisted in a full minute before the other, and very soon nothing was left to remind the passenger standing entranced upon the stern-walk that the life-saving process, just as it would have been carried out had a man fallen overboard at sea, had been gone through—nothing but the insidious smell of concentrated onions and verdigris caused by the Holmes' lights.

That night I retired luxuriously to my bed, scamping no detail of the nocturnal toilet, revelling in the steadiness of the cabin walls and floor, the power of the electric fan, the wide-open ports and the capacity of the wardrobe. The bunk, though wider than others I had known, was narrower than any shore bed—that was the only point where criticism was possible. But at ten minutes past two I awoke to find the ship grown skittish, and to be glad that the bunk was no wider. The wardrobe door had opened, and hit me on the head as I leant over to turn on the electric light, one bedroom slipper and one evening shoe were careering swiftly in unhallowed union beneath a chest of drawers and a tinkle of colliding glass proceeded from the shelf above the washing-stand. A kindly coast no longer protected the ship, which was now fairly launched upon a four days' stretch of uneasy ocean. For a moment the heart of the passenger sank. No omnipotent stewardess was here ; only a maid who might be *hors de combat* the whole time. Seasickness on board a man-of-war is as out of place as goloshes in a ball-room or a caterpillar in a salad —incongruous, unpardonable, revolting. She would not succumb. So she switched off the light and resolutely went to sleep.

My husband brought in my early cup of tea next morning, since in spite of heroic efforts, Emily had been physically incapable of dressing herself. This was not a pleasant day, and what interest it contained for myself was due to one sense only— that of hearing ; for my eyes were closed, food gave me no solace, I felt distinctly uncomfortable, and my smelling-bottle had emptied itself into the recesses of my dressing-bag. So I lay still and listened. The cabin-door sentry had a cold, and I numbered his sneezes with lively compassion and longed to send him out a cinnamon lozenge. The wind was now right astern, so the steering-engine was extremely noisy ; the sea splashed against the ship's side, now more, now less violently, but it was no good counting the seconds between the biggest splashes in the hope of finding they occurred at regular intervals, for they did nothing of the sort. Prayers on the upper deck at 9.15 a.m. gave me food for surmise. The band played the men to their devotions with a jiggy march that sounded like Sousa. The ceremony lasted about three minutes, and then the music struck up once more, stopping finally so abruptly in the middle of a bar that, as I did not know and could never have guessed that prayers had been read at all, I could only suppose some strange naval version of " musical chairs " was being enacted. Then there were the officers in quest of an appetite for lunch or dinner who took constitutionals on the poop, and by dint of counting very carefully I was able to tell to a nicety how many paces it took to cover the distance from after-bridge to stern—so many from just overhead to the stern and back, and so many seconds to count before the footsteps, growing from pianissimo to fortissimo, returned to the spot immediately above my bunk.

Of course there were plenty of bugle-calls throughout the day, and the band (which was bad) played " The Roast Beef " before the ward-room dinner and " The King " when his Majesty's health was drunk. For two whole days I cultivated my sense of hearing, repeated the multiplication table, made doggerel rhymes, dozed a great deal and received nourishing food at intervals from the hands of a benevolent admiral. But I maintained unimpaired the dignity which seasickness infallibly destroys, and rose, pale but proud, on the fourth day of my voyage from the couch, erstwhile thought narrow, where two soft cushions had been inserted as wedges to keep me from rolling unduly. Under the after-bridge I sat that night in the gathering darkness, rejoicing in the steadiness of such a position, many paces (as I well knew from counting them) forward of the spot, haunted by screw and steering-engine, where I had lain so long. Thence I looked down into the brightly illuminated life of the upper deck. The band was playing a two-step, and to its brassy strains two junior officers, pipe in mouth, danced featly and with extraordinary seriousness. An auction of old papers and periodicals was going on in the ward-room, and barefooted bluejackets drew close to the skylight to listen to the voice of the charmer who bid up a bundle of London papers to 5s. 9d. Down from the fore-bridge to his belated dinner came the jaded navigator laden with charts. The wireless began to chatter in its dark closet, and the torpedo-lieutenant flew up the starboard poop-ladder, and nearly fell over my chair in the dark. Oddest sight of all, half a dozen marines, in training for some race, and clad in shorts and many-coloured jerseys, pattered barefoot round the upper deck. Presently the commander appeared, and to him I poured forth all the questions which had accumulated in my mind during the days of solitary confinement. How does one get into a lifebuoy ? How does one find the secret cupboard in it where there is food and drink ? What are a boatswain's duties ? Does a boatswain's mate grow into a boatswain automatically if he lives long enough, and where does he practise shouting orders before he has to start doing so professionally ? By what method are British naval bandsmen trained to play so badly ? Does the navigating officer ever go to sleep at sea ? Where is the canteen—and what is sold there ? I asked no questions about guns, torpedoes, or wireless telegraphy, for I know my limitations where science is concerned, but I wanted to know how the ship's company lives and moves and has its being, collectively and individually, what it eats, and how it is punished and rewarded. So it was late befoie my curiosity was gratified. and I reluctantly sought my cabin, there to find a pallid Emily, crushed but not broken, and pitifully anxious to efface the memory of past neglect.

Next morning there was firing to be done, and while the ship circled round and round with much clattering of the steering-engine I lay in my bunk and listened to the noise of the guns. Luckily, they were not making all they can, for they were being fired not in naked majesty but with tubes containing small bullets inside them, and the voice of the largest was no worse than the bursting of a paper-bag, while the smallest reminded me of the opening of the sort of soda-water bottle that has a glass marble in its throat. Sitting up in bed I felt as though I were trying to balance myself on a gigantic and unruly air-cushion, for the ship had next to no way on and wobbled ridiculously. But this was over by noon, and she proceeded with a fair amount of *aplomb* upon her way until darkness set in. By that time I had earned credit by dining with some appetite in the fore-cabin, and mounted to the poop with augmented self-respect to be present (by special permission) at the night-firing. I am entirely incompetent to describe with accuracy what passed. At any rate, I know that the target is dropped overboard, and the searchlights on both bridges pick it out and keep it visible. It is only a canvas-covered frame in the shape of a cross that bobs about on the waves on its edges, and never seems to get damaged, though apparently hit dozens of times. By half-past ten the firing was over, and the target had been hauled on board, a part of the entertainment at which I was not invited to be present. They said that targets frequently provoke angry passions conducive to intemperate language by their clumsy fashion of getting on board; hence my exclusion from the final scene. Next morning the voyage came to an end, and, though I was dressed before the ship anchored, my presence on the poop was not desired. As I left the ship shortly after breakfast I caught sight of the commander, followed closely by a personal suite consisting of a bugler and a boy with a megaphone. I longed to know what they were going to do, and where and how they would do it ; but one thing had been carefully impressed upon me by my husband, and that was *never* to talk to anyone but the chaplain when a ship is coming, or has just come, into harbour.

CHAPTER XXXIII

HOBART

It was both cold and wet when my husband and I disembarked at Hobart in January, 1909, and, as the horses and carriages had still to be landed, we walked and trammed to the western end of the town, where Newlands, the house taken for us by the Tasmanian Government, was situated. Everything was dripping in the garden and shrubberies, and the house felt damp and cheerless when we entered it. The aroma of too-domestic cats and dogs was heavy in the hall and passages, and until we had found a pleasant little upstairs sitting-room, undarkened by a verandah, and had been comforted with tea and a crackling wood fire, our spirits drooped. Next day sunshine, widely-opened windows and a sentence of banishment on the four-footed retainers of the house restored our serenity, and the discovery of great bushes of sweet-scented verbena, geraniums six feet high, and a group of large mulberry trees laden with fruit in the pretty old-fashioned garden aided the reaction.

The Governor of Tasmania, Sir Gerald Strickland, and Lady Edeline Strickland were old acquaintances, since the former (now Governor of New South Wales) had been Colonial Secretary at Malta while we were in the Mediterranean in 1897—1900, and their genuine and unexacting kindness during our Tasmanian holiday added much to our comfort and pleasure. They were admirably conscientious in the performance of their public duties, and their bevy of little daughters, ranging from five to twelve years old, were as sweet and pretty as a spring garland.

The southern part of the island is smiling and beautiful, and it is hard to reconcile such peaceful surroundings as those of Hobart with the memory of such horrors as, through the cruelty or mismanagement of the early Governors and their subordinates, were permitted to exist while it was yet a penal settlement. I tried to read that painful book " For the Term of his Natural Life," but flung it from me before I had half read it, and abandoned myself to the charm of the Tasmania I could see, with its blue mountains and sparkling sea, great trees, spreading apple orchards and snug farms.

It was a lazy holiday for me, and I had good company at Newlands for the greater part of it, for my husband's sister, Sister Bridget of the Kilburn Sisterhood, who needed rest and refreshment, came from her Melbourne school to spend her leave with us. When she left I had Phœbe's companionship, and during her visit a naval officer's wife, who had nearly succumbed to cold and exposure when " bushed " on Mount Wellington in the freezing night mists, came to us for rest and nursing.

There is a little " season " at Hobart which coincides with the squadron's summer visit, and as it is a favourite hot-weather resort with Sydney and Melbourne people there were plenty of gay doings while we were there. Each of the ships used to go over in turn to do the gunlayers' test-firing at Norfolk Bay, about forty miles east of Hobart, but boat races, picnics, dances, and " sing-songs " were of agreeably frequent occurrence, and a considerable number of naval (matrimonial) engagements were foreshadowed, or actually embarked upon, during these pleasant months. No wonder the Australian station is beloved by sailors. No wonder that many a harassed officer " batter-fanging " about the Channel looks back regretfully to the years he spent between Torres Straits and Dunedin, the Leeuwin and the Southern Seas. And it was not only the dancing and racing, the boating and picnicking that proved so attractive. There was sport, so dear to sailormen, so rare in these days of concentration in home waters, to be had, from red-deer stalking in the South Island of New Zealand to duck-shooting on the Black-Soil Plains, and shark fishing in out-of-the-way Pacific islands.

CHAPTER XXXIV

OCCASIONAL RHYMES

WHEN I was five I believed I could " make up poetry." Perhaps this belief was encouraged by the playing of a game invented by my eldest brother. We three little ones, Charley, Bob and I, separated by a long gap from our elder brothers and sisters, used to sit on the low wide steps at Parknasilla, our home in Kerry, and Alfred used to say " Give me a rhyme for *diminution*," or " *catacomb*," or " *mannikin*," and the first child who found a rhyme he considered sound was commended. I was proud when I gave *Lilliputian* as a rhyme to *diminution*, but I had been hearing expurgated and simplified stories of Gulliver, and the word was ready in my head.

However, my first acknowledged effort to " make up poetry " met with such derision from my young brothers that I soon abandoned my ambition. All I can remember of my *magnum opus* are these lines, written before I was six :

> " When the tide is gently flowing
> And the breeze is softly blowing
> I love to sit upon a rock and think of olden times."

Not until 1898 did I try again. Then I composed two appropriate valentines destined to mystify and gently annoy a junior lieutenant and the sub. of the

Hawke. But my husband intervened, calling them " anonymous communications." This made me extremely cross, for I had always believed that anonymity in valentines was not only admissible but desirable, and I was not soothed when the commander, to whom I had confided my disappointment, deprived me of the better of the two, touched it up (greatly to its detriment), and despatched it as his own composition to Mr. Beaty-Pownall ! I again retired from the flowery field of poetry, and not a rhyme did I achieve until the year 1907, when I *dreamt* a very queer one. This is how it ran :

> " I am in prison, and he is dead—
> Both of us broke, my complexion fled ;
> For ever and ever it will be said
> ' They should never have mar-ri-ed
> Since they had no butter to put on their bread.' "

Then I became conscious, but before I was fully awake this *coda* hopped into my brain :

> " But this is the truth (which I scarce dare utter),
> We had really no bread to put under our butter."

The composition by " unconscious cerebration " of these tragic lines, which might very well describe the fate of two reckless young people who had started life on £200 a year and a motor-car, did not stimulate me to further effort. My discouraged Muse remained mute until I had been several months in Australia, when something—lying awake at night, I think—led me to occupy myself with rhyming, and

OCCASIONAL RHYMES

Mr. Share, Private Secretary to Lord Northcote, was the subject of my first serious effort. All of us at Admiralty House, to say nothing of Mr. Share's other innumerable friends in Australia, felt actual distress as the fear of losing him along with his chief developed into certainty, so my verses were far from being a mere exercise in rhyming.

Kind Mr. Share !
Beyond compare
For manners bland and debonnair,
I wonder if you ever swear,
Or do you always " grin and bear,"
Good Mr. Share ?

Keen Mr. Share !
Your secretar—
ial duties are performed with rar—
est tact and skill and patient care,
And all you do is on the square,
Straight Mr. Share !

Wise Mr. Share !
Your *savoir faire*
Would soothe the very sulkiest bear,
And lure him smiling from his lair,
Offering his claws for you to pare,
Cute Mr. Share !

Dear Mr. Share !
We'll tear our hair
And robes of ashy sackcloth wear
If it turns out that you must fare
To England back. We cannot spare
You, Mr. Share.

July, 1908. Sydney.

215

Captain Leslie Wilson, R.M.L.I., A.D.C. to Sir Harry Rawson, was going to have a birthday in the autumn of 1908—the sort of birthday which can be celebrated by a cake of moderate dimensions, since quite a small number of little candles would suffice to encircle it—and in a moment of expansion I threatened him with an " Ode." I regret that *serve her* is inadmissible as a rhyme to *Minerva* and *sailor* to *failure*, but only purists will be pained. There is not a grain of flattery in the sentiments expressed ; in fact, I only regret that I have not attempted a second part, dealing epically and appreciatively with Captain Wilson's election as Unionist member for Reading and his more recent departure for the Dardanelles as a lieutenant-colonel in the Naval Division.

> When he was born, so fair was he,
>   Mars, Venus, Neptune and Minerva
> Came down the peerless babe to see,
>   And asked his mother could they serve her.
>
> Mars vowed that he should join the Guards,
>   But Neptune wanted him a sailor ;
> They wrangled, and 'twas on the cards
>   The boy's career would be a failure.
>
> But Venus, who of Love is Queen,
>   Swift interposed to stop the fighting.
> " Make him," she cried, " a Red Marine,"
>   And got the gods' consent in writing.
>
> Then she herself the baby took
>   And taught him various ways of smiling ;
> Minerva fetched a pretty book
>   Which made diplomacy beguiling.

OCCASIONAL RHYMES

Mars personally supervised
His military education,
And Father Neptune minimised
The horrors of " initiation."

.　　　.　　　.　　　.

Thenceforth the lucky Leslie throve,
Gentle yet strong ; sincere though wily.
Birds, beasts and human beings love
Him dearly—but respect him highly.

August, 1908.　Sydney.

In the following verses on my friend, Mrs. Gordon
Wesché, I endeavoured to describe the typical
Australian woman as exemplified in her remarkable
and delightful personality.　I called them

LINES ON HER AUSTRALIAN FRIEND
BY AN ENGLISHWOMAN.

Australia's great and rich and fair ;
Jewels of price are common there,
But Phœbe's one a King might wear.

She is as witty as she's wise,
And has the brownest black-fringed eyes
That ever woke to sunny skies.

Eyes that can see beyond to-day
To far horizons, and their ray
Lights up new lamps along the way.

Hunger, fatigue, heat, cold or wet
When Phœbe's with me I forget.
Far in the background they are set.

And if I'm bored, or cross, or glum
I telephone and bid her come,
Whose laugh would cheer the deaf and dumb.

There's nothing Phœbe cannot do.
She'll break a horse, or patch a shoe,
A page of Browning she'll construe,

Turn an old gown, or make a pie,
Or make a speech, or knit a tie,
And never, never will say die.

Then she's a safe perennial source
Of facts concerning every horse
At Flemington or Randwick Course.

Times and *Spectator*, both she reads,
And comments on the Empire's needs.
Mistrusting words, she dotes on deeds.

My friend, of course, is " native born,"
While I'm " imported "—term of scorn—
And two years hence, far off, forlorn,
Phœbe in absence shall I mourn.

Christmas, 1908. New Zealand.

Though I was somewhat humiliated by finding the above described as " doggerel " in the *Sydney Herald*, it served as the text for a most interesting article by the editor himself, who had no idea that the verses were mine. They had been published in the *Spectator*, but the title as I have given it had been changed to " To a Colonial Girl." Now the adjective *Colonial* was barred and banned, expurgated from my vocabulary and extracted from my brain when I left England for Australia in February, 1908, so the gratification I derived from the acceptance of my verses by the editor of the *Spectator* was sadly discounted by their disastrous label.

OCCASIONAL RHYMES

The following verses, written during a short holiday in the Blue Mountains with Phœbe and Commander Bowring, were the result of high spirits at a high altitude.   But some part of the *Boadicea* joke leaked out later, and I was asked point-blank one day *if my daughter was really christened Boadicea !*

BOADICEA.

Once on a time there *wasn't* a girl,
Of British maidens the choicest pearl,
Almost too good and too pretty to live,
And possessing all gifts that the gods can give,
        Whose name was Boadicea.

She was five feet five with a figure neat,
She had capable hands and slender feet,
Her chestnut hair was wavy and long,
And each word she spoke like an angel's song—
        This fancy-bred Boadicea.

She was invented, and christened too,
At Medlow Bath in the Mountains Blue.
There I evolved her ; for sponsors three
She had Phœbe the Wise, the Commander and Me,
        And we called her Boadicea.

Never a daughter at all had I
Till Boadicea stepped out of the sky,
And now I'm as proud of her beauty and grace
As any real mother could be in my place
        Of a genuine Boadicea.

I'd like her to marry, and yet I should love
To keep her for ever—my treasure trove.
To whom shall I offer her lily-white paw ?
To whom shall I make myself mother-in-law ?
        Who shall have Boadicea ?

> She merits a husband wise and kind,
> And if he were rich I should not mind ;
> But if the Commander should come to woo
> I'd give him my blessing and daughter too.
> > *He* should have Boadicea.

October, 1908.   Sydney.

Commander Bowring's comments on this rhyme were of a somewhat jeering nature. He thought Boadicea might prove an expensive and unserviceable wife if she ever materialised, so negotiations were dropped, though, happily, without any straining of relations.

Lord Chelmsford's nose appeared over my horizon in 1909 and inspired the following humble tribute :

A VICE-REGAL NOSE.

> Elizabethan poets sang of eye-brows,
> > And Buonarotti sculped the beard of Moses ;
> Phrenologists descant of low or high brows,
> > But I, for my part, set great store by noses.
>
> Six months ago, a calm and sunny morning
> > (Of peaceful rule a most auspicious omen),
> Brought New South Wales a Governor, adorning
> > All that he touched, and Chelmsford his cognomen.
>
> Leaving the *Cooma* for the *Powerful*, cruiser,
> > He and his consort met th' assembled Navy ;
> Then, to the guns which banged a " How d'ye do,
> > sir ? "
> He landed and drove off to take his davy.
>
> Myself, so far, I'd carefully absented,—
> > I had been told, indeed, to take things coolly—
> But at the swearing-in I was presented,
> > And made my curtesy willingly as duly.

OCCASIONAL RHYMES

Proud though his port, His Ex.'s glance was kindly,—
　　Humour and wisdom blent in its expression—
His voice alone would make one serve him blindly;
　　But this is not the whole of my confession. . . . .

It was his *nose* that fairly bowled me over,
　　So finely chiselled was it, so fastidious,
One to command success in King or lover,
　　And make one think all other noses hideous.

November 28th, 1909.　Sydney.

His Excellency received this tribute in the kindest spirit, and replied in a letter which included a verse as modest as it was brief :

Oh, why apostrophise my nose ?
　　'Tis battered and 'tis all awry.
Had you been privileged to see my toes
　　Your verse would then have made the angels cry.

Miss Talbot, to whom the following verses were written, came out from England in 1909 as the accredited emissary of the Victoria League, and was spending Christmas at Lord Chelmsford's country house, where we were her fellow guests. Her great ability and charm, combined with her kindness to me when temporarily blinded through my own carelessness, impelled me to write the following verses in her praise. Several days of confinement in a dark room gave me an opportunity for composing what all who know Miss Talbot will recognise as a well-merited, if imperfect, eulogy:

RECOLLECTIONS OF AN ADMIRAL'S WIFE

To M. T.,

OF THE VICTORIA LEAGUE.

Years, full and many, of my life had passed
    Ere the converging ways
Brought us together at a halt, to last
    A few refreshing days.

Far had you journeyed, to the Empire's good
    Devoting heart and mind ;
Waking the power that lies in womanhood,
    Forging the links that bind.

I was a sundered link, by hazard thrown
    On a Pacific strand,
And you the smith to weld such links in one
    Flawless, resilient band.

Lessons you taught me. Though you never preach,
    Inspiring things you say,
And you can soar to heights I fain would reach ;
    But mine are wings of clay.

Sanguine, yet sane, your creed ; and broad, not
      long,
    And when we disagree
I hardly dare to think you can be wrong,
    So wise you seem to me.

Yes, you are wise—a serpent to beguile,
    With just a dash of dove—
Making your list'ners think as well as smile,
    And work as well as love.

Your hand has virtue ; and when grinding pain
    Has got me in its clutch
I think of you and long to feel again
    The cordial of your touch.

OCCASIONAL RHYMES

Gath'ring fresh laurels for VICTORIA'S grave
    Your very soul you spend,
Daughter of Empire, you, and Duty's slave,
    And Australasia's Friend.

New Year, 1910. Sydney.

Mr. William McArthur, late M.P. and Liberal Whip, was, owing to business losses in Australia, living and working at Sydney for the greater part of our time there. We used to have one-sided political discussions, for I was the disputant and aggressor and he could never be " drawn," no matter what provocation was given him. So amiably careless, so disconcertingly detached was his attitude, that I addressed this rhyme to him as Gallio :

TO GALLIO McARTHUR.

The only rhyme for Gallio
That I can find is " Tally Ho ! " *
And that is really odd because
A better Whip there never was
Than Gallio McArthur. You
Controlled a Liberal pack that knew
And trusted you when all was " blue."

* (I'm told the Huntsman, not the Whip,
Cries Tally Ho ! Excuse the slip.)

I think your day must come again,
Since sunshine follows nights of rain,
And famine heralds years of ease.
Yours, then, the " crop " succeeding *Pease*,
And one whose name my mem'ry slips ;
For, Gallio, you were Prince of Whips,
And cheered your crowd of cranks with quips.

1910. Sydney.

The rest of my rhymes written in those three good years, 1908—1911, are either too scurrilous or too intimate in their character for reproduction here.

I was, however, the recipient of many specimens of unpublished amateur verse ; some simple to baldness, others so intricate as to be quite un-intelligible, and a few full of feeling but lacking in form and polish.   But I am certain that the following will find admirers.   It was written by a little girl of eleven at Miss Clarke's school at Wahroonga who was as pretty and frisky as she was clever, and if a small black kitten with blue eyes had composed these lines I should have been scarcely more surprised :

ODE ON LEAVING ABBOTSLEIGH, WAHROONGA.

O Abbotsleigh, thou Hall of Learning great,
  How can I leave thy sheltering walls for aye
To sail my barque upon the sea of Fate ?
  I can but groan and sigh.

My heart doth quail and tremble at the thought
  Of leaving thee and going forth alone.
Alas !   I have not loved thee as I ought,
  And now my time is gone.

No more thy well-worn passages to tread,
  No more to slam each sadly-battered door,
With date-befuddled head to go to bed
  No more !   No more !

KATHLEEN MCKAY.

To conclude this Miscellany I give the following extremely ingenious alphabetical catalogue of British

OCCASIONAL RHYMES

Possessions written by Mr. E. S. Smithurst, of Sydney.

PAX BRITANNICA.

For the Boys and Girls of the Empire.

Where the brave old British emblem flies in sunshine or
    in storm
British boys and girls will gather, British hearts are leal
    and warm.
Round the world the flag is flying; island, continent,
    and sea
Greet its crosses, learn its lessons, all it means for you
    and me.
Fair Australia, Britain's daughter, dwells beneath the
    Southern Cross,
Keeps the Empire's honour stainless that it may not
    suffer loss.
Grim old Aden guards the entrance of the Red Sea's
    southern shore,
And Ascension stands an outpost where Atlantic surges
    roar.
In the West Bermuda's islands Britain's ships of war
    maintain ;
And the negroes of Barbadoes tend the waving sugar
    cane ;
Whilst Bahama's myriad islands in the sultry tropics
    stand,
Where Columbus and his sailors first descried the
    Western land.
In the East, where precious timbers, rubber, rice and
    spices grow,
High above the fierce Malayan flies the flag in Borneo.
With her reign of terror ended ancient Burma lies at
    rest ;
Mandalay's a queen barbaric, silks, and rubies on her
    breast.

On the plains of BECHUANA and the wild BASUTOLAND
Peaceful 'neath the flag of Britain Afric's native warriors
    stand.
See where rising in her greatness CANADA, the Western
    Queen,
Shows her wealth of mine and forest, golden grain, and
    pastures green ;
See where facing the Antarctic, Table Mount its forehead
    rears,
And the CAPE, with " Good Hope " waiting, looks
    towards the coming years.
South of India's dusky millions CEYLON shows her myriad
    charms,
Christian, Buddhist, Hindoo, Moslem, worship 'neath her
    stately palms.
Now in CYPRUS' isle for freedom the oppressed no longer
    cries,
For the Crescent Flag is lowered and the Red Cross
    banner flies.
DEMERARA'S turbid waters, ESSEQUIBO'S tide is rolled
Through the lands of lovely orchids o'er the sands of
    shining gold.
Now by Britain's arm protected EGYPT'S ancient land
    grows strong,
And the fellaheen are sheltered after centuries of
    wrong.
Swept by storms, the isles of FALKLAND stand to guard
    Magellan's Pass ;
FIJI, like a gem, lies basking mirrored in a sea of glass.
Like a crouching lion watching, GIBRALTAR guards the
    way
Where at dawn the British bugles herald the approach of
    day.
And where GAMBIA and the GOLD COAST front the long
    Atlantic waves
Britain's flag has been the emblem for the freedom of the
    slaves.

On the breast of Canton River ships of every nation
  throng,
Britain keeps her watch unfailing where the flag flies
  o'er HONG KONG.
With their wealth of timber laden, northward see the
  vessels pass,
Teak, mahogany, and sandal, cut in British HONDURAS.
INDIA'S wearied millions resting from the long-continued
  strife
 Neath the British " raj " are waking to a fuller, freer
  life.
With a mighty treasure ransomed, Britain set her
  captives free
In the isle of fair JAMAICA, in the Caribbean Sea.
Where the Indian Ocean opens from fierce Bab-el-
  Mandeb's Straits,
On KURIA'S barren islets, guarding life, Britannia waits.
Here at LAGOS, on the Slave Coast, 'neath the flag all
  men are free ;
There the LEEWARD ISLANDS shelter from the storms the
  Carib. sea ;
And the nation's highway guarding—Britain to the
  Eastern land—
Rock-bound MALTA, fair MAURITIUS, in the central
  oceans stand.
Westward, fruitful MANITOBA, with her harvest greets
  the day ;
In the east the peaceful trader dreads no more the fierce
  MALAY.
Hand in hand Britannia's daughters throng to greet their
  kith and kin ;
NEW SOUTH WALES and fair NEW ZEALAND 'mid the
  nations entrance win ;
NEWFOUNDLAND and NOVA SCOTIA, strong with northern
  breeze and blood ;
And NATAL whose sons and daughters firm in time of
  danger stood,

Long NIGERIA's tropic forests owned the Arab slavers'
    wiles,
British law now reigns triumphant o'er four hundred
    thousand miles.
Proud ONTARIO on the lakeland stands her growing
    trade to meet,
And Niag'ra, queen of waters, pours her tribute at her feet.
'Mid the brothers now united for all purpose high and
    great
By Bloemfontein's sparkling waters sits in peace the
    ORANGE STATE ;
Where the commerce of the nations through the Red
    Sea gateway pours
PERIM keeps her lonely vigil by the grim Arabian shores ;
And PAPUA, looking southward o'er the narrow Austral
    sea,
Sees her pearlers, and gives promise of a nation yet to be.
Nature lends her glowing orchards, fruitful plains and
    fields to deck,
And St. Lawrence rolls his waters by the shores of proud
    QUEBEC.
QUEENSLAND, who can tell her future, wealth of promise
    past belief ?
And her long-drawn coast lines guarded by the mighty
    Barrier Reef.
In the ages yet to follow men shall tell the wealth and
    fame
Of RHODESIA proudly bearing her great Empire-builder's
    name.
By the world's great Eastern gateway SINGAPORE sits
    throned a Queen,
Where the argosies of commerce by her busy wharves
    are seen.
ST. HELENA's rocky fastness saw ambition's banner
    furled ;
He who died an island captive craved the empire of a
    world.

Golden grain and precious fleeces SOUTH AUSTRALIA'S
    wealth declare ;
And the SEYCHELLES' coral atolls wave their palms in
    tropic air.
Off the fiery Gulf of Aden, lonely, see SOCOTRA stand ;
In the ancient realm of Sheba Britain rules SOMALILAND.
From her mountain height TASMANIA sees her fruitful
    vales below ;
Westward, TRINIDAD lies basking in her orange orchards'
    glow.
On the rolling veldt the TRANSVAAL sees her flocks and
    herds increase,
And, her days of trekking ended, cultivates the arts of
    peace ;
O'er the lands of tropic forest whence the Nile its journey
    takes
Wide UGANDA owns our sceptre 'mid the great Nyanza
    lakes.
See the State, the world reminding of the glorious
    Empress-Queen,
Proud VICTORIA through the ages still shall keep her
    memory green.
And her wondrous younger sister—in the future none
    more great—
With her wealth of field and forest, WEST AUSTRALIA'S
    golden State.
Where three mighty Pow'rs converging threaten future
    war's alarms
WEI-HAI-WEI, with frowning bastions, stands as Britain's
    " place of arms."
X, the emblem of the unknown, shall remind us, if you
    please,
How the flag bears peace and goodwill to unknown,
    uncharted seas.
For the hope of earthly treasure men will dare nor
    count the price,
See the YUKON cities rising in a land of gold and ice

Where through many a blazing village toiled the slave-
   train from afar
Now the Moslem bows submissive to our rule at
   ZANZIBAR.
Such the lessons since the story of our island race began,
May the Brotherhood of Britons bring the Brotherhood
   of Man.

EDWARD S. SMITHURST.

January, 1910.   Mosman, Sydney.

CHAPTER XXXV

LAST MONTHS AT SYDNEY

THE public mourning which followed the death
of King Edward put a stop to the winter gaieties of
1910, and, as the flagship was still away cruising with
the new crew she had brought from Colombo in the
previous February, I found myself alone at Admiralty
House on my return in May from Victoria and
South Australia, with time to devote to the serious
business of collecting money for furnishing the
Seamen's Institute and floating the recently-formed
Bush Book Club of New South Wales.

In aid of the Seamen's Institute I held my first
(and only) drawing-room meeting at Admiralty
House, and, anxious as I was that it should be
financially successful, it went desperately against
the grain with me to beg for money in cold blood

under my own (temporary) roof.   When I had made an official statement of our needs from my seat at the end of the billiard-room, the short pause that ensued struck actual terror to my heart.   What if nobody should respond ?   But I need not have trembled.   In a few minutes the generous audience, perched all round the room on the high settees, were eagerly offering gifts in money or in kind ; our object was secured, and the Institute became some six months later as attractive and comfortable within as it was solid and dignified without.   Once more I had reason to bless the cheerful givers of Australia. Since that day in May, 1910, thousands of seafaring men and boys have found a pleasant haven on Circular Quay.   The beautiful little chapel on the top storey welcomes them on Sundays, and through- out the week they may find at the Institute hot coffee and other light refreshments, writing materials and stamps, cubicles with easy and clean-sheeted beds, and a dozen other relaxations and delights in addition to the aids to thrift and temperance furnished by the Chaplain and his lay helpers.   The officers and men of the Merchant Service now, more than ever, deserve well of us " who live at home in ease."   At Sydney they get their deserts.

Wise management provides in such an establish- ment so overwhelmingly powerful a rival to the grog-shop or saloon that one would like to see in all ports of any magnitude just the same judicious combination of creature comforts and mental and moral stimulants.   What seafaring men and boys

want is a home, not a reformatory, or at best a
Sunday School.   It is not easy to provide under one
roof the instructive and the truly agreeable ; something approaching to home life, but ordered and
made more inspiring by the supervision of an
acceptable sky-pilot.

One day Mr. Allen Pain, Chaplain to the Sydney
Seamen's Institute, took me off in his launch to a
big iron sailing ship recently arrived in the harbour,
one hundred and four days out from London.   I
scrambled up the ship's side by a rope ladder of
peculiar detachment whose wooden steps sloped at
odd angles, and was perforce lifted over the bulwarks
on to the rusty iron deck below.   The apprentices'
berth was to my inexperienced eyes a dreadful
place, but I was told it compared favourably with
those of other ships.   I thought it rather like a wild-
beast's lair—dark and stuffy, with grimy blankets or
railway rugs on the narrow bunks, no washing
appliances, no room to turn round in, and one little
slab for a table.   No wonder we wanted to give the
apprentices, most of them boys of gentle birth, a
taste of comfort when they arrived at Sydney ; and
not only the apprentices but the officers and
crews.

Not long ago I asked a friend of mine who had
recently left the Merchant Service whether Noble's
descriptions of ship life in his *Grain Carriers* were,
as some people maintain, too luridly coloured.
" Not one bit," was the answer. " I was an
apprentice for four years in ships of the same class,

on the same route, and when I came back finally to England and my mother met me at Liverpool I was almost ashamed to face her, for I felt I had become a wild beast from living among wild beasts. . . . I shall never entirely get over those years. On our last voyage we had worse weather than usual rounding the Horn, and one of the men fell from aloft in a gale of wind and shattered his leg below the knee.   The skipper was dead drunk in his cabin and there was no one but a deck-hand (who usually acted as butcher) to amputate the leg.   We broke into the skipper's cabin, stole half a bottle of brandy, and made the poor chap drink it off.   And then *the butcher sawed the leg off with a rusty meat-saw.* It didn't save him, though ; mortification set in, and he was dead in two days."

Besides the Seamen's Institute the Bush Book Club of New South Wales, born in 1909, needed endowment, and six months later we had a big meeting at the Town Hall with a view to intro-ducing its claims to public notice.   In recommending its establishment I was unfortunate enough to call down a heavy shower, if not a storm, of criticism upon my head by saying that if Australians in the Bush had more opportunity for reading they would cultivate the imagination in which they appeared to me deficient.   What made me say this I am not quite sure.   Possibly I argued that so practical a people as Australians must be deficient in imagina-tion ; and I knew for a fact that educated people in the back-blocks languished for want of anything beyond the daily or weekly papers to read. From the number of letters I received from strangers in the Bush who had heard of our desire to provide them with books I learnt that hundreds of people were longing for the books they could not afford to buy. Of these letters I give one expressing in words both vivid and convincing the sentiments of all my unknown correspondents. The writer subsequently started a Bush Book Club centre at Barringun, and her letter describing the solemn function which took place when the first parcel of *twelve books* reached Barringun by mail-coach was far too pathetic to be amusing. The little group of hungry book lovers " gave three cheers for Lady Poore and the Bush Book Club before they separated." Few incidents connected with our life in Australia have touched me more than this.

" Barringun,
" Via Bourke,
" *May 1st*, 1910.

" DEAR LADY POORE,

" At the back o' beyond—' Back o' Bourke '—I read with much pleasure of your interest in those on the Salt Bush plains and those in the silent, solemn sombre Bush. I am in accord with all that you have said, and as far as my experience goes none have ' blazed the track ' that you have taken. The School Library may do a little good in some places, but in many they are dead institutions.

" I am the wife of a Sergeant of Police living on the Queensland border, and was previously a State-school teacher. My heart often aches when I see so much mental starvation. Mostly the children in the West-

Nor'-West are bright and hungering for illustrated books
—natural to those whose reading powers have not been
cultivated.

"People without imagination who cannot feel the
glamour or romance of the Bush are never likely to make
literature. They must be a little intoxicated by the
wine and roses of life to see the ineffable glory and
sweetness of nature as seen in the trees, the flowers, the
birds and insects. Here there is endless scope for
poetic genius, for imagination and fancy and all that
combines to make a deathless word-picture of nature
under new conditions.

"I like poetry wild with war, hot with love or all
glowing with scenery, but I would rather write one little
song that a child or peasant might sing and feel than a
very miracle-poem of abstraction and profundity.

"I cannot speak too highly of these brave, hardy,
independent Western people who have so few advantages and where one finds so much lost talent. I live
where Will Ogilvie spent some years and wrote:

'That's where the wildest floods have birth
Out of the nakedest ends of earth—
    At the Back o' Bourke,
Where poor men lend and the rich ones borrow—
It's the bitterest land of sweat and sorrow—
But if I were free I'd be off to-morrow
    Out at the Back o' Bourke.'

"Let us hope, Lady Poore, that your movement may
bear fruit and that in the years to come an immortal
epic like 'Paradise Lost' or another 'Faerie Queene'
may be the proud boast of Australians. The children
of the West-Nor'-West are now in the formative stage,
and the opportunities you are anxious to afford may be
powerful when they reach the reflective and executive
periods of their existence.

" In conclusion I beg to ask if I may become a member of the Bush Book Club ?

" With grateful thoughts from one on an ' outpost,'

" I remain,

" Dear Lady Poore,

" Very respectfully yours,

" K—— D——."

Five years have passed since the Bush Book Club of New South Wales found its feet, and now it has no less than three hundred and seventy branches in the State. It pays its way, not by the subscriptions of readers, as these are necessarily low, but by the voluntary contributions of books and money of those able to give them.

For the modest endowment secured to the Club the theatrical company who were my travelling companions between Marseilles and Adelaide in 1908 were largely responsible. To them and to the officers and men of the flagship the Club actually owes its start in life. Three hundred and fifty pounds may not be a vast sum, but many a merchant prince has begun life with but a tithe of it, and few merchant princes have given greater happiness with their money than has been secured to the bookless people in the Bush of New South Wales by the help of the Navy and that Musical Comedy Company. The entertainment they provided was so well patronised by Sydney people that our enterprise was safely launched in 1910. It has not been I, but others, who have methodically carried on the work then started. The Club has now a number of powerful friends in addition to the voluntary workers who censor, mend, cover, pack and dispatch the books. Professor Edgworth David, of Antarctic fame, is one of its supporters, and Mrs. David is its president. Captain Bean, Australian " Eye-witness " with the Commonwealth Forces in the Mediterranean, is another good friend. He is the author of several books dealing with various phases of life in Australia, and one in particular—" On the Wool Track "—I read over and over again with increasing pleasure, for he knows the Bush, and the rivers and the coast of New South Wales as few men do ; or perhaps I should say he has the great gift of imparting his knowledge on these subjects as few men could.

CHAPTER XXXVI

LAST MONTHS AT SYDNEY—*continued*

OF course I ought not to have undertaken the presidentship of the New South Wales Optimists, for in doing so I was flagrantly disregarding Sir Harry Rawson's advice not to " spread " myself, but when Mrs. Curnow, a light-hearted and intelligent lady of eighty, begged me to do so I was ashamed to refuse. Sir George Reid was our Patron, and at our initial meeting the Town Hall was packed with both optimists and pessimists eager to hear him speak. It fell to my lot to " introduce " him to the audience, and I think the situation amused him as much as it did me. That I, a mere accident, " imported for three years' service in the Commonwealth," should introduce the big man and brilliant orator to a gathering of his own countrymen was comic, if not absurd.

A variety of definitions of optimism were offered at that and subsequent meetings. Our venerable founder said gracefully. and truly that it was " The process of distilling the best and sweetest out of life and sharing it with others."

When I had to speak in public on the subject I generally confined myself to warning my hearers against a false or lazy optimism, and I should have quoted a letter from Moore, the poet, in this connection had I been sure that his words would not have horrified my hearers. He wrote : " All things are possible with God, as the old lady said when she hoped to win the first prize in a lottery *although she had omitted to take a ticket*."

The optimists came in for a good deal of chaffing criticism from the less serious newspapers, and I dare say we deserved it, but it is just possible that chance seeds of optimism sown in 1910 may be bearing fruit in these sad years of war and suffering. The unconquerable—I had almost written incorrigible—cheerfulness of the Australian wounded in Egypt was the theme of a letter to me from one who is a helper in an Alexandrian hospital. She writes : " I love these Australians. They *insist* on getting better when the doctors give them up." That is a fine optimism. I now think with something like shame of the advice and warnings I, as a sort of amateur Priestess of Optimism, dared to give in the speeches I made at Sydney in 1910. Only those who have themselves endured with courage and sweetness heavy sorrows and disappointments and long periods of physical pain are fit to preach the gospel of Optimism ; and the chances are that such people will not preach, but set a silent example.

The following oddly pathetic letter from a struggling optimist came to me during our Sydney campaign.

" O. P.,
" c/o Newtown P.O.

" To LADY POORE.

" MADAM,—As I am an Australian, perhaps you will excuse the liberty (if it is a liberty these labour times) of writing to you, but I am a self-appointed member of your Optimistic Club, and I can assure your ladyship that the conditions of my life have not been conducive to optimism as I have had great trouble ; but I can manage at least ' one smile a day ' genuine. Also an old lady of seventy or thereabouts belongs to your society. She also has risen above more than ordinary grief and is hopeful of good, but I would like you to suggest some badge or motto for use on letter paper so that it would symbolise hope and cheerfulness, assumed or real, even when we have the toothache.

" Yours respectfully,
" h. O. P. e.
" c/o Newtown P.O."

239

CHAPTER XXXVII

LAST MONTHS AT SYDNEY—*continued*

SEPTEMBER 14th, 1910, was our silver-wedding day and I think Phœbe was responsible for warning Sydney of its approach. As I was dressing that morning I saw from my window a particularly glorious garland shining between the fore and mainmasts of the flagship and wondered why I had not heard that a *Powerful* officer was to be married on our wedding day. Then it flashed into my mind that this silver-spangled laurel wreath was displayed in our honour, and I rushed into my husband's room to call his attention to the pleasing phenomenon. When I went downstairs I found the sideboard covered with boxes and letters, and a strange silver bowl filled with roses standing in the middle of the breakfast table ! There were all the things I wanted, and had long coveted, and others I had not so much as dreamt of possessing. The presents from the officers of the squadron were ostensibly for me, etiquette forbidding their being offered to the Commander-in-Chief, but I knew full well they were *ours*, not *mine*, and that doubled their value. There were presents from individuals and presents from groups and communities, including our own faithful servants—among them two delightful watercolours by Miss Gladys Langer-Owen—and I could not eat my breakfast for looking at them all, even if I had not had a lump in my throat that felt as big as the graceful *repoussé* " Armada " jug which was the Captains' and Commanders' gift. And then there was a big silver basket in which, among other flowers, I found seventeen little bunches of forget-me-nots from seventeen girl friends who had by their enjoyment of our parties enormously increased our own.

The " silver-bridegroom's " present to his " silver-bride " was a pendant of black opals and diamonds, which made the large and useful silver salver I gave him look very prosaic by comparison.

Long before I had sufficiently gloated over our new possessions I had to be off to an important committee meeting, but I have rejoiced now for five years in all that day brought us, and kind thoughts of the givers are for ever inseparable from the gifts that are daily used or worn.

The *Powerful* went to Port Phillip (Melbourne) for target practice as soon as the Randwick Spring Race-week, with its closely packed gaieties, was over, and my husband's letters for the first few days were full of the maddening vagaries of an extemporised target and the startling changes of weather which made the work tedious and difficult.

The *Terra Nova* with Captain Scott was at Port Melbourne at that time, and I give here some extracts from my husband's letters referring to the explorer and his ship's company.

" *Oct.* 17.—Captain and Mrs. Scott dined with me last night. He is a nice, straightforward, pleasant *gentleman* with a twinkle in his eye. I hope you may be able to be of some use to Mrs. Scott if she comes back from New Zealand viâ Sydney after her husband has started for the Antarctic. Who do you think is the skipper of the *Terra Nova*? Mr. Evans, one of the old *Hawke* midshipmen ! He came to dine too, most cheery and full of delight at going to the South Pole, for he is to be one of the shore party.

"To-morrow I go to inspect the *Terra Nova* in the morning and then she sails for New Zealand. All their people have dined in the wardroom to-night except one, Captain Oates, Inniskilling Dragoons, now a full-blown A.B., who had only a flannel shirt and a pair of trousers patched with a piece of red table-cloth to wear, so he was shy.

"*Oct.* 18.—Yesterday I went on board the *Terra Nova* and saw everything. They seem very cheerful. Except the scientists, Captain Oates and an Indian Marine man, all of them are naval people. Several of the men are old Antarctic hands, fine-looking fellows, too. I asked one big bluejacket (a petty-officer by rights, but they are democratic in Antarctic circles and are all A.B.'s) how he liked going back, and he said, ' Oh, I don't know, sir ; I thought I'd like to see the end of it.' We gave them a cheer as they sailed, and I think if pluck and determination can do it they won't leave much of the South Pole to be found by anyone else."

Before crossing to New Zealand Captain and Mrs. Scott spent a short time in Sydney, and when they left for Lyttelton, whence the *Terra Nova* sailed, the burden of financial anxiety pressing upon the great explorer's shoulders had been considerably lightened by the donations of Mr. S. Hordern and other Sydney magnates interested in the expedition.

On her return from New Zealand after bidding her

husband good-bye, Mrs. Scott passed some days with me at Admiralty House. I had been ill, and was still so feeble a convalescent that I worked myself into a fever of nervousness before she arrived. It seemed to me, and I do not think I was far wrong, that her position was almost as painful as that of the wife of a man condemned to die at some unknown date in some inaccessible spot unless a reprieve, scarcely to be hoped for, should be obtained ; but when she came her self-command and cheerfulness made me feel I had been behaving like a hysterical schoolgirl.

When the flagship came back from New Zealand early in January, 1911, my adieux to Sydney had to be said, and this was no easy matter. However, there was no help for it, and when the Lady Mayoress invited me to a farewell gathering of my friends at the Town Hall I pulled myself together as best I might and tried to keep before me the example of Lady Northcote as I had seen her on a similar, if far greater and more important, occasion. But it was difficult to be brave, and I knew that my words of thanks for the beautiful bracelet and ring of Lightning Ridge black opals set in diamonds with which the Lady Mayoress, on behalf of the ladies of Sydney, presented me, were spoken in a voice which was half a croak and half a whine. I have often wished I could do it again and do it better, for I could not manage to utter what was in my heart. It is only on such occasions that I wish myself a man and unaffected by that " determination of tears to the throat " which defeats the old-fashioned woman's bravest efforts to maintain coherence and self-control when she is treated with particulàr kindness. Shortly before this the Ladies of the Seamen's Institute Committee had given me as a token of their regard a large heart-shaped black opal of unusual depth and velvetiness set as a brooch and " fringed " with diamonds. The occasion of its presentation was less public than that previously referred to, and, words entirely failing me, I travelled round the circle of good friends and most faithful coadjutors and heartily kissed each member of it. The Chaplain—the only man present—escaped by a miracle.

PART III

ENGLAND, 1911—1916

CHAPTER XXXVIII

THE first section of my homeward voyage was made in the *Powerful*, and I was so sorry to leave Sydney that I actually did not much care whether the sea was rough or smooth. The voyage to Hobart only represented to me so many miles put between myself and the home where I had been so happy for nearly three years.

The Tasmanian Government had provided us with a charming house on the Brown's River Road, and the few weeks we spent there in January and February were, so far as I was concerned, nothing more than a rest-cure. Phœbe, who accompanied me, needed repose as much as I did after watching over me during my illness at Sydney, and together we walked and drove, gathered shells on the shore and played patience. I was fortunately absolved from all social and philanthropic duties, and when my husband returned to Sydney in the flagship to hand over his command to Admiral G. King-Hall I thought I was quite strong again. But I was not. Of the sufferings and discomforts endured on the voyage from Hobart to Colombo I will say as little as possible. I fell ill the day our ship left Hobart, and when we reached Fremantle my husband wired to Perth for the principal doctor there. He had just finished his rather discouraging diagnosis when the Governor, Sir Gerald Strickland, arrived with Lady Edeline Strickland to see me, and at the same moment the son of my father's caretaker at our old official home in Limerick appeared with his wife and a magnificent bouquet. The ship was very full and mine was only a two-berthed cabin hardly suited for the reception of an Excellency, but both the Governor and Lady Edeline insisted on coming in, and no sooner had they left than Robert McMahon, his wife and the bouquet more than filled their places. Though I was feeling the reverse of cheerful and my appearance was enough to warrant my visitors in thinking this meeting our last on earth I could not but be amused by the situation as I lay in my comfortless little berth " receiving company." But I was far from ungrateful.

When we arrived at Colombo I was ten days worse, and my memories of Ceylon are all painful. From Galle Face the Colombo doctor sent me to Kandy, whence another doctor hurried me up to Hatton. There I spent ten weary days in a private hospital while my husband nobly " stood by " in a country hotel whose roof was haunted by both rats and snakes. I felt such a marplot. We had meant to spend a whole delightful month in Ceylon with our boy whom we had not seen for three years, and now all our plans and his were spoilt. All I saw of the island was viewed from the window of a train or of a sickroom, and on the 30th of March I was taken down to Colombo and put on board the P. and O. *India.*

I cannot help smiling now when I think of one special anxiety which perplexed and agitated my mind when I was at my worst. I had in my cabin-trunk two small-sized white ensigns forming part of the dress of Britannia which I had, before leaving Hobart, contemplated wearing at the customary fancy-dress dance on board ship. Now I greatly desired to be wrapped in these flags should I be buried at sea, but I could not bring myself to ask my husband's consent, fearing that such an indulgence would be contrary to all precedent, and it would have been in the highest degree mean to work on his feelings by using my last breath to make such a request. The newest of P. and O. house-flags, or even the highly respectable blue ensign, would never have contented me. I wanted only the very best flag in the whole world for my shroud.

The convenient symbol * * * will sufficiently describe my subsequent experiences which, though mercifully mitigated by the comforting presence of Phœbe, were highly unpleasant.

After an exceptionally severe tossing in the Bay we landed at Plymouth on the morning of April 20th, a truly gilt-edged spring day, and got safe home to Winsley the same afternoon.

CHAPTER XXXIX

MOVING ON

By the first days of July I was considered well enough to attempt a short visit to London. It was not a great success, for the noise made my head ache without ceasing, and the heat was almost insufferable. One night I dreamt I was a night-watchman at the Zoo. Standing on a high tower I was encompassed by a crowd of all the birds and animals which hoot, grunt, bray, bark, low, shriek, roar, bleat, neigh and whistle ; and the din was nerve-rending. I woke to find it was not yet midnight and that half the motors in London were carrying away the audience after a concert at the Albert Hall, while I lay quaking on my bed on the third floor of a house at the Park end of Queen's Gate !

It was on Saturday the 8th of July that I returned to Winsley, and my husband gave me all Sunday for rest and refreshment before breaking the un-welcome news that he had been offered the Nore Command. It was unwelcome because neither of us was ready to start work again, and we had been much looking forward to a reasonable period of quiet enjoyment in our own home. But the Powers at the Admiralty had been very good to my husband all through his service, and it would have been a shabby act to refuse the billet just because he wanted a longer spell on half-pay, or because we were not drawn to Chatham.

An odd thing happened while we were still at Winsley. I had begun to read Lord Rosebery's "Chatham" on board ship shortly after leaving Hobart, but I was soon too ill to interest myself in anything more exacting than the mildest of novels. When I was well enough to tackle it again I sent for it to the library, but on hunting it up in June to send it back to Cawthorn and Hutt I found it so badly stained with ink all round the edges of pages and cover that to return it was out of the question. No enquiries elicited any explanation or solution. No one had seen it in the contaminating company of a leaky stylographic pen, much less an ink bottle. It was a mystery ; and when my husband told me we were going to Chatham I looked with a superstitious distrust at the mourning edge round Lord Rosebery's book and wondered what bad luck our new move was going to bring us. Alas ! there was mourning enough at Chatham before we left there.

CHAPTER XL

CHATHAM

A WEEK before I joined my husband at Chatham, where he had relieved Sir Charles Drury on August 29th, I was thrown out of the dog-cart and alighted with some violence on my left knee. It was nearly four months before I could relinquish my crutches, six before I could walk without a stick. While I was still lame influenza bowled me over, and forced me to retreat to Winsley and do a month's rest-cure. So it was not till March, 1912, that I actually took up the duties and pleasures of which my life at Admiralty House was, in somewhat unequal proportions, composed. After Sydney it all felt very flat and looked very ugly. Cold winds and heavy rain, gritty dust, a new and shadeless garden and a muddy estuary (which I always thought smelt of cabbage-water) offered a poor exchange for the year-round sunshine and flowers and the unfading and unfolding beauties of Sydney Harbour.

Chatham is an ugly place, with scarcely an outstanding feature, save its Town Hall, to break the squalid monotony of its streets. On the west it immediately adjoins Rochester, its far more dignified neighbour, one High Street merging imperceptibly into the other. Eastward lies Gillingham, a modern town of small, new houses, useful and undistinguished, which shelter the families of thousands of sailors and dockyard men ; but a broad stretch of rough grass, known as the Lines, separates its row upon row of red brick and stucco from Chatham, and forms a valuable airspace and playground, burnt up and dusty, or swept by wind and rain (and always paper-haunted), for the dwellers on both sides of it.

There are four sets of barracks in Chatham : one

for the Royal Engineers, one for a Line regiment, one for the Navy, and one for the Royal Marine Light Infantry ; and most important of all its " Establishments "—its *raison d'être*, in fact—His Majesty's Dockyard. Upon all these centres of activity the great and admirably-planned Naval Hospital looks down from the far side of the Lines, magnificent in its spaciousness, and enclosing lawns and flower-beds of a vigorous gaiety astounding and unaccountable where distracted gardeners, poor soil, and extreme exposure to every wind that blows might be expected to furnish only borders of the hardier weeds, edged with storm-proof oystershells.

Behind high blank walls the Dockyard spreads itself along a muddy estuary, and on five days of the week the clang and whirr and thud of the machinery behind those walls make the neighbourhood trying to all but the incurably deaf. At certain hours the hands, pallid and grimy, pour in or out through its gates in such crowds as block traffic and embarrass the average wayfarer by presenting front, rear, and flanks all equally impervious to his passage. Strings of tramcars await the outward-bound tide at the gates, swallowing all they can contain and moving heavily away, and hundreds of bicycling mateys, regardless of its rules, add to the perils of the road. If one should be lucky enough to find oneself in the neighbourhood of the Naval Barracks when the Dockyard empties itself into the town, it were wise to seek shelter within its gates and so escape the enveloping hordes which deviate not one hair'sbreadth from their route for man, woman, or child ; no, nor would they for an angel with a flaming sword if he tried to bar the way.

Inside the barracks' grounds one can pause to draw breath and inhale the sweetness of its well-protected rose-garden, lingering perhaps to read the inscription on the monument erected close by to the memory of French prisoners of war who died during their detention on St. Mary's Island more than a hundred years ago—an inscription which, for simplicity and good feeling and style, could hardly be bettered.

> " Here are gathered together
> The remains of many brave soldiers and sailors,
> Who, having once been the foes, afterwards the captives,
> of England,
> Now find rest in her soil,
> Remembering no more the animosities of war or the
> sorrows of imprisonment.
> They were deprived of the consolation of closing their
> eyes amongst the countrymen they loved ;
> But they have been laid in an honourable grave
> By a nation which knows how to respect valour and
> sympathise with misfortune."

It is surprisingly easy to lose one's way in Chatham Dockyard, and as its various roads and passages, penitentially cobble-stoned, are unnamed, it takes a stupid person some time to learn its geography. Alluring notice-boards, white, with clear black lettering, attract the stupid person, but as they only bear the cryptic words, " Whistle and go slow," they are not really illuminating. Still, there are policemen to be met with—members of the Metropolitan Force, than whom none are more helpful and indulgent towards an obviously pacific female—and, directed by one of them, the wanderer in search of an exit may proceed westward between piles of well-seasoned timber—oak, teak, and pine —each balk inscribed with its name and grade; past the prim little Georgian houses inhabited by dockyard officials and known, unofficially, as Harmony Row; past old Admiralty House—the big new one looks on to the Lines—with its dignified Adams ceilings and chimneypieces and its shady, terraced garden; and finally out through the turreted red-brick main gate, bearing the Royal Arms emblazoned in red and gold over its central archway, into the dreary colourless town.

No one ever goes to Chatham for pleasure save the guests at the Sappers' or Marines' balls and concerts, and we very soon found that people who came down from Town on business just did their business and went back as quickly as possible.

In the course of his lecturing tour in 1913 Commander Evans of Antarctic fame came to stay with us, and a very cheery and entertaining guest he was—one of the eternally young who get and give so much pleasure in their way through life. He had been a midshipman in the *Hawke* in 1897—8, and his iron muscles and determined character made him a decidedly awkward handful for the senior members of the gunroom mess who desired to " deal faithfully " with him. That discipline was necessary in his case is proved by a story he told us at Chatham. He was a very troublesome little boy at school and, as ringleader, actually ran away with two others, remaining uncaptured for three days and nights. Then supplies failed, and the party were rounded up by the police as vagrants and consigned to the nearest workhouse. The expulsion from school of all three followed this escapade. However, Commander Evans was invited on his return from the Antarctic to lecture at *this very school* and was introduced to his audience with a great flourish of trumpets as their most distinguished old scholar! Commander Evans found the temptation to tell the story of his expulsion irresistible, and the joy of his youthful hearers can be imagined.

Foreign attachés sometimes lunched with us before or after a visit to the Dockyard, and when foreign men-of-war came in the senior officers would dine with us. Among the latter I cherish a specially friendly recollection of a Swedish captain and lieutenant, who by their frank enjoyment of it turned an ordinary dinner-party into a *succès fou*.

We always danced after dinner, and only those of our guests who had never danced before stood out. Lame men, fat elderly ladies, a Doctor of Divinity with admirable silk-stockinged legs, all danced the Lancers, and people who protested they would certainly become giddy circled successfully round the room. It did us all good, and when I got over my lameness I enjoyed the exercise as much as anyone, for the ballroom was all that could be desired and we had a really excellent band directed by a bandmaster who took infinite pains to please us.

The Lords of the Admiralty were generally content when they visited Chatham in our time to send someone to write their names in our book on the last morning of their stay, but on one occasion Mr. Churchill called upon me at teatime. He was extremely polite and quite unsmiling, but so hot and dishevelled that I wondered what he could have been doing to get himself into such a state. Whether he had been acquiring first-hand knowledge by shovelling coal in the stokehold of a Dockyard tug or climbing telegraph poles I forbore to inquire, but whatever his occupation, the lieutenant who accompanied him had obviously not shared it, for he was as cool and trim as possible. At no time has Mr Churchill been considered a successful exponent of the sartorial art, but the story goes that once, at least, he arrayed himself on an occasion of importance in the uniform of an Elder Brother of Trinity House. This was during an official visit to France, and to the question of a puzzled French officer who inquired what rank and service the uniform represented, the First Lord is reported to have made the astounding reply: " Je suis le Frère Ainé de la Trinité."

CHAPTER XLI

PLEASURE AND PAIN

As time went on and I made or renewed friendships, and created or revived interests, I became to some degree acclimatised and grew reconciled to my lot at Chatham. Still never a day passed but I thought of what I had left behind at the Antipodes : of the swift and boundless kindness of the people, the genial climate, the multitude of roses, the scarlet of the coral-tree, the blue of the jacaranda, the scent of the brown boronia or the taste of " billy " tea. Or it was the spaciousness of the Bush and of the great untrodden sea-beaches that came back to me, or the rush of a " larrikin " boat through the waters of Sydney Harbour on a Saturday afternoon. Yes, I was very homesick for Australia.

It was a great pleasure to welcome friends from Australia at Admiralty House, and as all the Staff had been out there, they were in complete sympathy with us. " She is *very* dark, certainly, and very foreign-looking," was the comment of an English girl on one of these guests whom she saw at a dance at our house, and the speaker was quite evidently under the impression that our dark-eyed friend was an aboriginal—a " black gin," in fact.

I must confess that my own ignorance of the geography of Australia was lamentable before I went there, but at least I had the excuse of having been at school in the days when the map of that continent was very nearly empty. Still, at no time did I imagine the bulk of its population to be black, and I had fortunately had special opportunities of meeting Australians after my marriage since many naval officers have found wives among these attractive exotics.

Ignorance as regards Australians is very marked in the untravelled Briton, who is curiously prejudiced against them, and I was almost as much amused as I was annoyed by the conversation of two richly ill-dressed and peculiarly unattractive elderly women whom I once had for travelling companions between Chatham and London. They were evidently old friends who had not recently met. " And how does John's wife get on ? " asked one. " Oh, well, you can't expect much of a *colonial*," was the answer, " and the worst of it is, she seems to glory in being an Australian instead of keeping her mouth shut about it. What I say to her is, ' What may do very well for the colonies isn't good enough for England. . . .' Give me England ! Now I was in Switzerland last summer, and when I got home I felt sorry I had spent my money on the trip. There was nothing there—*nothing*, I assure you—to compare with the view from the cinderpath on the East Cliff at Margate." (At least I think this was the spot named by this experienced traveller.)

But, after all, it is not the majority of English people who have occasion or means to visit Australia, whereas the enormous preponderance of Australians regard a visit to England as either necessary or desirable, and generally achieve it. However much I may permit myself to jeer at the ignorance of the untravelled English man or woman with regard to Australia and the Australians, I find their attitude infinitely ·more pardonable than that of those apostates among Australians who, having made their fortunes in their own country, from which many of them continue to draw their revenues, abandon it for ever, eliminate from their talk all reference to Australia, and from their hearts all affection for the great country of their birth. This is an exasperating form of snobbery which makes me sick.

September, 1912, brought our boy home to us for a six months' holiday after four years and a half of rubber planting, and it was good to see his colour and muscle gradually returning as the autumn and winter wore on. At the end of January Phœbe arrived from Sydney, and, as she made her head-quarters with us, there was plenty of life and laughter at Admiralty House until April came and Roger sailed for Singapore, taking with him a good half of the gaiety. Then, in spite of a three weeks' holiday at Winsley in sunny May weather, I found myself sliding steadily down the hill of health till June arrived, bringing me physical pain hitherto undreamt of. Surgeons, nurses and all the para-phernalia of severe illness took possession of the house, and the admirable Phœbe watched over us all. To her everyone looked for direction and comfort, and she never failed. It was she who helped me to make my will, and how we laughed over it! I had just become possessed of two charming trinkets which I grudged leaving to anyone *because I had not yet worn them*. Of course I knew I was very ill, but not until I was convalescent did I realise how nearly the pendant of old paste and the long chain on which widely-spaced beads of pale amethyst were threaded had become the property of my tall nieces, Clarissa and Rosaleen.

I had been getting so tired and springless, so intolerably old, with a face that had become as grey as my hair, hands that shook and bones that were positively obtrusive. I felt in fact that I was not worth keeping unless I could be " done up as good as new," and it never occurred to me that, being what I had become, I should be seriously or inconveniently missed did I fail to recover. In this frame of mind I welcomed with a kind of rapture the arrival of that brilliant surgeon Mr. Sherren and the incomparable anæsthetist who accompanied him.

.   .   .   .   .   .

I am told that the only words I said when I came partially to myself were, " Is it fine ? " That seemed to matter tremendously, for the 21st of June was the day fixed weeks before for the annual fête of the Friendly Union of Sailors' Wives, and hundreds of women with such children as they were unable to leave at home were to assemble in the Barracks grounds in their best summer rig and enjoy themselves from 2.30 to 6.30. The nurse told me it was fine, and then my brain ceased from troubling.

A long convalescence is a weary thing for patient, nurses, servants, relations and friends ; and months passed before I was fit to take up even a few of the threads which, though not broken, were lying untouched in my little loom of life. But the 1st of October came at last, and it was a memorable day for me, since on it I returned from Winsley to Chatham after a period of seclusion which had become almost intolerable—ten weeks made up of long, empty, headachy days and still longer restless nights ; of putting two and two together in a feeble brain and making three of them ; of climbing up the traditional two steps to fall back one. Phœbe had left us in August to our great regret, and her place as comforter, adviser and referee had been taken by another Australian friend than whom no one could have been more kind and tactful. If I wept, as I regret to say I frequently did, she never told me I ought to be ashamed of myself as I was really getting on famously, but petted and consoled me instead till I laughed at myself for being such an old goose ; and laughter is better than drugs any day. When this Antipodean guardian angel left us to return to Australia in January, 1914, it was a black day for all at Admiralty House.

CHAPTER XLII

THE COMMANDER-IN-CHIEF'S COXSWAIN

TWENTY-ONE years ago I had a Turnover in the *Globe* entitled " The Captain's Coxswain." It was written at Bermuda when my husband commanded the *Tourmaline*, and one of his brother-captains told me it was extremely good. Becoming vain of my small achievement, I let another captain's wife know what I had done, and, to my annoyance, she claimed the ideal coxswain whom I had sketched as her husband's, whereas he was founded on our Reynolds and embellished and altered only to avoid detection. Nothing would persuade her that she was wrong. It was Wilson and no other to her, and I should have been flattered since Wilson was her *beau idéal* of a coxswain.

Since those days I have had more than one coxswain for a friend, but none to compare with Reynolds of the *Tourmaline* until Morgan arose to remind me of all a coxswain can be.

Morgan is a chief petty officer and wears the peaked cap and single-breasted jacket of his rank. Tall and slight, but well set up, active yet dignified, decided yet deferential, forgetting nothing and anticipating every contingency, Morgan was a priceless adjunct to our household. He was of it, yet outside it. Devoted heart and soul to my husband, who was always his first thought, he could yet give his attention to such comparative trivialities as sick hens, the vagaries of our electric installation for heating and lighting; and the introduction of my young nephew to rifle shooting, to the outer mysteries of the dockyard or the steering of the barge.

And what an admirable chauffeur he was! As a gunnery man he was at home with machinery, and all that a 15-h.p. Fiat touring-car is supposed to do, and much more, did Morgan get out of the one he drove for us. He coaxed her up the hill from Lynmouth to Lynton when its surface was bad and people ran after him to say the ascent was impossible, and at Chatham he threaded his way steadily through streaming hordes of nonchalant dockyards-men, dodged irresponsible dogs and hens, crazy cows, cats deliberately bent on making trouble, and unattended babies with such consummate skill as created in me a confidence which I had never any reason to regret.

With the men under him Morgan had a short way and a successful. He stood no nonsense, and judged with perfect justice the conscientious slow-coach and the bustling slacker. And he was the soul of faithful economy. If he thought we were using too much electric light he let us know it. When I found the cover of the footwarmer in the landaulette was wearing out I suggested its being sent " somewhere " to be fitted with a new one. Morgan was horrified. He would make a cover for it himself. Would he buy a piece of thick Kidder-minster? *Buy* it? Oh, no; he could *find* a piece that would do. He did "find" a piece, though I could never discover where or how, and next day the foot-warmer was neatly and becomingly arrayed in a carpet jacket of a pattern familiar to all ward-room officers.

When I was crippled for a time no one took charge of the fore-handles of the carrying-chair with such skill as Morgan, and woe betide the " wheeler " bluejacket if I was tilted or slewed so as to cause me alarm or inconvenience.

In his management of the poultry yard Morgan showed positive genius. Feathered fowls had been entirely outside the radius of his activities until I invited him to be the guardian of eighteen hens in the disused moat between Admiralty House and St. Mary's Barracks; but, after a brief yet intelligent study of a treatise on poultry-keeping published by the Board of Agriculture, he started with a good courage, and never were hens more faithfully dealt with in sickness and in health. Broody birds were punished with " 10 A." (a naval punishment consisting of limitations in rations and leave), which means that they were placed comfortlessly under a barred crate and kept on short commons till they repented and " returned to duty." Sitting hens were treated with the utmost consideration, chicks skilfully helped out of hard-shelled eggs, delicate ones cossetted in a basket placed over a 15-candle-power electric light, cramped legs rubbed, and patients with unclassified ailments successfully treated according to the dictates of Morgan's own strong common sense.

When the time of our departure (incorrectly believed final) from Chatham approached I was in doubt as to the transport of such hens as we wanted to establish at Winsley, and supposed they should be packed in crates and despatched by rail to Bradford-on-Avon. But this scheme found no favour in Morgan's eyes. It was expensive and risky. He would himself convey them in the touring-car which was to go to Winsley. This, with infinite skill and precaution, he accomplished. Twelve hens and a cock and one hen with fourteen chicks travelled under his care a hundred and fifty miles. He was bothered at first because the cock would insist on crowing, and he " kept thinking it was the horn of a car coming up behind." Halfway he halted to feed and water the party, but eight hours and a half after leaving Chatham he had them all safely at their journey's end, and not one of them had turned a feather. Indeed, two of the more conscientious had laid eggs on the way ; unlike the oft-quoted Roman Emperor, they did not have to say " I have lost a day."

Morgan often took me out for short airings when I wanted to clear my brain before a committee meeting or needed more and fresher air than that surrounding Admiralty House ; and, sitting beside him, I could ask for advice, enlightenment or fair comment on matters which perplexed or merely interested me. I shall never forget the way he rapped out the words " If he *does* come there'll be another Mutiny at the Nore " when I told him I had heard a rumour (unfounded, as it turned out) that a certain Admiral was to be my husband's successor.

Morgan was never too busy or too tired to undertake an errand or a diplomatic mission, and the "dinner-hour," which I was early taught to respect, signified less than nothing to him when he had a "job of work." Even the charms of Miss Morgan, who entered this life in the first month of the war and proved a most entrancing study to her father, could not distract him from the path of duty or tempt him to neglect a wish or caprice of mine.

A well-known naval chaplain whose habit of startling his congregation by what some of us considered *enfant terrible* remarks from the pulpit was a hero of Morgan's. " He mayn't be polished, and perhaps he shouldn't make people smile in church," said Morgan ; " all the same I've seen a church next door to empty when the parson preached Saint Paul—cold. Now *he* gives you modern heroes, men you can understand about and try to copy, and there's barely standing room at a voluntary service. At Bermuda men would go the length of shifting their clothing and ask for leave to go to evening service at the Dockyard Chapel when he preached. And time and again I've heard men say, when unnecessary bad language was flying about, ' I say, old Trunky wouldn't like that.' (It's on account of his big nose we call him Trunky ; perhaps I oughtn't to have let it slip out.) And as for the Marines, they fair worship him."

Morgan writes an excellent letter with pith in

every one of its short sentences. I never saw the remarkable document which he posted up asking irresponsible persons to abstain from feeding the hens when convalescent after fowl cholera, but I have the paper headed " Rules for the care and maintenance of the house-bicycle " (at Winsley) which he compiled, and it is a model document.

Morgan left Chatham when we did and is now a Master-at-Arms in a very responsible position. He had occasion to return to Chatham on duty a few months after our departure, and while waiting with his car in High Street he took a glance into the photographer's window where a large portrait of my husband was displayed. To quote his own words, " It bucked me up so to see the dear Admiral's face that I nipped into a jeweller's shop and bought a brooch for the missus."

How I miss him, with his ready wit and capable hands, I cannot say. Sometimes I feel I must go and live near Morgan since the exigencies of the Service necessitate his presence in places far removed from Winsley.

CHAPTER XLIII

SOCIAL ASPECTS OF CHATHAM

BEFORE we went to Chatham I had indulged in visions of long drives in spring and summer into the beautiful country outside, of eating strawberries in the gardens of kind people and coming home laden with flowers, and perhaps even plants, for my own big, ugly garden. These visions did not materialise to any great extent. Kent is not New South Wales, nor yet Devonshire, nor have its inhabitants the characteristics which make a stranger welcome within its borders. The fact is that it is too close to London and all that London can give. I can count on the fingers of one hand the Kentish people who took any interest in us, and four out of the five were " friends of friends." There was no special reason why we should inspire interest, but no one had told us that one must live seven years in Kent before the inhabitants consider one's claims as a neighbour, and even then may decide to ignore them. When we realised that Chatham was, to all intents and purposes, neither socially nor, generally speaking, philanthropically in Kent at all, it was something of a surprise. My head may have been swelled, it is true. It certainly dwindled to the dimensions of a common pin's when I found of how little worth we were outside the port of Chatham. One or two people whom I met at the houses of mutual friends explained that they really could not call upon me owing to the perils of street traffic in Chatham, while others seemed to think it natural that I should dispense with the customary formalities and call upon them first. But this really did not provide me with a satisfactory grievance, for, as it turned out, I had neither health nor leisure for making distant expeditions. To have two or three houses to go to where one is sure of a cordial welcome is to be truly fortunate, and this was our happy lot. The most beautiful of these was Lord Darnley's, Cobham Hall. There we met people who had done, or were doing, notable things ; we heard delightful music, and the atmosphere, moral, material and intellectual, was of the kind which invites the shyest rosebud to unfold and mutes the peacock's scream.

Admiralty House itself was both spacious and comfortable, and its garden presented difficulties which engaged, and usually defeated, my well-meant efforts. The country outside Chatham when the cherry orchards were in bloom was indeed lovely and reminded us of Caldecott's famous picture-books. There was the same gay blue sky across which sailed plump, silver-tipped clouds of purest white ; mist and spray of cherry blossom wreathed the deep-red cowls of the oast-houses, and sedate sheep lay and snowy lambs gambolled upon the emerald turf. Such is the picture I carry in my mind of the Garden of England in springtime.

We were very lucky in having good friends among the various " Heads of Departments " and their wives. General and Mrs. Ronald Maxwell * were at Government House and Colonel J. Capper † and his wife at Brompton Barracks. Brigadier-General and Mrs. Kennedy (nicknamed for good reason " The Brigadearest and The Brigadarling ") reigned

* Now Sir Ronald and Lady Maxwell.
† Now Major-General Capper.

at the Marine Barracks, and three successive Surgeons-General—two of them very old friends of ours and all good comrades—presided at the Naval Hospital; while at the charming old Admiralty House in the Dockyard we found Admiral and Mrs. Nelson Ommanney and left Admiral and Mrs. Anson. The unlimited kindness showed us by Commodore Erskine * and later Commodore Gaunt † and all their subordinates at the Naval Barracks made us forget that there was no supporting flagship for us to rely upon as we had always relied upon the *Powerful* in Australia.

At Sheerness were Sir Cecil and Lady Burney, Rear-Admiral and Mrs. Dundas of Dundas and Captain ‡ and Mrs. Prendergast.

Anyone who has ever lived in a naval and military centre will understand and appreciate the comfort to be derived from being as happily placed as we were. Official dinner-parties are robbed of their terrors when one is secure of a congenial partner, and the burden of business is immeasurably lightened when it is shared by those who understand and respect one another.

We were fortunate also in that my husband had the same flag-lieutenant, Lieut. F. C. Fisher, who had been with him for three years on the Australian Station, and when he was promoted in June, 1912, Lieut. C. F. Danby—an old *Powerful*—was just

---

* Now Rear-Admiral Erskine.
† Now Rear-Admiral Gaunt.
‡ Now Rear-Admiral Prendergast.

leaving Dartmouth College and at liberty to take his place—a very happy chance. There was no " second choice " in the case of any of my husband's Staff. Those he invited to join it accepted with the alacrity which is a testimonial any commander-in-chief must appreciate, and in this case all were old shipmates, or station-mates, and knew both of us at our worst as well as our best. We owe to Captain P. H. Colomb (flag-captain), Paymaster in Chief W. Le Geyt Pullen (secretary), Commander—now Captain—H. W. Bowring (flag-commander), and the two flag-lieutenants above mentioned many pleasant hours, much peace of mind, and all the comfort and support tried friends, long and closely associated, can afford. Mr.—now Commander— Danby married a fortnight before war broke out, and by so doing added to our intimate circle a member of whom we were all justly proud.

CHAPTER XLIV

SAILORS' WIVES

So it came about that I was very sorry to leave Chatham when the 15th of July, 1914, came. I had had an opportunity of working with, and for, that section of society which above all others interests me—sailors' wives and families—and had learnt a great deal about them. When one considers that among the lower " ratings " money is never plentiful and often scarce, temptations numerous and ill-health too common, the steady courage and devotion which distinguish the men's wives and mothers are worthy of warm and wondering admiration. There are black sheep, no doubt. Where are there not? But I often ask myself, " How many of us, brought up in comparative luxury, carefully educated and liberally amused, would stand the strain of separation, indifferent health and almost constant pecuniary difficulty as these women stand it? How many of us would have the grit and endurance to keep clean, kind and respectable under such conditions as theirs? " It is true that they possess the best husbands in the world—husbands who will scrub the floors, do the washing and mind the children without losing an iota of their manliness; but when these husbands are at sea there are long periods of loneliness which there is little to mitigate, and if a woman is fairly young and passably good-looking she must lead the life of a recluse if she is to escape the damaging criticism of her neighbours. The wonder to me is that the enormous majority should be so steady and so faithful considering the snares spread for them in any of the great naval ports.

I was surprised when a very good woman, a religious devotee, argued that I was wrong in aiming at *amusing* the men's wives at our winter teas rather than *improving* them. It seemed to me that a " good laugh " was what they chiefly needed. " If they want amusement " (observe the " if ") " they can go to the music-halls," said my friend. Yes ; out into the streets in the dark winter evenings, and late home again, to spend sixpence, or maybe a shilling, on a seat and listen to the veiled, or unveiled, vulgarity of one " turn " out of three

Unco' guid women are so often wanting in the imagination which their weaker sisters frequently possess. They are mentally incapable of putting themselves, as it were, inside the skins, seeing with the eyes and feeling with the hearts of those whom they seek to benefit. They give others that which they honestly believe those others *ought* to want, and shelter themselves behind the commandment, " Do unto others as you would they should do unto you." I have myself sat facing the horses in an open carriage on a bitter day, giving the finishing touches to what was only an incipient cold so that a blindly unselfish woman might have the satisfaction of giving up to me the place I did not want. She, meanwhile, sat where I longed to be, with her back to the horses, growing greener and greener—a mistaken martyr. What these self-sacrificers never learn is to " study others," as an old servant of ours used to say. Many wise and kind people are able to appreciate altruism even in its most un-attractive forms, but when it is merely the outcome of a calculated effort to " acquire merit " by per forming so many " kind actions " *per diem* regardless of consequences, it strikes me as nothing less than intolerable, and I want to bite the importunate hand that overfeeds me and kick away the intrusive footstool pushed under feet that only wish to rest upon the carpet.

The actual horse-power wasted annually in giving help to people who do not require it, or giving the wrong sort of help to those who are in need, would move mountains.

A certain important and well-known society which has for its object the improvement of wives and mothers of the humbler sort does excellent work in some places, but I have never found it in my heart to join it for the reason that the majority of its instructors are to a great extent in ignorance of the actual conditions in which the instructed lead their lives, and are not prepared to study those conditions patiently and sympathetically. I was once present at a large meeting of this society at Malta and was privileged to hear a lady address the assembled soldiers' and sailors' wives as follows : " You must remember, dear friends, that it lies entirely with you to keep your husbands from the public-house. If, when they come off duty, you are always smiling and neat, with nicely brushed hair and a pretty ribbon at your neck, they will want to stop at home." The speaker was credited with a private fortune of fifteen hundred a year ; she lived well outside the thickly-populated, and then not too sanitary, town of Valetta, and she went home every summer to escape the heat Her straight black hair was *raked* back from her sallow face into an unbecoming knob, and her blouse of salmon-coloured silk was everything a blouse should not be. . . . I wondered how much of his time her husband managed to spend at the club or in the mess.

The following historical remark of an old woman to her companion, overheard as they made their way home from a similar meeting at Fulham Palace many years ago, shows that people of the class which suffers from our well-meant but often unintelligent attempts at their improvement find it hard on their side to understand the circumstances of their " improvers " : " Now I wonder 'ow the Bishop's lady do manage when '*er* ole man comes 'ome drunk ? "

I have long thought that district nurses, doing either general or maternity work, are perhaps the most powerful social missionaries in existence. Their practice is qualified by only a modicum of preaching, no more indeed than a pointed hint here and there, an unrehearsed object-lesson in nursing or in invalid cookery at the patient's house, and, where absolutely needed, a good " dressing down " to the careless and dirty. They spread the gospel of adequate ventilation far more successfully than anyone else can do, since they prove the need and benefit of fresh air by actual daily demonstration as they go their rounds. They are themselves so bound by the regulations of their profession that the slightest trip, or slip, on their part is noted by the authority to whom they are immediately responsible. Indeed, I have often pitied maternity nurses for having to fill up so many forms and returns dealing with registration and other matters when they are themselves tired out by long and anxious attention to serious cases. Yet, when I remember the cruel and needless loss of life among mothers and infants not so many years ago owing to the carelessness and insobriety of nurses, the ignorance and folly of mothers and lack of proper supervision by Government, I cannot but be glad of the regulations which protect both nurses and patients in the present day.

The wife of a commander-in-chief must know herself to be an object of considerable interest to the wives of the subordinate officers in the command. She is blamed and criticised freely, but on the other hand the smallest kindness she performs is apt to be magnified into a noble deed, and this not only by flatterers, who are easily recognised. This being so it should not be hard for her to gain the confidence and enlist the help and sympathy of the wives of officers. I well remember hearing the late Admiral Sir H. Grenfell say, *à propos* of the wives of certain commanders-in-chief : " Lady Dash always used every ounce of weight given her by her position and personal charm in the right way, and people were ready to do anything for her ; Lady Blank, on the other hand, attempted to boss and dragoon the officers' wives, which only made them grudge the help they gave her and rejoice when she left the port."

It was not only the men's wives but the officers'

wives whom I learnt to know at Chatham. The fact that comparatively few of the latter live in or near the port gave me better opportunities for making their acquaintance than I should have enjoyed at Portsmouth or Devonport, and I found among them friends who will, I know, remain friends to the end of the chapter. One of them, a lieutenant's wife, combining *savoir faire* in an uncommon degree with boundless beneficence, divides naval officers' wives into three categories :

(1) The anxious, loving, clinging creature who takes no interest in the rest of humanity when her husband is ashore and weeps while he is afloat.

(2) The wife who intends to have a good time and regards her husband's profession chiefly as a means to that end.

(3) The normal wife who neither borrows trouble nor steals pleasure.

A good many officers' wives do not join the Friendly Union of Sailors' Wives on the grounds that its visitors are regarded by the men and their wives as busybodies. No doubt some of them answer to this description, but it should be remembered that nobody compels the women to join a society of which visiting is well known to be the main object. Many ladies are shy of becoming visitors, and quite naturally so, until they find how welcome they are made. Then they enjoy it so much that they become positively enthusiastic and soon learn to help the men's wives in a hundred ways which cost them time and thought, but in material no more than a few postage stamps, an occasional illustrated paper or a bunch of flowers. The visitor solely bent on improving those she visits has mistaken her vocation. She is apt to be inquisitorial, and her didactic methods will bore, if they do not actually offend, her victims. She will come across plenty of difficult or disappointing people, but, if she realises that she can learn fully as much as she can teach in the course of her visiting, she will be acceptable as well as useful.

A well-founded criticism of certain officers' wives as visitors comes from the officers themselves. This is that ladies use their personal influence with their husbands to obtain promotion or special indulgences for the men whose wives they visit. It is perhaps unnecessary to say that officers are even more to blame in the matter if they yield to such petticoat persuasion. For myself I can only say that one or two salutary snubs from my own husband, reinforced by actual, and sometimes painful, experience, have kept me from indulging in so reprehensible a practice. I have been appealed to, while at Chatham and elsewhere, both openly and anonymously, to interfere in service matters and petition " my dear husband " to give more leave to married men, or hasten the re-employment of others dismissed their ships for good cause ; but my invariable reply, when reply was possible, has been that my husband rightly would not tolerate my intervention. I must, however, confess to having in several instances appealed privately to commanding officers of ships with more or less happy results. That there are two sides, and sometimes more, to every question is not commonly apparent to women of all classes.

While writing about sailors' wives and their friends and helpers I should like to point out that above all others Miss Weston and her staff of ladies possess and use such expert knowledge as makes their work both acceptable and successful. Their hearts are as fully engaged as their brains and hands, and there is discipline and system in all they do, side by side with sympathy and understanding. The work of the Royal Naval Friendly Union of Sailors' Wives is necessarily the work of shifting amateurs ; that alone puts competition or comparison with Miss Weston's out of the question, but we amateurs can be useful also, and can make the lives of those among whom we live easier and brighter. For my own part I owe much to Miss Weston personally and to several of her coadjutors, since whenever I have turned to them for advice or information I have received it promptly and found it valuable. That Miss Weston's Sailors' Rests attract a larger number of men than Sailors' Homes managed by naval men and enjoying a permanent endowment shows how strong a hold her methods have upon the Navy. The men may drink beer at a Sailors' Home but none at Miss Weston's Rests, yet the absence of the official element at the latter more than compensates for the lack of beer, and the practical interest taken by Miss Weston in their wives and families appeals to them very strongly.

I hated saying good-bye to my friends, officers' wives and men's wives alike, when the time came. An opportunity for doing so was given me shortly before I left Chatham when the summer treat of the Friendly Union of Sailors' Wives took place in the Barracks grounds, and yet it was not possible to express half the gratitude I felt for the unvarying kindness and goodwill they had shown me. Our senior member, wife of a warrant officer, gave me a great sheaf of Madonna lilies from her own garden, and then the branch as a whole, represented by Mrs. Anson, presented me with a beautiful (and genuine) Queen Anne writing-table as a souvenir of our friendship. To the bottom of its top drawer is screwed a brass plate bearing an inscription which modesty forbids me to reproduce here, but when I am feeling very useless, or old, or sad I look at it and take comfort in the thought that, deserving or not, I have enjoyed the confidence and affection of many sailors' wives.

CHAPTER XLV

EARLY DAYS OF THE WAR

I SAID good-bye to Chatham, as I thought for good, on July 15th, and though I could not but be glad to exchange its dingy streets, dusty grass and smutty air for the fresh peacefulness of Winsley, I departed with a heavy heart.   Although my husband had still four years on the Active List of his rank I felt it was good-bye to the Navy for me, good-bye to the life which, with all its ups and downs, I had found interesting and delightful for twenty-nine years, and I was not only sad but rebellious, for I felt there was a good deal of life in me still and I did not want to have my harness and my shoes taken off and be turned loose in a green paddock for the rest of my days.   The following week I spent in a desperate effort to quell this internal rebellion, and repeated over and over again to myself, " The trivial round, the common task *must* furnish all I *dare* to ask," so that by the time my husband arrived on leave, as eager as a schoolboy home for the holidays, I was able to smile naturally and expatiate with him on the many charms of an inland home.   But on the 25th the newspapers made us very uneasy, and as we sat down to dinner on the 28th a telegram arrived which decided my husband to return at once to Chatham.   He left by a midnight train, and for the next week I lived in a sort of nightmare in which fears predominated over hopes, and lost all the serenity I had taken such pains to acquire.   The very clocks seemed to tick " War, war—war, war " as I sat alone in the evening, and I gave up trying to be cool and collected on Wednesday, August 5th, when I read in the morning paper that war with Germany had been declared.   But I was thankful England had played the game.   After half an hour of indecision I resolved to return to Chatham in defiance of my husband's wishes, for I simply could not remain away from him and my sailors' wives. I had only fifteen shillings in cash in my possession and the banks were all closed, so I drove into Bath, taking with me an aquamarine and diamond pendant and a black opal pin (both my own exclusive property) and offered them to Mr. Mallett. I felt rather shy and ridiculous as I waited in the " Octagon " among all the beautiful gems, silver and furniture until he was at liberty to speak to me ; but he was very kind, and, as he was naturally quite indisposed to buy anything at such a moment, I gladly accepted his offer of five sovereigns in return for my extemporised cheque and returned home triumphant. I had telegraphed earlier in the day to a private hotel at Gillingham (Chatham), and was relieved to find I could be taken in there with my maid on the following day, for I could not under the circumstances expect a welcome at Admiralty House, where the staff were all in residence and only a " nucleus crew " of servants manned the establishment. More modern wives than myself may find my reluctance to return uninvited incomprehensible and picture me a cowed and broken-spirited woman. This is very far from being the case, but my husband and I have always considered one another's views and wishes, so it went against the grain with me to do otherwise. I wrote to break the news of my unauthorised return, knowing full well he could only receive my letter too late to stop me. Then I remembered that it might be impossible to motor through the very military counties of Wiltshire and Hampshire without some kind of passport, so I begged a neighbouring J.P. to concoct one, making it apparent that I was returning to Chatham *on duty*, *i.e.*, to take up my duties as President of the Soldiers' and Sailors' Families Association (Naval Branch) there. I was quite sorry its production was unnecessary, for it was an interesting document. However, we were stopped twice ; once at a railway bridge near Odiham, and once in a narrow road not far from Andover, where we were directed to draw up to let a long string of A.S. Corps wagons pass. It was late and dark when we reached Gillingham, and I was glad to find a hospitable note from my husband awaiting me : " Come to lunch to morrow, and you shall be scolded and forgiven. Your rooms are ready."

Next morning, after a talk with Mrs. Anson, Vice-President of the two societies whose work was to be so important during the war—the Soldiers' and Sailors' Families Association and the Friendly Union of Sailors' Wives—I went to the Town Hall where the Mayor of Chatham had permitted both committees to establish themselves. I found that the local committee of the Charity Organisation Society under Mrs. Day had already flung themselves into the breach and were helping us with heads, hearts and hands—and badly we needed them, for in peace time the naval branch of the Soldiers' and Sailors' Families Association at Chatham is a mere skeleton worked by the President, Vice-President, and Honorary Secretary (a naval officer). The Executive Committee met but rarely, and as it consisted almost entirely of ladies who were also members of the Friendly Union of Sailors' Wives Executive, I thought then, and still think, it would have been better to amalgamate the two societies for the period of the war. In the Friendly Union of Sailors' Wives rooms goodwill and confusion reigned and I wondered when, if ever, we should be ready for all emergencies —never if it had depended on myself. Fortunately good organisers and devoted workers were not wanting, and a start had already been made with the business of registration. A continuous stream of men's wives came in by one door, gave their names and all necessary details concerning themselves and their husbands to ladies in the registration office, and passed out by another door. By the time this part of the work was completed we had nearly six thousand names on our books.

CHAPTER XLVI

EARLY DAYS OF THE WAR—*continued*

WHEN I returned to Admiralty House from Winsley, I found all the staff " living in." The billiard-room had become the chart-room, and on the very day war was declared my husband started a newspaper depôt in the ball-room. Here papers, magazines and books were collected, sorted and made up into parcels for ships and hospitals by a party of girls under the leadership of Miss Pullen, the Secretary's daughter. The girls came every day, rain or shine, and until we left Chatham they worked like trumps. Two of the bandsmen went daily to the railway station with a handcart and brought back heavy loads of reading matter from all parts of the United Kingdom, while local friends dropped their contributions into a basket at the front door. I never knew or dreamt that so many daily, weekly and monthly publications (secular, religious, and irreligious) existed. Ladies' fashion papers, parish magazines of ancient date, Christian Science papers, Spanish illustrated weeklies, children's magazines and the grimy sweepings of many lumber-rooms arrived ; also numerous packs of cards so darkly thumbed that they had to be burnt. But there were many regular contributors and others who sent us quantities of capital stuff, and every day the parcels made up by Miss Pullen and her staff of girls (the eldest may have been twenty-one, the youngest thirteen) were put into sacks and sent down to Sheerness. The bulk of the newspapers and periodicals went to the Nore Destroyer Flotilla, while the books were given to the three naval hospitals at Chatham. Perhaps the noblest gift we received was ten years of *Punch* sent by a London clergyman. We had the numbers bound in nice fat pale-grey volumes and they were presented to the big hospital on Christmas Day.

Our house was, of course, shorn of all the extras which make the difference between a " residence " and a home, for all our own gear—pictures, china, silver, and a hundred little joys and comforts—had gone to Winsley early in July, and there wasn't a cushion, or a flower vase or a book in the house when I returned.   It was perfectly impossible to make the rooms look pretty, and I did not struggle to do so. We soon got accustomed to the heavy and serviceable Government spoons and forks and the uncompromising solidity of everything.   Half a dozen sixpenny vases held the flowers we found indispensable, and a kind and thoughtful friend sent over from her house at Rochester some sofa-cushions which were very welcome.   We left only a few servants at Chatham when we went home in July—as my husband had expected to turn over the command to Sir Berkeley Milne on August 29th—and we had dismissed the *chef*, so our establishment was of a decidedly scratch description for the five months we remained on after war broke out.   An A.B.'s wife presided in the kitchen and very well and wholesomely did she feed us.   Meals occurred at the usual hours, but my husband and the staff came to them when they could and left when they must, regardless of ceremony.   They were badly off for fresh air and exercise, and my husband wore a brown path on the east lawn, which became a sort of quarterdeck where he tramped up and down for a few minutes at a time on the days when business was particularly heavy.

We had interesting visitors from time to time at

Admiralty House.   Commodore Tyrwhitt, whom we had known since he was a very young lieutenant in the *Cleopatra* in 1893, dined with us just after the Heligoland fight at the end of August, and of all that he told us the fact that seemed to be of the greatest personal interest to him was that it should have been his friend Captain Wilmot Nicholson who came out in the *Hogue* and deftly and quickly in pitch darkness towed the disabled *Arethusa* into port.   Captain Nicholson himself dined with us not long after, on his return from Holland, whither his rescuers had taken him when the poor *Hogue* was torpedoed.   If ever a man hungered and thirsted to " get a bit of his own back " from Germany, it was he.   Captain Fullerton and Commander Snagge, commanding two of the monitors which did such valuable work at Nieuport, were also welcome guests, but no one had time or inclination at Chatham for entertaining or being entertained in the first months of the war, and these glimpses of valiant and interesting people were for me as rare as they were thrilling.

My own day's work started with letter writing till 11, when I went to the Town Hall till lunch time. After lunch I contrived to get an hour's rest, and if there was no need to go again to the Town Hall, I took a short walk or drive, visited one of the hospitals, or went down to the Dockyard to see the ships in for repairs, if anyone was at liberty to escort me.   I rarely went on board a ship, for petticoats were decidedly out of place, but I did visit the *Arethusa* and one of the shallow-draught " veterans " back from Nieuport. The submarines lying alongside inspired me with the deepest interest combined with an invincible repugnance. The spirit of the officers and crews of these engines of death, compounded as it is of moral and physical courage, strikes me as being without parallel even in peace time ; in war the risks and responsibilities are multiplied a hundred-fold. Only a few weeks before war broke out a friend sent me a Limerick composed by a young " scientific " officer. It ran as follows :

> " There was a young man who said, ' D—n !
> I suddenly see that I am
> Only able to move in a predestined groove ;
> I'm not ev'n a 'bus—I'm a *tram*.' "

He and his fellows have been released from their bondage since he wrote that rhyme. That the limitations to which it refers have vanished in the stress of actual warfare no one who knows anything of the Navy can doubt.

There were generally more letters to write before dinner, and after dinner I played a solitary game of patience before going to my bed, where I resolutely read a novel in the hope of distracting my mind from the horrors of war, the anxieties and sorrows of my friends and the little problems and complications which every day brought me, but the Dockyard noises and the relieving of sentries round the house, to say nothing of the frequent rousing of my husband (whose room was next to mine) when urgent business required his attention, made it difficult to get sound or prolonged sleep.

It was not only my work that occupied my thoughts on these lengthening autumn nights. Roger had been invalided from Perak after a very serious attack of malarial pneumonia and I had established him at Winsley in September to undergo the long and weary cure prescribed by Sir Ronald Ross. It seemed hard to abandon him to even the kindest of nurses and neighbours, but my course seemed plain to me, and the success of the cure rewarded him for his patience.

Roger * was gazetted a temporary lieutenant in the Field Artillery on November 30th, and we had a visit from him at Christmas time when he managed to get a few days' leave. Thus in seven years he had been successively a sailor, a rubber planter and

* Roger Poore, Lieutenant R.F.A., was killed instantaneously by a piece of heavy shell while Observation Officer for his battery in the front trenches near Ypres early on Sunday morning, September 19th, 1915, aged 29.

Major A. E. Erskine, his Battery-Commander, wrote of him : " It was not only we gunners who realised what he was made of. He was twice called upon to act as Observation Officer in the trenches in a stiff fight, and every infantryman I came across who had had anything to do with him spoke in admiration of his pluck and his determination to do what he had to do however thick the shells were falling. He died as he would have wished, periscope in hand, observing for his battery in the thick of the fight—a glorious example. . . . I personally feel his death more than I can say. He was always the greatest help to me ; at all times cheery, he worked as strenuously as any man could. The Battery deeply deplore his death, for he had won the affection of his men by doing something every day to increase their comfort, and you could see how much they liked him by the way they worked for him under the most trying circumstances."

Lieut.-Colonel W. B. Browell, commanding 48th Brigade R.F.A., wrote : " The whole of the Brigade under my command mourn the loss of your son. I myself was very fond of him. . . . We have had a very bad time in a dangerous part of the line ever since we came out in May, and have lost heavily in officers killed and wounded."

a soldier, and I liked to think that his early experience as a sailor would make him a better soldier than his short military training alone could do.

CHAPTER XLVII

DANGER, NECESSITY AND TRIBULATION

OF course as time went on overworked ladies broke down, and there were little jars and misunderstandings, inevitable where all were amateurs and many anxious and worried about their husbands, but we were most fortunate in having capable civilian volunteers to help us. Long hours were worked whenever there was much to do. From 10 a.m. to 9 p.m. was not an unusual day early in the war, when disasters came thick and fast among Chatham ships, but as time went on and our organisation improved the strain was lessened, and the ladies themselves realised that exercise, regular meals and sufficient sleep were all necessary if efficiency was to be secured. For them lawn-tennis and golf stopped abruptly; running up to town to shop and see a matinée became almost impossible, and dinners and bridge parties were unheard of. Chatham, at any rate, was not long in finding out that we were at war; its character was completely changed, its ugliness forgotten, and its intense vitality, threaded though with heartrending reminders of grief and loss, its most salient feature.   Night and day the Dockyard throbbed with the beating of a thousand hammers. The white-faced mateys seemed inspired as they went about their tasks of constructing, refitting and repairing.   Their energy and enthusiasm were every bit as fine and important as the valour and dogged resistance of their brothers at the front or in the North Sea.   They worked, and still work, with the unquenchable ardour which no money can buy. When they repaired the battered plates of the *Arethusa*—" saucy " indeed—and her destroyer children, after the Heligoland fight, their hammers rang with as martial a note as any bugle, and in a space of time unparalleled for shortness the work was completed and the little grey ships once more took the bleak road to the North Sea, as staunch as before and keener than ever ; live things all of them and restored to power by the spirit and skill of the very men who a month or two earlier so gladly left and so reluctantly re-entered the Dockyard gates.

The civic life of Chatham, centred in the Town Hall, became identified, or at any rate interwoven, with the work we had to do for the wives and families of our soldiers and sailors.   What had hitherto been to most of us merely the main junction for tramway traffic was suddenly transformed into the hub of our day's operations, and the Mayor and his staff became the generous and long-suffering hosts of no less than three ladies' committees.   Members of these committees with anxious or puzzled faces passed in and out ; soldiers' and sailors' wives—many with babies in arms and little children trailing behind them—penetrated to the committee-rooms to obtain pay and advice, or lingered round the notice boards at the doors. Besides registering names and addresses, the ladies of the Friendly Union of Sailors' Wives occupied themselves in cutting out useful garments and distributing mourning, and they were always ready with consoling and cheering words for the inquirers who drifted in and out, nervous, restless, torn with doubts and fears as to the safety of their men.

The uninitiated public did not, and do not yet, understand that ships of the Chatham Division are not manned from Chatham only, but from the eastern half of England (including London) and Scotland, so that our widows and orphans at Chatham amounted to only a few hundreds after we had been five months at war. In those months *nine* Chatham ships were sunk, while at Portsmouth the loss of the *Good Hope* and *Bulwark*, and at Plymouth of the *Amphion* and *Monmouth* were the only heavy trials that befel the wives and families in those ports. The first Chatham ship to go was the *Pathfinder*, and we had twenty-one poor widows on our list. They had not been left long in suspense, but when the *Hogue, Cressy* and *Aboukir* were all torpedoed in one group thirteen days of racking suspense elapsed before full and authentic lists of the lost could be published, and every day of those thirteen days hundreds of wives and mothers came down to look for news with faces growing hourly more lined and haggard, their eyes dimmer and more sunken from want of sleep and the gradual draining away of hope. " Brave " is no adequate word for them. Tears there were, but no hysterical ravings. A piteous dignity was theirs that none who strove to comfort them will ever forget. A *Hogue* baby was born twenty-four hours after her father was drowned, but her mother refused to believe that all was not well. On the eleventh day I saw her sitting in her kitchen nursing the little creature and still contriving to smile, but next morning brought the official announcement that her husband was among the lost, and she smiled no more.

" He is such a grand swimmer," said a wife who could not think herself a widow, " and I know he would swim, if it was a hundred miles, to get home to me. Seven years married we've been and never a cross word. . . . Hush then, baby, or I'll tell your daddy."

Up at the Naval Hospital the good-natured flowers went on blooming till the frosts of autumn cut them down ; hundreds of beds awaited the wounded ; surgeons and nurses were ready and tons of " sick comforts " stacked wherever space could be found. But only a handful of wounded and injured came until the disastrous attempt to relieve Antwerp early in October provided occupants for the half-empty wards. Up to that time the casualty lists for the Chatham Division had been mainly lists of drowned.

CHAPTER XLVIII

COMMITTEE WORK

THESE were strenuous times for us all, and during the first few weeks I found myself ejaculating at intervals : " *Please*, God, let me keep well ! " To break down at such a time would have been unpardonable, and yet it was necessary to risk breaking down, for, though I knew quite well others would be able to do my work better than I could, there were not too many of us at Chatham, and I felt I had a trust and desired desperately to fulfil it adequately. A verse from a poem by C.L.G., which appeared some months later in the *Spectator*, expresses exactly what most of us, whether fighters or only helpers, have felt all through the war :—

> " And if I had ten lives to give,
> Far sooner would I risk the giving
> Of every one of them than live
> And lose all reason for my living."

I visited each of my two committee-rooms at first twice, and later once, every day. The Soldiers' and Sailors' Families Association (Naval Branch) Case Committee sat daily with Mrs. Anson as chairman during the first months of the war, and every day each case that came before her was investigated and reported upon by our visitors. The women in receipt of help would either come themselves to the Town Hall to take their weekly money or it would be brought to them, if they so preferred, by one of the ladies. There was never an hour's avoidable delay in helping them and no undesirable publicity was given to their need. Some of the widows were so young and pretty and looked still younger in their weeds. Poor things, they were wonderfully good and patient, though their faces were often grey with suffering and ravaged by tears and want of sleep. I well remember one little widow, an Irish Catholic from Cork, whose husband, a reservist who had been very comfortably off before the war broke out, was one of the missing in the three cruisers disaster. He had only come off the sick list the day his ship sailed and could not have had a chance in the cold water of the North Sea ; but we tried to comfort her when she came to us for news, tried to inspire her with a hope we could not ourselves entertain, and with tears rolling down her cheeks she whispered, "God is good." Wives and mothers, summoned from distant parts of the United Kingdom to see patients *in extremis*, were met at the station, and, if the ladies of the Friendly Union had no room in their own houses, lodgings were found for them. Among the reservists' wives there were many who knew nothing of the Navy and had never in their lives undertaken a long journey. Some of these, dazed, fatigued and broken in spirit, were met in London, safely convoyed to Chatham nd taken up at once to the hospital in the car of one of our members so that no precious time should be lost. All of us who had cars used, as far as possible, to send back to their homes those of the Chatham wives who had learnt from the Town Hall lists that they were widows. Some were in ill-health, some worn out with suspense, but I only saw one whose self-control had completely deserted her, and she was soothed and taken home by the kind and capable professional nurse who had given us her services in this painful part of our work.

Many of those who came for news or for payment to the Town Hall had no money for tram and train fare and had walked far with a baby in arms and little children clinging to their skirts, and these we used to invite into the Friendly Union of Sailors' Wives committee-room to have a cup of tea and a buttered bun. Indeed, tea was almost always going, and to some of the very anxious or very sad it brought at any rate a modicum of creature comfort not wholly to be despised.

But much bitter and unfair criticism was directed at our methods of administering relief by persons whose politics were of the sort that constrain a man to be up against capital, law, order and good manners and make him think the wearing of a red tie of more importance than either cleanliness or godliness. Gradually this hostility died down, and I confess that we heard with the greatest satisfaction that our principal local critic had met with a well-deserved rebuff whilst spouting cheap socialism from a street platform in Gillingham. A party of recruits coming from a cinema show gathered round to listen to his eloquence, but when he began to speak disrespectfully of the King they up-ended his platform, shooting him and his supporters off it as they did so, and marched them down the street to the tune of " Rule, Britannia."

CHAPTER XLIX

SICK, WOUNDED AND DROWNED

THE wounded from the *Arethusa* and her attendant destroyers were, from Commander Hope down, the most astonishingly cheerful and plucky patients, but when the men wounded in the Antwerp fiasco were brought to hospital, exhausted and suffering from the long jolting in springless vehicles to the place of their embarkation, a great depression fell upon the spirits of the semi-convalescent occupants of the wards. Nothing, however, could daunt some of them. Of these one boy of eighteen, desperately wounded in the knee, was twice operated on and suffered tortures. One night he begged the nurse to bend down so that he might whisper to her. " I'm in hell, nurse," was what he said ; and that was the only time he complained.

Marner, of the *Arethusa*, whose arm had been amputated at the shoulder, was another patient in whom I took a special interest. He was ship's cook, and when he was hit was wearing a cotton jacket in the pocket of which he had eleven shillings and fourpence. But the surgeon who performed the first operation (a second followed in hospital) had cut away the blood-stained garment and it was thrown overboard, *money and all.* So when Mrs. Marner went to see her husband in hospital he impressed this fact upon her, and told her to go down to the ladies at the Town Hall and tell them about it. I was in the Soldiers' and Sailors' Families Association committee-room when she arrived and told me the story. Her pretty grey eyes, fringed with thick black lashes, were blurred with tears, but an irrepressible smile shone through when she showed me her husband's portrait in an illustrated paper, and I heard afterwards that the whole ward rejoiced whenever she went to see Marner in hospital, so plucky and so merry was she. Of course we gave her the eleven shillings and fourpence, though at this moment I could not give my reasons in writing for doing so were Sir James Gildea to require them.

My husband particularly wished me to see and speak to *all* the patients in our hospitals who were equal to talking, whether they were sick or wounded, for the natural tendency of visitors was to take notice only of the wounded, and it frequently fell out that the men injured in action received all the sympathy and all the gifts. A poor Highland boy, suffering from appendicitis, whom I asked my maid— a Highlander herself—to visit, said to her regretfully, " Nobody cares to talk to me. I'm only sick." I found that little square cushion-shaped bags of lavender covered with pale blue satin were much liked by the patients, and as my Winsley lavender crop was even bigger than usual in 1914, I had about 150 of these to distribute. They were nice to handle, small and sweet, and could be slipped under the men's pillows, and I don't think anything gave me greater pleasure than their acceptance by the patients at the various hospitals for soldiers and sailors, Belgians and British.

The loss of the *Hawke* on October 15th brought a fresh wave of sorrow to Chatham. So small a proportion of officers and men were saved; and I shall not easily forget the pathetic sight which met my eyes a few days later as I got out of the car at the Town Hall. A handful of dispirited-looking men, wearing short, thick leather jackets over their uniforms, were straggling past on their way to the Naval Barracks. Motor omnibuses had been in readiness there to fetch them from the station, but the hour of their arrival had been incorrectly telegraphed from London, so the *Hawke* survivors walked. Though it was none of my business I followed the chief writer in charge of the Naval Information Bureau at the Town Hall when he went out to take their names, and I asked one of them if I might not send up at any rate some of the party in my car. " Perhaps *he'd* liked to ride," was the answer—and the man to whom I spoke pointed to one of his shipmates—" for he's pretty shaky." " Would you care to go ? " I asked. " No, 'm, thanking you very much. They'd think I was sick and put me in hospital, and I want to get off home on leaf." So on they tramped, and my heart ached for them, for they had none of the honours of war—no band, no admiring crowd, no cheering.

Apart from the loss of her officers and men, we regretted the old *Hawke* herself as though she had been human. We never loved any ship as we loved her. But she can never be a forlorn and battered coal-hulk like the poor little *Tourmaline*, my husband's first captain's command. The *Hawke*, at any rate, is the coffin of brave men.

The *Hermes* was the next to go—the sixth Chatham-manned ship torpedoed—and mercifully the casualty list was a short one. But on the very next day the grievous tragedy of the *Good Hope* and *Monmouth* was enacted thousands of miles away, and the delay in obtaining particulars which followed had strained the fortitude of hundreds of wives and mothers to breaking point before the official announcement of their loss plunged Portsmouth and Plymouth into mourning. To our own household the loss of a midshipman in the *Monmouth* brought lasting sorrow. An officer and a gentleman—so small, so straight, so keen—had gone down fighting in those wild, far-off waters.

Our next naval disaster had about it no thrill of excitement, no glamour of battle. The *Good Hopes* and *Monmouths* could cry *Morituri te salutamus !* to the country for which they gave their lives ; but the officers and men of the *Bulwark* had no time to say one word, no reason to strike one blow. She blew up at eight o'clock on the morning of November 26th, just after the colours were hoisted, and *nothing* was left of her above water but two little humps of twisted metal. The wind was from the west, and we heard nothing of the explosion at Admiralty House, though we were only four miles away, but before I was out of my room the heart-sickening news was brought to me.

Although the *Bulwark* was Portsmouth-manned the injured survivors and the dead bodies recovered from the wreck were, of course, taken to Chatham Naval Hospital; their relations and friends came to visit or identify them there and their sorrow was ours. The Captain, Guy Lutley Sclater, was my husband's old shipmate of happy *Hawke* days, and had ever since remained a staunch and valued friend. His body was one of the earliest found, but the ring he was wearing was the principal means of identification, while Captain Morton's was known by the name on his clothing. The sea is most merciful when it carries out of reach at once and for ever the human tabernacles of those dear to us. To remember them as we have known and loved them is the happier lot. Of the few survivors of the *Bulwark* some were doomed from the first and lingered for a few hours or days, eased as far as might be of their pain by whatever method wise and humane surgery could devise. One wife was summoned from Scotland to see her man before he died. " *He* knew *me*, but *I* didn't know *him*," she told us. " His face was so dreadfully burnt I could hardly see it for bandages—only just his eyes, and they looked so strange."

And day after day fresh flotsam and jetsam escaped from the sunken ship; more bodies were recovered, and papers, clothing and books washed ashore. A constant watch was kept, and all service or personal relics were taken to the Naval Barracks, where they were dried and catalogued. The mother of a drowned cadet who visited me at Admiralty House showed a brave front, talking calmly of her loss and surprising me by her wonderful self-control. When we parted at the station she said, " I hope I am brave; I try to be; but when I saw his little waistcoat——"; and for a few moments she gripped my hand and could not speak. Nor could I. The poignancy of her tone as she said the words " *his little waistcoat* " I shall never be able to forget.

A friend of mine, whose daughter was widowed by the *Bulwark* explosion and left indifferently provided for with three little children, said to me on the day following the disaster, " I could better have borne to lose my own husband. I *cannot* bear my daughter's grief."

CHAPTER L

VISIT OF THE KING AND QUEEN

It was on the 3rd of October that the King and Queen visited Chatham and lunched at Admiralty House. Their decision to do so had only been announced to my husband on the previous day, and the terms in which their intentions and wishes were conveyed were so considerate that I had neither time nor temptation to become the victim of stage fright. But I was fully sensible of the honour that was being done to us, and wished most ardently that the house was more fit for their reception and that our late excellent *chef* was not, for all I knew to the contrary, fighting " somewhere in France." However, the A.B.'s wife, reinforced by a man from Barracks, kept her head and sent us in an eatable meal of the simplest description, and, perhaps because I am not at heart a Martha, I never troubled my head over possible and unavoidable deficiencies, either during the meal or after. Friends had lent us flower vases, silver dessert dishes and cushions ; willing fingers arranged the flowers, and the Admiral Superintendent's daughters arrived with a cartload of ferns in pots with which to fill the empty fireplaces. All had done their best, but it was a humble and sketchy best. Besides ourselves and the staff only the Surgeon-General had been invited, and as soon as lunch was over their Majesties, with Lady Desborough and Sir Colin Keppel who were in waiting, drove off to the R.N. Hospital to visit the men wounded in the Heligoland fight. To my great delight the King and Queen granted my petition that they should pause for a few moments outside the Town Hall on their homeward way so that the ladies of our two committees might have the satisfaction of seeing them. I telephoned the good news to the

Town Hall, asking that the Mayor, to whom we were so deeply indebted for the quarters we occupied there, might also be informed, and later in the afternoon found myself standing on the pavement in front of that building, flanked by committee ladies and backed by Mayor and Aldermen, when the royal car drew up. In obedience to their Majesties' wish I presented the Mayor and Mayoress and Mrs. Anson ; there was a cordial shaking of hands, a few kind words, and the car was off again. . . . But the effect was magical. The pall that had hung over us had been lifted for a moment ; Chatham had felt the royal sympathy, clasped, as it were, the kind hands of King and Queen in its sad hour, and smiled through tears. Unlucky is the country that has nothing more picturesque—nothing more tangible—than a Republic composed of a pack of elderly gentlemen in frock coats as the outward and visible sign of supremacy. (My apologies to France.)

The wounded men at the hospitals, both naval and military, had been heartened and uplifted by the royal visit, and their Majesties had driven quite slowly across the lines where thousands of soldiers, new and old, were massed so that they too should be cheered and encouraged by the interest shown in their doings. It was indeed a great day for Chatham. As I turned away after watching the royal car out of sight a thin, white-faced little woman, whom I did not remember to have seen before, spoke to me. "Wasn't it *splendid* to see them!" she said. "While I was looking at them I forgot me 'usband was at sea."

Inside the Town Hall I found the Mayor and a little crowd of municipal authorities and their wives waiting to thank me for the great honour and pleasure I had been lucky enough to procure for them. I almost think they would have made me an alderwoman then and there out of sheer gratitude had I suggested it. But my debt to them was, and is, so great that it will never be discharged in full. Many a quarter of an hour of their time have I taken up, many a kindness have they done to our committees and to our poor sailors' wives ; but, from the Mayor himself down to the charwoman who kept the committee-rooms clean, I heard not a single complaint, although we overran the building and never hesitated to appeal for information or advice to the various officials.

CHAPTER LI

CHEERFUL MOMENTS

AMIDST the general gloom of those days there were some joyful surprises. One lady, visiting, as she supposed, a widow, was greeted by a beaming face when the door was opened, and behind the happy wife a big man in a fisherman's jersey and wide trousers, given him by some kind-hearted Dutchman at Ymuiden, blocked the little passage with his small son clinging tightly to his hand.

Two bluejackets standing outside the Town Hall found their own names in the list of lost under the heading of H.M.S. *Aboukir*. " But we're alive, Bill, ain't we ? " asked one. " That's right," said Bill, firmly, " no mistake about it."

A troubled party of three Scotchmen applied to the ladies at the Town Hall for news of the son of one of them. They had received a telegram from him, " Safe, Chatham," but his name was not to be found in any list, and they were as puzzled as they were anxious. However, one of our Friendly Union of Sailors' Wives Committee had chanced to hear that two young fellows had got into trouble just before their ship—one of the three cruisers—sailed and were confined in the Detention Quarters, and it occurred to her that one of them might be the missing son, so as delicately as possible she made the suggestion that the seekers should enquire there. And there, sure enough, he was : " Safe," and " at Chatham." The three men returned to tell their informant of their success and asked her to accept 5s. for the purchase of fruit for patients in the Naval Hospital — a very acceptable thank-offering.

The morning after the Hospital Ship *Rohilla* was wrecked off Whitby the mother of a young sick-berth steward on board her came to us almost beside herself with anxiety to ask for news. The boy's name was not in the first list of saved, and I wired to Whitby

x 2

for information respecting him. At seven o'clock that evening a telegram came from the boy himself announcing his safety, and a few days later I heard from his own lips the story of his escape. He was a good swimmer and, after being nearly suffocated in the crowded charthouse where the survivors were gathered, obtained leave to try to swim ashore. This he succeeded in doing, and staggered, bruised and spent, on to the esplanade, without, of course, a stitch of clothing on him. An elderly lady in the crowd, quick as thought, slipped off her flannel petticoat and handed it to him as he fell exhausted. Eager helpers carried him up to an hotel, where everything was done to restore him, but, to his lasting regret, he never saw his benefactress again. If she should chance to read this book she will know that he was not ungrateful. Before we parted he said, with a heavy sigh, " It's an awful thing to be an only son. I wish my mother had half a dozen. Then she wouldn't worry so about *me*."

Two entertaining child - stories which deserve chronicling came to me from Winsley.

Archy, aged only three and a half, but already thinking deeply about the wickedness of the German Emperor, had been punished by his nurse for *spitting*, a sin which she considered to have been directly prompted by Satan.

Archy : " Nannie, are there bad angels as well as good ones ? "

Nannie : " Yes, darling ; when you are naughty the bad angels are making you so."

Archy : " Have the bad angels a master, like the good ones ? "

Nannie affords full information upon which Archy reflects.

Archy (two hours later) : " That bad gentleman, Nannie—Mr. Satan, that you were telling me about —is a German, I s'pose—and spits. *God, of course, is English.*"

Later on Archy was going as Cupid to a fancy dress children's party and, much interested in his wings, remarked to Nannie : " When I get my wings on I'm going to fly up to heaven and ask God to drop bombs on the Kaiser."

The conduct of the war was made specially interesting to us by the fact that most of the Admirals commanding afloat were personally known to us, while Lord Kitchener, Sir John French and Sir Horace Smith-Dorrien had crossed our path more than once.

For my own part, I had made the acquaintance of Sir John French shortly after I left school when he was a subaltern in his old regiment, the 19th Hussars, quartered in the South of Ireland. Now that between thirty and forty years have elapsed I may be pardoned for narrating an amusing incident which occurred in those days.

My sister and I were invited to tea with Major Coghill, commanding at Limerick the squadron in which Mr. French served, and as our host showed us the way to his own quarters he silently pointed to a notice pencilled on his subaltern's door : *Non Licet !*

I knew enough Latin to translate the laconic prohibition, and I also knew the pretty girl whose name, though spelt differently, was pronounced *Licet*, so I gathered that Mr. French was in the eyes of his C.O. too young to contemplate matrimony at that period of his career.

Sir Horace Smith-Dorrien commanded a battalion of the Sherwood Foresters at Malta in 1899, and my husband and I knew him well, which statement will convey to his innumerable admirers that we liked him very much. One day when he was lunching with us on board the *Illustrious*, I confided to him that I was in the grip of a *migraine*, and begged him to forgive me if I was stupid to the verge of imbecility. His sympathy was at once aroused in a special degree, for he had been for years the victim of these sudden and annihilating visitations, and he then and there prescribed a far stiffer whiskey and soda than I relished. But it cleared away the partial blindness, and the arrested circulation in my brain started work again. We discovered that day that my initials— I. M. P.—spelt his own early nickname, acquired because he was very far from being a model child, and later on, before he sailed for South Africa, where his name carried with it a guarantee for all that was swiftly efficient in warfare, he gave me his photograph, upon which " Imp to I.M.P." is written.

In return I presented him with a much-bent silver coin for luck and a little case of sticking-plaster with this verse, which, though poor enough, was the best I could produce :

> " The plaster in this little case
>   For scratches, cuts on hands and face,
>   Is specially intended.
>   Friend, when you're fighting overseas
> No wound be yours more deep than these,
>   And none less quickly mended."

Sir Horace maintains his high position among the small group of undethroned heroes and unchanging friends who have helped to make our lives both happy and interesting.

CHAPTER LII

PROFIT AND LOSS

WORK is certainly the best anodyne for sorrow, and we were all glad at Chatham to have plenty to do. My daily walks to and from the Town Hall were often very wet and muddy when the downpour of December set in, but I welcomed the exercise, and as it was the feet of thousands of promising recruits that churned the mud into stiff brown butter and made walking detestable I could not complain. No doubt everyone has noticed one effect of the war, for it is so extremely obvious. It is the general cessation of grumbling over trifling inconveniences, small ailments and domestic worries. If one is cold one remembers that the men in the trenches or in the North Sea are far colder. If one is ill one's illness is as nothing compared with the sufferings of the wounded. If one's train is an hour late it is because troops are on the move. If one's cook gives warning it is not worth fretting over. If one's investments do not pay there are plenty of people who have no money to invest and a hard struggle to keep going at all. The great griefs and trials around us dwarf the lesser ills that flesh is heir to, and if sorrow comes to one's own door one must accept the unwelcome guest with fortitude, neither expecting nor exacting the same measure of sympathy or condolence which before this era of great national trial our every grief evoked. The hardest lesson to learn is that one's nearest and dearest is, after all, only one man in a multitude, one life to give for the Empire if need be.

As a set-off to the heavy losses which befel Chatham in the first months of the war, we had matter for rejoicing in the Australian success in the Bismarck Archipelago, the *Königsberg's* internment by the *Chatham* in East Africa, the good services of the smaller ships of the East Indies Squadron, and the fall of Tsing-Tau. But the *Sydney's* exploit in destroying the gentlemanly but piratical *Emden* and the revenge of Admiral Sturdee in the Falkland Islands were the big naval events which stirred us most.

Captain Glossop of H.M.A.S. *Sydney* is our very good friend, and well do I remember our first meeting when I landed at Garden Island to attend service in the Dockyard Church just after my arrival in Australia. He was then commander of the little *Prometheus,* and as we talked I reminded him that his ship was known for good cause as the *Promote-Us*, and wished that she might bring luck to him. As a matter of fact, she did not do so as promptly as might have been desired; but there can be no doubt that his exceptional knowledge of Australians and the Australian Station obtained for him the command of the *Sydney*, and gave him the opportunity of so greatly distinguishing himself as the captor of the *Emden*.

Mingled with our rejoicings over Sir Doveton Sturdee's victory was the inevitable pang of regret that ships such as he brought into action had not been available at Coronel; and when we drank Sir Doveton's health we drank also to the glorious memory of the *Good Hope* and *Monmouth*, outranged, outclassed, wiped off the face of the ocean—but lost, not captured.

Our life was lived to the accompaniment of dock-yard hammers and the voice of the drill sergeant. Thousands of recruits were drilling on the lines and in the barrack squares, recruits who learnt their duties in as many days as they would have required weeks before the war. It would have been hard to beat those of the Royal Engineers for intelligence, physique and zeal, and it was a delight to watch the drummer-boys (all sappers' sons) on the parade ground—heads up, shoulders back, martial to the tips of their toes and proud to bursting point. Even the brand-new recruits, being marched into Brompton Barracks from the railway station, *marched* : and as they got their uniform piecemeal—here a military cap over mufti, there a khaki tunic over blue serge trousers and tennis shoes—each one turned, by a transformation almost as magically swift as Cinderella's, into a fighting man ; lean, keen, alert, inspired.

Of some recruits who had joined a line regiment at Chatham Barracks we heard a very funny story. Regardless of their newly-assumed military obligations, they actually absented themselves from Chatham without leave and went hop-picking for several warm September days ! On their return they were not treated as deserters but as erring children, and now as made soldiers they must look back upon their little escapade with something like horror.

CHAPTER LIII

SAILORS' WIVES IN WAR TIME

In October we started fortnightly entertainments for the members of the Friendly Union of Sailors' Wives in the Central Hall at Chatham, where for the three preceding winters they had been held by the permission of Mr. Hall, the leading Wesleyan minister in the port. Though he was himself at the Front, he and all his staff were the means of our holding these little concerts in a spacious hall, where the wives were able to work for our Clothing Store, while superfluous and noisy children were amused in the lobby outside.   After the concert tea was carried round, and proceedings closed with the Hymn for Those at Sea and the National Anthem.   Mothers' Meetings were also held once a week *under expert management*, and, at these, Bible Classes and Health Lectures formed part of the programme.   They were very successful, and confirmed me in my belief that amusement and instruction for grown-up persons are best kept separate.   A serious lecture sand-wiched between a merry *potpourri* on the band and a sentimental song is too obviously the powder in the jam.   If a vote were taken I think it would be found that most people prefer their powders plain.   It seems to me that only persons specially qualified by training (or genius) to understand the habit of mind of their hearers, knowing them in their own homes in " working rig " and with the mask of company manners laid aside, knowing also their trials, their struggles and their temptations, have any right to attempt the instruction and improvement of their inferiors in social position and education.

Much has been said and written about clubs for sailors' and soldiers' wives during the war, and a great deal of money seems to have been subscribed for establishing them.   Time will show their value, but with a pretty intimate knowledge of the ways of sailors' wives gained in the thirty years of my married life, I am inclined to doubt their usefulness.   An admiral's wife is reported in the newspapers as having said when opening one of these clubs in London, that the women frequenting them *would be subjected to no rules and restrictions*—a risky system, if system it can be called. Why, even the most pious prelates at the *Athenæum* would give trouble if there were no rules to regulate their behaviour ! Nor, as far as I can ascertain, is there any black-balling ; all the men's wives, irrespective of character or antecedents, are eligible. Now the best class of sailors' wives are essentially " home-keepers " ; the worst prefer the public-house to any imaginable club, while the intermediate section may go and sample a new club, but I doubt if they will become constant participators in its benefits. I have heard that in one of the great ports a large number of the men's wives economised in firing by almost living at the clubs last winter. They neglected their homes and their elder children, and took the younger ones with them. Their excellent separation allowances already permitted a far greater degree of comfort in their homes than they had ever enjoyed, but far too many of them spent the money on such luxuries as fur coats (" separation coats " they were called in the shops where they were sold), and to very few of them did the idea of " putting by " occur. I hope that the establishment of Penny Banks, such as the *Friendly Provident Bank* that has been successfully run for twenty-five years in Islington, may become the rule in naval and military centres before long. The Penny Bank gives no interest, so the depositors are urged to put their accumulations into the Post Office Savings Bank when these reach the sum of £1. The War Loan should benefit by such savings. The money to be put into the Penny Bank is *called for once a week* by authorised amateur collectors, and sometimes half a dozen members of the same family entrust their pence to this peripatetic encourager of thrift.

To return to the clubs : our sailors' wives of the superior sort are rarely gregarious. One constantly hears them say, " I don't ' mix up ' with anybody here." Many among them have been domestic servants in good places and have learnt a refinement of thought and speech which disinclines them to make friends of their less polished neighbours, and there are numbers of such women in the great naval ports who have at most one real friend. These will not be likely to appreciate clubs where no qualification further than that of being married to a sailor is needed in their members. But they like well enough going to entertainments where they can sit in rows, and to these they generally go with a chosen companion. Though we of the Friendly Union of Sailors' Wives have made repeated efforts to foster acquaintanceship between the men's wives, we have generally found our attempts unsuccessful. After all, we, in our class, would not wish the wife of the Lord Lieutenant of the county or of the Bishop of the diocese to " prescribe " our friends for us.

CHAPTER LIV

WAYS OF HELPING WIDOWS AND ORPHANS

ONE day in November, as I sat in my own den nursing an obstinate and devastating cold, a note was brought to me which fairly took my remaining breath away. It was from the Naval Barracks, and enclosed a cheque for £107 to be spent for the benefit of the wives and children of men in the Nore Command. The money represented the weekly contributions for the first three months of the war from the officers at the Barracks. Visions of all that so large a sum might accomplish (we were not rich at Chatham) floated before my watering eyes, but it was not easy to decide how best to spend this windfall, and I consulted my husband and his staff before concluding that what was specially needed were the means to get a number of war widows and their children out of Chatham, where rents are high and morals less so, and back to their old homes. Beyond that I was very anxious to help a few *ante-bellum* widows and orphans to emigrate to New South Wales, which had been my home for three memorable years. The Commodore and officers unanimously decided that the money entrusted to me might be expended on these objects, so I was free to form my committee of ladies at Chatham and begin negotiations with the emigration authorities of New South Wales. The " repatriation " part of the scheme was started at once, and certain sums received from individuals and from the ship's company of H.M.S *Bacchante* (earmarked for the benefit of widows and orphans of the *Hogue, Cressy* and *Aboukir*) were at our disposal for this purpose.

I had already received letters from Sydney informing me that warm-hearted people in the State of New South Wales were anxious to adopt as many as 250 orphans of the war, and I had been obliged to reply that our war widows were being so liberally pensioned that they refused to take advantage of any such offers. Not one would part with a single child, although we had already received many offers of adoption from various parts of the United Kingdom. Now it seemed such a pity under-populated Australia should have no opportunity of doing a kindness of the sort that equally " blesseth him that gives and him that takes " that, after discussing the matter with my advisers on both committees dealing with our wives and families, I decided to write and ask New South Wales to accept a small " consignment " of *ante-bellum* widows and orphans—unpensioned and struggling with the help of the relieving officer for a bare existence—and find homes and work foi them. Theoretically it is wrong to send hard-working women and healthy children out of England, more particularly when war is making havoc of our population. But, as a matter of plain fact, these women and children, whose cause makes no sensational appeal to the well-to-do and secures no eloquent advocate in Parliament, are losing health and courage in the struggle to live on less than the irreducible minimum. The war has not augmented their earnings, and it has enhanced the cost of necessaries by 25 per cent. They are in piteous straits, for the wave of generosity which has cast up money, clothing and Christmas presents at the feet of our amply-pensioned war widows and orphans has brought nothing to them.*

CHAPTER LV

THE *CALLIOPE*

ON December 17th occurred one of the great events of my life. I launched the cruiser *Calliope*. The Admiral Superintendent had invited me a year earlier to launch a submarine, but I have always felt, and still feel, so cordial a loathing for this sort of craft that I refused. Such underhand and devilish engines of destruction should never have been adopted by civilised nations, and I am strengthened in my prejudice against them by hearing that the great Pitt himself expressed similar views in language quite as strong, though, naturally, of superior eloquence.

---

* Since the above was written, a little company of "Pilgrim Mothers" and their children have been sent out to New South Wales, the greater portion of their passage money having been contributed by the congregation of St. James' Church, Sydney.

The *Calliope*, however, was a slightly larger *Arethusa*, and belonged therefore to a family I already loved and admired. It was a great piece of luck for me that she bore neither a city's nor a county's name, but was called after the Muse of epic poetry. No highly-placed Government official's wife, nor yet the wife of some important member on the Ministerial side of the House, was specially indicated as the correct person (geographically) to perform the launching ceremony, so I, who had no stronger claim than that of being the wife of the Commander-in-Chief at the Nore, came into what I am pleased to consider my own. The ceremony was private for reasons of State, and, besides our own small party from Admiralty House, only the Dock-yard officials and their families were gathered on the launching platform. I hit neither the Chief Construc-tor nor myself on the thumb with the mallet ; I broke the bottle with such unnecessary zeal that bits of glass and splashes of wine flew back in our faces, and I had just time to wonder what would happen if the ship were to " hang," when, slower than the minute hand of a clock, her nose began to recede from us ; then quicker and ever quicker till she glided off the ways and took to the water—a real live ship and my own godchild. I might have said in christening her, " I name *this ship*," but Admiral Anson gave me leave to use the second person, and, as ships to me are persons, not things, I said, " I name *you* His Majesty's Ship *Calliope*, and may God bless *you* and all who serve in *you*."

The Admiral Superintendent had impressed upon me beforehand that the launch would be shorn of the glories and excitement usually attending such an event. But not one of the launcher's perquisites was lacking ! (1) a bouquet of long-stemmed pink carnations tied with my favourite colour ; (2) a carved casket and tools of beautiful design and exquisite workmanship ; (3) a broad sheet of white satin on which were printed three separate poems, all of considerable merit, written by the Dockyard Poet. I could not mark my connection with the *Calliope* by presenting her with a service of plate, but her first captain (Captain Tweedie) accepted a cherished Chinese *Netsuka* as a mascot, which I sincerely hope may bring luck to the ship and all who serve in her. Now she is a flagship, like her elder sister, the *Arethusa*.

CHAPTER LVI

FINAL DEPARTURE FROM CHATHAM

WE had just got back to Admiralty House after church on Christmas morning when the thrilling news that a Taube was in sight brought us out into the garden, where we spent an hour watching its manœuvres against a provokingly patchy sky, fog-banks obscuring it for several minutes at a time.

The aircraft defence guns crackled all round us, but so far as any of the watchers could judge, the Taube received no damage of a material nature and passed finally out of sight in the direction of the North Foreland. The papers next day had a great deal to say about hostile aircraft over Sheerness and the warm reception they got there, but never a word about the " Battle of Chatham," which we thought very unfair. It certainly was interesting to see a Taube at fairly close quarters, and her appearance was no doubt intended as a menace to the mouth of the Thames, but a real disaster which befel Chatham that day was not due to the Germans but to the fog. Since no leave was being granted, the wives and children of the men in the ships at Kethole Reach had been invited to eat their Christmas dinner on board, but the fog was too dense at the hour fixed for the start to admit of their making the trip. It gave one a pang to think of their bitter disappointment. No preparations for dinner at home would have been made, and very likely their kitchen fires were already out when those who would have been such warmly-welcomed guests on board the ships returned disheartened from the place of embarkation.

There was a good deal of business to attend to during the days following Christmas and many good-byes to say, and on the 30th I took leave once more of the staff, bade adieu to my co-workers at the Town Hall and departed regretfully from Chatham, a place which had become unexpectedly dear to me during the three years and four months of my sojourn there.

And yet I was more resigned to go than in the previous July, because I had at any rate *lived* every hour of the first five months of the war, and was tired enough when I reached Winsley to need the rest offered by quiet nights and monotonous days. I had also strengthened friendships already begun and been fortunate enough to make new ones. One takes plenty of short cuts in the land of friendships as well as in *le pays du tendre* in war time.

It was on the 1st of January that my husband handed over the Nore Command to Admiral Sir George Callaghan, having held it longer than any previous Commander-in-Chief for just a century. His last morning was saddened by the grievous news of the loss of the *Formidable*. The paramount naval authority was long in learning that our fleets at sea required an adequate escort of destroyers. It may have been an act of genius to improvise a sort of Naval Brigade of several thousand men for service ashore, but the saving of several thousands of *trained* men's lives afloat would have resulted from a short apprenticeship in the school where that oft-despised instructor, Experience, teaches.

It was frequently asserted in his praise, by critics as well as apologists, that to Mr. Churchill's foresight was due the fact that the British Fleet was kept mobilised after the " Naval Exercises " of July, 1914, so that it might be immediately available in the event of war. Considering the European situation he could have done no less. If lunch is in progress and a hostess hears that an influx of unexpected guests is probable she will not tell her servants to clear the table and carry the food away as soon as she and her family have done eating.

It has also been said that the mobilisation itself was an improvisation consequent on the murders at Belgrade. Can the British public suppose that a naval mobilisation on a great scale can be " got up " in a few days, like theatricals in a country house ? And now that the authentic story of the " Stand fast " business is known the obvious comment is this : That what in the First Lord would have been an act of commonest prudence becomes, as the doing of Prince Louis of Battenberg, an ample refutation of the insinuations published in such newspapers as cater for persons preferring highly-spiced inaccuracy and innuendo to plain truth or unmarketable silence.

CHAPTER LVII

COMMUNICATED TO THE EXCOMMUNICATED

My husband has become a captain in the Wiltshire Regiment, since, although his name heads the Active List of Admirals, no suitable employment could be found for him in his own service, and idleness in this critical period of his country's history appeared to him intolerable. His duties as officer in charge of a recruiting sub-area of Wilts occupy him fully, and I have found some work to do for the War Office Egg Collection for sick and wounded and the Malta Hospital Comforts Fund. But my duties do not render me independent of external interests, and letters from people more fortunate than myself, in that they are in the stream while I am in a back-water, help to beguile days without sunshine and nights without peace.

Among my correspondence are some letters from a naval surgeon, and in one of them he thus describes his sensations while his ship was in action :

" We had been out sweeping the seas again and again before we caught the German Fleet. Of the action I saw very little—only a few smudges of smoke on the horizon in the early morning. The rest was a nightmare of horrible noises, alarms and mortal wounds. For the first hour and a half I sat at my station with nothing to do but wait, which was very trying. Then, after the —— fell out and the three German cruisers devoted their fire to us, our casualties came pretty thick and fast. After that I forgot all about the action, and it had been over for $1\frac{1}{4}$ hours before I knew we had finished.

" We were lucky in one way. Our killed were killed outright, whilst the wounded did not have anything very shocking in the way of injuries.

" The mental aspects of war are very interesting. I am not a psychologist, but I distinctly remember the day when it dawned upon the ship's company that somebody was attempting to kill them. The knowledge that they were attempting to kill somebody came later.

Previous to this, war had been a matter of service routine and almost like very realistic manœuvres. The period between the two stages was very horrible and my own personal experience of it I look back to with a feeling of shame. But we were all the same, and as I suppose we are all just the normal healthy men you meet every day, neither particularly courageous nor particularly cowardly, probably the same phases were gone through in other ships. In fact, I know it was so in one ship at any rate.

" I'm afraid this sounds like awful rot, but perhaps you can gauge the feeling when one starts out to find out whether one is brave or cowardly and one finds one is neither."

Later on a complaint reached me from a visitor among our wounded, some of whom had turned restive under a douche of tracts. It does not seem fair to send a man who has lost both legs for his country a sermon entitled " The Wounds of Sin," nor is it justifiable to stitch stiff cards covered with condemnatory texts on to the " comforters " destined for our sailors in the North Sea. Well-meaning egg collectors for naval and military hospitals decorate their eggs with texts. " Just as I am " was written on one, and " All things are possible with God " on another. These seem to indicate a slight degree of uncertainty in the donors' minds as to the contents of the eggs.

Better than a hundredweight of tracts are the little cards sent out by the Chaplain of the Fleet to our men. These are of thin cardboard and measure 3 inches by 2 inches.

Slip this inside your cap.

A SAILOR'S PRAYER.

Heavenly Father, forgive my sins, and strengthen
    me in all that is right.
Grant me help to carry out my duties faithfully
    and bravely.
Bless and protect the officers and men of this ship.
Shield all I love from harm in my absence.
      For Jesus Christ's sake.   AMEN.
From the Chaplain of the Fleet.   Aug., 1914.

Now and then the censors must be cheered by
finding a pearl, and one cannot grudge them the
refreshment, for their task must be as boring as the
going through of examination papers with the hateful
sense of being intruders and spies superadded. One
poor censor, a chaplain, felt himself grossly insulted
on finding in a letter from a man to his wife the
following sentence : " I send you Postal Order for
10s., but you may never get it as all our letters have
to pass the censor."

So great a number of funny yarns from the Front
have been going the rounds that one fears some are
ben trovati, or at any rate, touched up, and some are
hackneyed, while others have appeared in comic
papers and thereby become common property. I
will, therefore, only give two in the hope that neither
may be a chestnut.

Some English Tommies finding " *Gott mit uns* "
scrawled on the wall of a farm evacuated by Germans,
wrote underneath, " *We've got mittens too.*"

A Scottish lad of sixteen, wilfully determined to

fight the Germans, falsified his age and twice enlisted in different corps, only to be ignominiously retrieved by his mother.   A third attempt was successful, for he joined the Black Watch and got to the Front. Sent back to a base hospital suffering from a strained heart, he found himself in the care of an Australian nursing sister.   He arrived in shorts and with neither kilt nor any other item of the distinctive insignia of his regiment.   " Sister," he said confidentially, " I'd like ye to see me in me full dress," and produced from his pocket a grimy portrait of himself arrayed in the complete panoply of the smart Highlander. " But," objected " Sister," " you never expected to wear the sporran at the Front ? "   " Where else, Sister ? " asked the puzzled boy.   " Ye'd never look for me to be wearing it ahint ! "

The efforts made by naval officers to keep their men actively interested, and therefore in good health and spirits, are admirable and unremitting.   In some ships they compete for what is called a " Part of the Ship " cup.   The competition includes all possible sports, and is held every six months.   Other ships start newspapers, and in some Limerick-making is popular.   Here is an example of the latter which hails from the lower-deck of the *Duke of Edinburgh* :

> " There is a young person called Fritz,
> And outside this harbour he sitz.
>   When out to sea we go
>   He runs a torpedo—
> To date he's not got any hitz."

" We are becoming keen agriculturists on board," writes a certain commander. " Everyone has his own crop of mustard and cress in his cabin, and on ' make and mend ' afternoons " (Thursdays) " intensive culture is practised on the quarter deck with the aid of a magnifying glass, so as to make the most of the very inferior article known as the sun up here. We have a flower show on Saturday and shall sing harvest hymns on Sunday. The doctor was a bad last at one of our shows, having tried to grow his plants on the very best sterilised and iodoformed cotton-wool, and the sub. was disqualified under the ' frightfulness ' bye-law for having sown his seeds on an ancient and grubby blanket, though they did well. Do you, as a practical gardener, know of anything that will thrive on fog, distilled water or condensed milk ?   Mother can only suggest canary seed."

Another officer, engaged to be married, writes: " I have taken a house which I have never seen, and bought an Airedale which I have never seen to look after the house—and the wife I have not yet got ! It is all a great query."

A funny, yet pathetic, incident was described to me in the following words by the young mother of a first baby whose father, commanding a destroyer, got into Dover the day after the little boy was born: " A——— rang up, and *the nurse pinched ' Edward ' and made him squeal to his father down the telephone.*"

On August 4th, 1914, a certain British squadron put to sea from a certain port " veiled in the northern mists." It was then quite certain that war would be declared with Germany during the night. There was great excitement on board, and nearly everyone had made his will. Suddenly the sound of heavy firing was heard right ahead. It was only the defence forces trying their guns, but the authorities could take no risks, and " Action " was sounded off. The first lieutenant ran down to his station in a compartment below, and on the way met the captain's steward in a state of great perturbation. " Is this a ' dummy run,' sir? " he asked, " or shall I take the captain's cockatoo down below ? " It *was* a " dummy run* ! "

More than one Maltese ward-room steward has shown himself unmoved by the din of battle. One has been immortalised in *Punch ;* another hastily relaid the ward-room table of a certain destroyer on being told that German officers were being picked up by one of the ship's boats, and greeted captors and captives impartially with the customary " Breakfast just coming down, sare," when they went below. A third was killed bearing a tray laden with cups of steaming coffee in the middle of the Heligoland fight because, in defiance of all prohibitions, he put the comfort of the *Arethusa's* officers before his own safety.

A cruiser torpedoed in the bows made her way into harbour with her watertight doors opening up as she went. The bos'n, looking down the hatch, realised that all below was blown away. Dismayed

---

* The term " dummy run " is used to describe the first run *past* the target when a ship is doing prize-firing. The ship steams past the target without firing to let the gunlayers see what the target looks like.

by the devastation, he exclaimed in tragic tones, "All me stores is gone!" (A bos'n has charge of certain ship's stores.) Then he ran aft to his cabin and, returning laden with books and papers, flung them all down the hatch, remarking with a sigh of relief as they disappeared: "And all me accounts too!"

A messman rescued from another torpedoed cruiser was wearing nothing but one of Gieve's life-saving waistcoats when picked up, but he firmly clasped under one arm a bundle of account books. Unlike the bos'n, he counted these his chief treasure, and when he was asked why he had burdened himself with them answered, "Sir, they're my life's work."

The sailors' identity discs bear in abbreviated form the religious denomination to which each man belongs. One of the *Duke of Edinburgh's* men is reported to have complained that he had *C. of E.* instead of *D. of E.* on his disc.

In another ship an indignant Scottish stoker asked to see the Captain at that psychological moment on a Sunday morning when all hearts may be opened and all desires made known to the commanding officer. "It's like this, sir," he explained. "I gave my religion as Free Church when I joined this ship. Free Church is what I've always been, an' Free Church I'll die. But the commander, he says to me, ' Free Church,' says he, ' that's no church at all. I'll have no *free-thinkers* in this ship.' "

It is said that a naval chaplain, still full of the excitement of a mine-laying expedition, turned a phrase which occurs in the prayer read every morning on board ship, " Who hast compassed the waters with bounds " into *Who hast compassed the bounders with warts*, but I suspect the officer who sent me this story of having invented the slip himself.

CHAPTER LVIII

COMMUNICATED TO THE EXCOMMUNICATED— *continued*.

FROM friends both English and Australian I hear plenty of war stories illustrating the cheerfulness, the pluck, the resource and the endurance of the men accustomed from boyhood to fight with flood, fire and famine in the Bush. After so severe a training in independence it would be absurd to expect them to become in a few months mere cogs in the well-oiled machinery of a military corps, unanimous in intention, prompt in obedience, simultaneous in action and punctilious in matters of dress and address. All are irregulars except the Royal Australian Artillery. That their experience in this war will teach them the value of obedience, unanimity and punctilio is certain—they themselves admit that many lives have been lost through acts of undisciplined daring; but it would be a pity that in learning their lesson they should lose their power of initiative, their happy acquiescence in the inevitable as far as personal discomfort is concerned and their passion for surmounting difficulties. If only the surplus of energy and intrepidity possessed by the heroes of Anzac, living or dead, could at this moment be distributed among the lethargic, the selfish and the faint-hearted youth of England, the reinforcements at the disposal of the War Office would be worthy of advertisement.

Their common-sense is illustrated by the story of the storming of a hill at Gallipoli by a party of Australian soldiers. A stout major led the charge, but the pace was too hot for him. " Wait for me, men," he panted. But each moment of delay lessened their chance of success. " Look here, Major," said one of them, " it's your loss or a hundred of us. We're going on." And they took the hill.

Their wounded have been arriving at Malta absolutely destitute, as their kits are left at Gallipoli. A Tasmanian private, wounded in the arm, found himself in a Malta hospital with no uniform beyond his trousers. The men who were well enough and had adequate clothing were allowed out every day, but the Matron refused to permit the coatless and capless patient to take the air, as he desired to do bareheaded and in a suit of pyjamas. However, he bided his time. When the Colonel R.A.M.C. arrived at the hospital and had hung up his uniform coat and cap in the hall before donning his linen jacket the private " borrowed " them and strolled out of the gate, saluted by the sentries who should have arrested him.   Later in the day the coat was returned to its peg and no questions were asked ; but it was not hung in the same place next morning.   So our ingenious friend, with a trusted comrade to help him, carried off a Maltese orderly to the bathroom, stripped him and went out shopping in his nice cool kit. The orderly was later on indemnified by a present of cigarettes from the delinquent.

At Gallipoli Australians have bathed regularly under fire regardless of bullets zipping into the water around them, and a shell would only set them diving.

On one occasion an Australian finding himself detailed for sentry-go proceeded to make his task as easy as possible by removing his helmet and hanging it with his rifle on an adjacent tree.   A passing officer asked, not unnaturally, " And what may *you* be ? " " Oh, I'm a bit of a picket," drawled the sentry unabashed, " and what may *you* be ? "   " Oh, I'm a bit of a major " was the answer.   " Well," rejoined the sentry genially, " if you'll wait a jiff, I'll get my rifle and give you a bit of a salute."

A story that scandalises the ultra regular is told of an Australian private in Cairo.   As a certain General and his A.D.C. were getting into a motor outside Shepherd's, two English Tommies standing by saluted and stood at attention.   The Australian private, recognising the great man, crossed the road and said politely, " Excuse me, General, but I'd just like to tell you that some of our blokes have had a bit of pay owing to them for about six weeks.   I thought you wouldn't mind my mentioning it, and perhaps you'd have it put right." The General, being emphatically " one of the best," took in the situation at once, and answered, " All right, my man ; I'll have it seen to."

Everybody knows now that a number of wildly insubordinate Australian volunteers were sent back last winter from Egypt to their own country as incorrigibles. Inactivity had proved disastrous to one undisciplined Bushman in particular, but he would not be baulked in his wish to fight the Germans. Landed at Sydney with other undesirables, amid a hail of hisses far harder to face than bullets, he determined to get back and be in the fighting line somehow, and escaping from confinement stowed himself away on board a troopship. At Gallipoli he found himself " unattached," but he succeeded in commandeering a Turkish donkey, and day by day the outlaw went forth and brought in wounded men of any nationality, more often than not under a heavy fire. People who saw this poor Samaritan tell us that he had earned the V.C. *fifteen times* before he was killed by a stray ball. The Turks knew him, and would withhold their fire while he passed on his errands of mercy.

From Alexandria my niece, Mrs. Kenneth Macaulay, writes :

" I can hardly imagine wounds more terrible, and suffering harder to bear than one sees here every day. I think the Australians are quite delightful, and I am so glad you think the same after a much longer and wider experience of the Them. men have charming manners and are extraordinarily plucky in action, and, what is much harder, cheerful and patient and unselfish in hospital. We often write home for them, and their parents write such pathetically grateful letters. We have even had several invitations to stay with complete strangers in remote and unpronounceable places in Australia. They think us very ignorant for not having seen Sydney harbour. It seems that the Turks have picked up the phrase ' *Do* you know Sydney harbour ? ' and fling the question from their trenches to ours in Gallipoli ! "

I have myself been visiting Australian soldiers in hospital at Bath where they are undergoing treatment for ailments contracted at Gallipoli. Everyone must know that sickness is far harder to endure than wounds, but I have found among these men crippled with rheumatism, weak and shaken from dysentery, the same indomitable spirit, the same brave acceptance of fever, lassitude and pain which appears to characterise all those born under the Southern Cross. They are so patient " under their sufferings " that they surely deserve " a happy issue out of all their afflictions." Their letters from home have been few ; so few that months have passed without news of any description, and an old *Herald* or *Telegraph* from Sydney is read from the first line to the last.

To their suffering and bodily weakness is added the pain of exile. No matter how happy we try to make their Christmas it must be passed among strangers. Their time in hospital cannot be brightened by visits from their own people ; when convalescent they must go among strangers; when discharged as fit for duty they will depart unsped, unwept, unblessed by wife or mother.

CHAPTER LIX

CHRISTMAS THOUGHTS, 1915

THIS Christmas should be a season of Remembrance and Hope.

We are thankful for pictures of past happiness conjured up as we sit by firesides robbed of those who made other Christmases merry. Many of us are unable even to borrow the material out of which to manufacture mirth. But we possess something we had not before—a future enriched and vitalised by all the present has lost. We know that treasure has been laid up for us in heaven, and though the lustre of gold tried by fire and the gleam of gems cut by the Master Craftsman are often dimmed or obscured to our eyes by clouds of doubt or the darkness of regret, we can always see a few steps of the shining ladder which reaches from a sad and blood-stained earth to that glorious Treasury, and almost feel the clasp of strong young hands stretched out to help us in our slow and painful ascent.

There are some more lonely and sorrowful, more sick at heart and suffering than ourselves; some whose Christmas may be made more endurable by our poor efforts; the sick and wounded who can fight no more; the parents who had no son to give ; others who have given and never knew when or how their gift was accepted ; others again whose husbands or sons languish in a German prison. All these are worse off than are we, to whom sacrifice was sweetened by the swift glory of the end.

And there are wives and parents tortured by watching the slow extinction of a brilliant brain, the gradual but unrelenting decay of great physical strength or the wreck of nerves once like finely-tempered steel.

There are young widows, brave, yet unfitted for the long struggle before them, and lonely girls who cannot claim the dignity of widowhood.

But in all the Litany of the War, in all that long roll of those for whom God's comfort and grace are daily entreated, none are more needy, none more overwhelmingly forlorn than the women whose sons, husbands or lovers have remained deaf to their country's call.

NOTE

My thanks are due to the Editors of *The Spectator*, the *Westminster Gazette*, the *Cornhill*, and the *Evening Standard* (1907—1911) for permission to incorporate in this book portions of articles which have appeared from time to time in these publications.

I. M. P.

INDEX

INDEX